# HENRY'S CHAPEL

# GRAHAM GUEST

Sagging
Meniscus

Set in Minion with LaTeX.

ISBN: 978-1-952386-22-0 (paperback)
ISBN: 978-1-952386-23-7 (ebook)
Library of Congress Control Number: 2021944633

Sagging Meniscus Press
Montclair, New Jersey
saggingmeniscus.com

# CONTENTS

# HENRY'S
# CHAPEL

THE SCREEN IS DARK, but there's a sound, like wind, or a great rushing of air ... or a *huge* breath. It's a really, really long out-breath ... It's the massive exhalation of a colossal being ... and it goes on and on ... All right, it's tapering off now ... Now he ... or she is coming back in with it, inhaling—with intent, it seems—*trying* to draw a deep-deep breath. It, too, goes on and on ... Finally, it tops out and we pause ... then the out-breath begins again *but it immediately ramps-up to a super-high speed*, and the being's lips must be drawn into a tight circle because you can hear it, the pressure, escaping through the hole, and then with an even sharper spike in intensity and a final super-plosive "thwop!" we are spit out with tremendous force into a bright white light tumbling, head over heels, through the sky, blowing through cumulus clouds, we fly, like a humongous preternatural loogie, flipping and rolling and twisting and turning ... but now ... now, we're slowing down ... slowing down ... slowing down ... And now we're just falling, straight down, out of the clouds, down, down, from the illusory blues of heaven to the solid greens and browns of earth below, faster and faster ... fade to black.

We sit, now, in darkness and silence.

The idea, though, evidently, is that we were present in God's mouth as a gob of spit, which God then expelled. Birthed by expectoration, at first we flew ... or, more like, on the power of God's breath, we travelled through the air horizontally, briefly, then fell to earth; all of it, a pretty spectacular new twist on the old *fall of man* chestnut, I must say. It's also worth considering that angels have *fallen* too, and that *we*, the audience, the viewer, the voyeur, could be cast in the role of fallen angels, or even the devil himself, which would be pretty outrageous.

In any case, we must have passed out during the fall and are now slowly regaining consciousness because, while the screen is still dark, we can hear a chorus of cicadas buzzing electrically all around, stopping and starting all together as if on cue. This goes on for some time and to some not insignificant effect until finally, against the void, the words:

# LAWNMOWER
# OF A
# JEALOUS GOD

appear (in red). They hang there for a few seconds then fade out and are replaced by the words:

# PART ONE
## FAMILY PORTRAIT

Then all that evaporates, and in its place materializes a big bright blue clouded sky, a big blue-backed field of hundreds, thousands of frozen white bulbous tumors, perfectly evenly-spaced across an imperceptible matrix, stretching as far as the eye can see. We must be on the ground, on our backs.

We roll over, and before us, we see a mother and her two kids, standing in the sun in front of a small, one-story, yellowish brick ranchhouse; the little girl is holding her mother's right hand; the little boy, her left; the two kids are about the same size, and they're about the same age: probably two, two and a half—chances are they're twins. They are, all three of them, squinting and smiling severely, in that pained, almost demented way, into the sun. They move a little bit here and there: they scratch their faces; the kids pull on mother some; they'd rather be doing something else; but, for the most part, they stay that way as the title credits appear in one corner then another: Newton Boyles Anchoby . . . Chad Eamon Martin Blartz[1] . . . Uda Copenhagen . . . Gordon Ram Dicters . . . Byce Karen Egg . . . Candle Lux Endebrin . . . T.T. Grañulardo . . . Richmond Maurice Hamburger . . . Joff Christian Hoffman . . . Joss Christiana Hoffman . . . Johnson John Pennygrabbles . . . Rosé Pranderson . . . Candy Anne Robadge . . . Penelope K. Rick . . . Keekee Marie Sanchex . . . Becky Lynn Stubarb . . . and Lyle Lovett as Lyle . . . then, in the center of the screen: Written & Directed by Albarb Noella.

Actually, we don't *know*, at this utterly initial stage in the game, that the woman is the kids' mother. It's an assumption. But it certainly seems justified, if only provisionally, because, you know, we've seen this sort of thing before, many times, with the woman and the kids and the holding-of-the-hands in front of the house, and it just seems to almost always turn out to be mother and kids, does it not?

Mother is wearing blue bell-bottom jeans and a ridiculously easy to remove rainbow tube-top, tell-tale signs that we are in the late-sixties, early-seventies United States. She's young, mid-late twenties, and pretty, if also a bit paunchy and rural. The girl is wearing a white sundress with multi-colored flowers all over it, and the boy is wearing diaper-bloated blue jeans and a

---

[1] Apparently, Blartz had to outdo all the other actors by sporting four names instead of three or, god forbid, just two.

brown and white cowboy shirt. Both kids are wearing generic monochromatic shoes; whatever mom's got going on shoe-wise is invisible under the blue bells. They've all got brown hair— mom's, parted down the middle; the kids', rounded into bowls— and all their hairs appear to have been recently brushed or combed; mother's hair looks particularly clean and silky. Perhaps they are expecting company. Which points up another thing we can add about this, our casual redneck family portrait: it lacks a dad—not that it *has* to have one.

We hear what sounds like a car coming down a dirt road. We turn around and see a really big, brown, four-door, full-sized car, like a Cadillac or a Lincoln Continental, speedily crunching down the access road to our family's house. We can also see now that there's another house, exactly like theirs, in view down and off to the right, but that's it for houses in the immediate area. This, then, there can be no doubt, is a low-income, seriously rural situation out here. The car is trailing a giant rooster-tail of dust and dirt. Company is on its way; perhaps this is dad.

Taking everything together, though: the largeness of the car, its relative speed, its straining engine, the chomping gravel, and the whole rooster-tail thing, it's tempting to think that *whoever* is coming down the road is some kind of asshole, that all of this stuff signals the impending introduction of a cock-of-the-walk asshole-type character; and if we are, indeed, so beguiled, then we should, of course, not be surprised to feel, as an accompaniment, a pang of trepidation concerning the fate of our little trio (whom we've only just met but already kinda love), a sort of *here comes trouble* type concern.

On the other hand, we have to admit, any such thoughts and feelings would be infinitely less than logically or forensically derived, but, instead, the mere decoctions of loose-lipped intuitions inspired by our narrative pasts: little prejudices, really; little flexible prejudices which, if they turn out to be right, allow us to gloat, *We knew it all along*, and which, if they turn out to be wrong, conveniently vanish into memorial oblivion because there is nothing *inherently* or *necessarily* terrifying or terrorizing or asshole-bearing about big cars, semi-high speeds, and rooster-tails of dust and dirt; indeed, *all* the cars back then were big, and both saints and sinners drove them; and a little extra speed in any size car does not necessarily an asshole make: lots and lots of wonderful people drive a little too fast sometimes—and here, in this case, maybe it *is* dad, and he simply *cannot wait* to see his wife and kids again after a protracted absence; and isn't it just sewn into the very nature of driving down a dirt road, regardless of car size, to kick up a rooster tail of dust and dirt? That is, I mean, short of driving exceedingly and excruciatingly and unreasonably slowly, what's *any kind* of driver or car to do about kicking up dust and dirt when driving down a dirt road?

It'd be appropriate to point out here as well that, so far, there has been no musical soundtrack, only the sounds of the given situation against a backdrop of relative silence, and we have all experienced just how affective and powerful and biasing a musical soundtrack in film (or, perhaps, wherever) can be. One single ominous tone here would all but confirm that our incoming driver is, indeed, an asshole. That said, we also know how powerful relative silence can be. Remember Jim Jarmusch's film *Stranger Than Paradise*? Perhaps we have been so conditioned by the comforting hermeneutic presence of the soundtrack that, when confronted with relative silence, we become uneasy, and maybe *that's* what's going on here . . .

The sky is neither a northeastern, nor a northwestern sky: it's too flat and wide, and there's a diffuse yellow-brown blended into the blue that one does not see in northeastern or northwestern skies, but it's not yellow *enough* to be a southwestern sky; it's also too lush and treed to be the southwest; and it's neither lush and treed, nor rolling enough to be the east-southeast. So given all this: the architecture: the two small yellow-ish brick one-story ranch-style houses; the topography: flat; the flora: green with brown, decently grassed and treed with oaks and pines; and the flat, dead, globuloid cauliflower tumor-pocked sky, with its hurtful hot yellow-brown-blues, and I'm thinking we've got to be in Southwestern Arkansas, Northeast Texas, or Northwestern Louisiana.

The car stops. It's a Buick. The engine shuts off, the cloud of dust and dirt catches up to the car, rolls over it like a massive amorphous tumbleweed, then engulfs our onlookers, in automatic response to which all three close their eyes and bow their heads in a manner befitting those about to meet their lord and savior.

The car door opens, and, from our onlookers' dust-clouded perspective, what appears to be a woman's high-heeled pointy-toed shoe drops onto the ground next to the car, then a figure steps up out of the car and places on its head what looks like a woman's flared sun hat.

Tall, erect . . . maybe titless and pretty masculine, she stands inside the crease of the open door. Mother lets go of the kids' hands and walks through the cloud of dust to the woman. Mother and the woman kiss, passionately, which I'll wager we did not see coming.

The dust settles, they walk back over toward the kids, and now it's clear: the woman from the Buick is *not* a woman, but a thirty-year-old *man* wearing cowboy boots and a cowboy hat—and blue jeans and a dark red and white-trimmed cowboy shirt—and if that doesn't highlight that weird gender dysphoria of the cowboy, well . . . But so maybe it *is* dad then after all.

"Emily. Henry. I want you to meet someone *very* special. This is the man I was telling you about, okay? He's been gone a long time, but he had to . . . he had to go to war to fight for our country, in a place called Vietnam, a long way away, but, God willing, he came *back*. This is Royd, this is your *dad*."

Dad, or *Royd*, gets down on one knee, pretends to shoot Henry—"Pakew"—then unfolds the other three fingers and says, "Partner."

Which, while cute, we can't help but notice is not the most *affectionate* greeting ever, especially given the circumstances. Granted, this is the South, maybe even *Texas*, and these are *males* we're talking about here; but *still*, you'd think there'd be something more: a hug, a real, *emotional* expression of endearment of *some* sort . . . maybe a deal where Royd sweeps both kids into his arms and . . . *something*.

So, *despite* Mother's introduction of Royd as the kids' dad and our natural desire to believe her, we have to admit, we're, right away, not one hundred percent sure; something's a little off, and whatever it is, it seems to me, is building upon our first impression of the driver of the approaching car a few moments ago as being some kind of rooster-tailing asshole and on his unsettling ability to *shape-shift* from woman to man; and so *now*, when Royd goes and does something like the shoot-and-shake-hands thing with Henry, it wouldn't be *entirely* unnatural for us to read *irony* into the "Pakew" because *maybe Royd's's not joking about "Pakew" vis-à-vis Henry, you know?*

"Shake your daddy's hand, Henry," Mother says.

Henry just stands there, so Royd picks up Henry's right hand and shakes it, Henry's arm going up and down floppily, like a flaccid tortilla.

Royd lets go of Henry's hand and turns to Emily, opens his arms for a hug, and says, "And *you* must be Emily," which either corroborates our idea that there *is* a sex-based greeting distinction inherent to Royd and/or his culture, *or* it's a sign that Royd has some creepy need to get closer to Emily than to Henry and something is, indeed, already *way* not right.

Emily clutches Mother's leg tightly.

"Emily. Go on and give Royd a hug please for mommy."

Emily squeals loudly, desperately, now trying to disappear behind Mother's leg; and again, it's impossible to disambiguate the implications of this behavior: Emily's either very shy, or her unvarnished instincts are telling her that there's a predator in our midst; it was easy, however, to notice how Mother called Royd "Royd" and not "dad" when she asked Emily to give him a hug just now, which further bolsters our suspicion that Royd is *not* the kids' dad at all.

Royd stands back up and looks at Mother.

"Don't worry about it. She'll come around."

Royd walks back to his car. He opens the backdoor and pulls out a suitcase; inappositely, the suitcase is fairly small, and, like Emily's dress, it has little flowers, little multi-colored flowers printed all over it, all over a bright, light blue background. Clearly, this is a suitcase designed for a young girl. Royd smiles and carries it into the house.

It's a funny picture, but in what world is this the appropriate bag for Royd? If he's *really* just back from Vietnam, then where the fuck is his big green army-issue duffle bag or his big black trunk? Sure, maybe his duffle bag was lost or stolen or destroyed somehow on his return to the States, and he had to replace it at his first opportunity with the first thing he could find or with the first thing that presented itself to him; maybe he bought it at a garage sale or a dollar store, where it was all they had in the way of suitcases.

Then again, could be he *likes* little rose-covered suitcases, saw it in the window of a local dollar store, disposed of the duffle bag, and bought it for himself, but he's not gay, just super-comfortable with owning and toting homo-suggestive luggage. *Or*, he likes little rose-covered suitcases, saw it in the window of a local dollar store, disposed of the duffle bag, and bought it for himself because he *is* gay.

I jest of course. More likely—given all the intra- and inter-narrative signs—he's not just back from Vietnam *at all*, and the suitcase . . . well, I bet it belonged to a young girl he systematically raped and ultimately murdered, but now he keeps it as a souvenir and as a way to flaunt his superiority and flout the law.

W E ARE IN A DARK ROOM, watching a young boy sleep, on his back, from a few feet away. The words:

# PART TWO

## LABOR

appear for a few seconds then fade out. We do not know this boy; we have not seen this boy. Slowly, we move in closer until we're right up on him, right up in his face. We watch him sleep like this for quite some time. He, everything is perfectly silent and still. Suddenly, a woman screams from another room and the boy's eyes snap open. He jumps out of bed—wearing only his rounded baggy white underpants—leaves his room, and stands out in the hall in front of a closed door. Presumably, it's the door to the room from which the scream came.

The door opens. Royd comes out dressed and carrying his little flower-covered suitcase. Mother follows in her nighty, holding her big round stomach and moaning and breathing heavily. Obviously, she's going to have a baby very soon. The boy, it's safe to say now, is Henry, but he's bigger, older, maybe seven or eight; and, obviously, we have no information at the moment about what transpired in the five-to-six year gap between Royd's arrival and the present, and we have been given no explanation for the existence of this gap. Perhaps it will be important, something we'll try hard to fill, a mystery we'll strive to solve; or, it may be of no consequence whatsoever.

Royd and Mother go out the front door and get in Royd's Buick. Henry stands at the open front door. It's the same house as before, if there was any doubt. Mother rolls down the window. She's all sweaty and red.

"There's Cheerios and a bowl on the kitchen table, Henry. Your Uncle Avery will be down in the morning to check on you, okay?"

Apparently, Henry's not going with them; they're leaving him there alone. Or maybe Emily's there somewhere too, in the house, but—Mother tells Royd to go; they drive off up the access road; they're gone—where is Emily in all this commotion?

I T MUST BE the next morning. Henry's sitting at the kitchen table in his underwear eating dry Cheerios out of a bowl with his bare hands. There are Cheerios all over the table around the bowl. The words:

# THE KEY

appear then fade out, but not without raising a few eyebrows because, first of all, we all know it's well nigh impossible to feature a key in fiction and not have it be . . . well, *key*; but to actually step out and announce, in an episode or chapter heading like this, that we're about to have it *handed* to us: that's downright metafictional: a real viewer's-guide-type info-bomb alert; and I mean, I think we even have to be prepared for the possibility that we are about to be handed *the key to the whole plot* here.

We've been placed, immobilized, on the table, down a few feet from Henry, and are being forced to watch him shovel cereal into his mouth. He chews with his mouth open. He has nothing to drink. This goes on for a couple of excruciating minutes, during which our eyes and ears and thoughts naturally seek out other things to focus on.

We can see the living room to our left (Henry's right). There's a TV, a lounge chair, a couch against the wall, and a window that looks out over the backyard. The hallway that leads to the bedrooms and the front door is to our right (beyond Henry's left shoulder). The kitchen is to our immediate right, but it's mostly off-screen.

There's a knock at the backdoor; Henry gets up and opens it.

It's a man in a blue gas station suit (or, you know, a full-body worksuit, or jumpsuit), looking down at and pointing a shiny gold key where the lock would be but for Henry's sudden opening of the door. And there we have it: *a golden key, held by a man who does not live in the house to which the key fits but in whose possession it is nonetheless, such that he, at all times, has access—through the back door, no less—to its otherwise hidden interior.* The *holder* of the key, then, is *the key*; and the holder of the key must be Uncle Avery.

"Oh. Mornin' Henry."

Uncle Avery puts the key into his pocket. Henry just stands there woodenly. A stressfully long number of seconds passes.

"Well come on, buddy. Lemme in."

Henry steps back and lets go of the door. Uncle Avery comes in and sits down at the table. He's about five-ten, early thirties maybe, pleasant face and demeanor; the slight paunch plus the red nose and cheeks suggest alcoholic.

"All right, shut the door, Henry, and come on back in here and set down, finish your breakfast."

Henry shuts the door, gets back in his chair, and starts eating again.

Uncle Avery laughs.

"You always eat in your underpants? Ain't no big deal if you do, Henry, it's just ... and how 'bout a spoon ... and some milk?"

Henry eats a handful of Cheerios.

Uncle Avery looks left, into the living room, then looks back at Henry.

"So, what about the big news? You ready to have you a little brother or sister? You *did* know that's what's goin' on with Mother, didn't you?"

Henry stops eating and looks at Uncle Avery but does not respond. Then he goes back to eating more Cheerios.

Uncle Avery looks off into the living room again. This looking-off-into-the-living-room thing seems to be something he does when he needs to vent his disbelief and frustration and to recharge his patience. He looks back at Henry and forces a smile.

"Well, that *is* what's goin' on with Mother. The reason she's so big ain't because she ate too much and is just all *fat* now, Henry"—he laughs—"it's because she's *pregnant*. Do you . . . That means she's got a *baby* inside her. You were born thataway; I was born thataway; we're all born thataway. Do you know what I'm talkin' about? 'Cause whenever she gets back from Mrs. Smickers' in Kilgore,[2] that's what you're going to have, a little brother or sister."

Apparently, Mother and Royd have gone to one Mrs. Smickers' house to have the baby instead of to the hospital, so all we can think is that Smickers is some kind of midwife. Also notice—now that we're, as it were, *keyed in* to Uncle Avery's ostensible super-significance—that, while this is not quite tantamount to the birds-and-the-bees talk, it's something close to it, and it can't be completely insignificant that it's Avery who's introducing the subject to Henry, not Royd.

Henry gets down from his chair. Uncle Avery stands up.

---

[2] Kilgore, so you know, is a small town in East Texas, near Tyler, between Dallas and Shreveport, LA. *So*, some people *do* have the ability to determine geographic location by simply looking at a picture, and if you are someone who can do that, who has that talent, well, whether you know it or not, what you're looking for, the big determining factors, are the light, the vegetation, and the architecture. The biggest one, for me, though, is the light. Seems like there'd be a forensic application for a such a talent.

"Henry, why don't you git some clothes on and let's take a walk, down by the creek, do somethin' while we wait for Mother to git back."

Now notice here too the possibility that Uncle Avery is *blocking* Royd, that he is in a sort of denial of Royd's presence in the family picture. The reason I say that is, a couple or three times now already, he's described situations in which Royd clearly plays an important part but has neglected to mention or include him. Avery said, for instance, " . . . whenever *she* gets back from Mrs. Smickers' in Kilgore . . . ," not whenever she and *Royd*—or even *they*—get back from Mrs. Smicker's in Kilgore; and he said, " . . . while we wait for *Mother* . . . ," not while we wait for Mother *and Royd*—or *them*. And, come to think of it, we might add, in this connection, that he's got a concomitant *fixation* on Mother: Avery blocks Royd and fixates on Mother.

I know, and I can almost *hear* your eyes rolling at this point, but if you'll just stop and *think* about it with me for a second, I think you'll agree that all this sort of thing falls under the familiar heading of Freudian Slip. The Slip is an unconscious locution that betrays some otherwise hidden psychological disposition of its speaker. Here, the idea is that when Uncle Avery goes to talk about situations that involve both Mother and Royd, he conveniently focalizes on Mother and blocks out Royd. Why? Well, we don't know yet, but maybe he loves and feels protective of his sister, and he doesn't approve of Royd, but which, if true, I hasten to add, does not *automatically* mean that Royd is a bad person; it just means that Avery has his own issues with Royd, and with his sister; and the problem may lie largely with Avery.

On the other hand, unlike with Royd, we tend to immediately identify with Avery; he is, unlike Royd, immediately likeable: he's got a sort of a cherubic face and an overall country-good-guy demeanor; he comes off as kinda simple and cute in his blue gas station suit; he's been given a much more amicable name, obviously; and, probably most importantly, he just seems to really *care* for Henry, and *we* seem to *care* about *that*. So Avery's omitting Royd from his everyday articulations *does* tend to subtly feed, fairly or unfairly, our running intuition that Royd is (at the very least) an asshole.

Henry runs down the hall and back several times, oddly quietly, the hushed circular pointlessness of which suggests, along with a couple of other clues, that there might be something wrong with Henry, that he is, in some way, you know . . . slow. Uncle Avery stops him.

"Whoa there, buddy. We can do better 'n 'at. Come on."

Uncle Avery turns Henry around and they go down the short hall to Henry's room.

There are two beds in Henry's room, but only one's been slept in, evidently. It could be that Emily has spent the night at a friend's house or something, but now, more and more, it's beginning to seem as if something has happened to her, that she is, for one reason or another, no longer in the picture . . .

The floor is strewn with clothes. Uncle Avery goes to the dresser and pulls out socks from the top drawer, a t-shirt from the middle, and a pair of pants from the bottom. He knows right where to go for these things; he's done this before. He sits on the corner of the unslept-in bed.

"All right, come here. Arms up."

Avery puts the shirt on Henry, then the pants.

"All right, now how 'bout them socks and shoes."

Henry sits down on the carpet, Uncle Avery watching. Henry manages to get one sock on. Then he fumbles with a shoe. After a while, Uncle Avery puts on Henry's socks and shoes. Most kids at seven or eight can dress themselves and put on their own socks and shoes, can't they?

"All right. Come on, Henry. Good job," Uncle Avery says, and we cut.

W E'RE FOLLOWING ALONG behind Henry and Uncle Avery as they walk hand-in-hand down to the creek, accompanied by cicadas. It is a happy picture, a poignant portrait of loving avuncularity . . . if not *paternality* because, yes, there's definitely a fast-growing sense or suspicion that Avery is somehow more Henry's father than Royd.

They come to a big oak tree down by the creek and sit down under it. The oak is massive and provides, size-wise, a major landmark. We swing out over the creek and hover in front of them, looking at them, around them, beyond them. We can see that the big oak hangs over the creek about a hundred yards down from Henry's house and that it's about the same distance from the other ranchstyle house, which—it's suddenly obvious—is Uncle Avery's.

Uncle Avery starts throwing rocks into the creek. Henry throws rocks too, some of which go into the creek; some just shank off to the side into the grass.

"Y'all three is fixin' to be pretty busy with that new baby, Henry. I sure hope you don't forget about old Uncle Avery. You and Mother is all I got."

Now here again, if *that's* true: if Henry and Mother are all Avery's got, then we need to go ahead and accept, *right now*, that Emily is, indeed, out of the picture—well, probably not out of the film or story *all together*, but just no longer around as a present member of the family—because he'd've mentioned her just now if she were still around; surely, he'd have said, "You and *Emily* and Mother is all I got." were she still around. And now it goes without saying that somewhere within the five or so year gap between Royd's arrival and the present, there is important information about what happened to Emily.

Uncle Avery looks at Henry.

"You know what, though? I was thinkin' about gettin' me a dog. Maybe a bloodhound. Would you like that, Henry? Would you like it if I got me a dog?"

Henry smiles.

"Yeah, I bet you would . . . if I got me a dog. Well I tell you what, buddy," Uncle Avery says and sits up straight, "that's exactly what I'm gonna do. And you can come over and play with him whenever you want."

Uncle Avery lies back on the ground and puts his hands behind his head. Henry lies back and put his hands behind his head.

Uncle Avery closes his eyes. Henry close his eyes. Henry opens his eyes and looks over at Uncle Avery. He looks back up into the branches of the big oak and closes his eyes.

Then, slowly, we begin to rise up, into the big oak tree. Keeping an eye on Henry and Avery below, we rise up through the branches, *despite* the branches, as if we are some larger animal's prey being hauled up through the tree by the back of the neck[3] because the leaves and branches are giving way and cracking and snapping and snapping back into place behind us.[4] Soon, Henry and Avery are totally occluded.

We pass violently through the body, the heart of the tree with no point of reference, totally ensconced in a skein of branches and leaves, until finally we emerge from its crown; but we do not stop there; we continue to rise,[5] higher and higher above the big oak, up to a point maybe a hundred, a hundred

---

[3]Though I'm sure we're simply mounted on the end of a pole that's being pulled up forcefully through the tree.

[4]A cool effect.

[5]Must be by drone now.

and fifty yards in the air, where we stop and survey the whole setting below; and it's as clear and distinct as it can be: the two houses, Henry's and Uncle Avery's, and the big oak, together, form the three points of a triangle; then, as if on cue, the words:

# THE TRINITY

appear then fade out, and now we know not only *that* Uncle Avery is the key to the plot—or, even better, that he is its *prime mover*[6]—we also know *why* because we are obviously supposed to identify him, by way of his house, with or as the *Father*; Henry, by way of his house, with or as the *Son*; and Emily, by way of the big oak, with or as the *Holy Ghost* (i.e., that all-binding natural spirit and something or someone who's *both there and not*)—all of which, together with the knowledge that Henry and Emily are twins, imply the following momentous conclusions: (i) *Uncle Avery*, not Royd, is Henry and Emily's father; (ii) Henry and Emily are not Mother and Royd's children, but *Mother and Uncle Avery's*; (iii) this story, thus, at least on one very important level, is about *incest*; (iv) where Royd functions, at least on one level, as some sort of validating (albeit, of course, false) cover story; and (v) Uncle Avery is the "jealous god."

So yeah, it's a big moment—well, *for us* because Henry is not privy to any of these revelations[7]—but still, there's also no way it comes as a shock or any kind of huge surprise because

---

[6] It's *that but for which none of this would've happened.*

[7] A big instance of dramatic irony, of course. Now we get to enjoy the suspense of wondering and worrying whether Henry will be able to figure any of this stuff out for himself.

it was set up for us so frequently and conspicuously; and not only that, but aren't these backwoods southern stories just totally notorious for pulling the incest card? I mean, it's a massive *cliché*. So maybe the only surprising thing here is that this *big reveal* takes place so early on in the film . . . Then again, maybe not on that too because a film is only an hour and a half: it's got to move along—and at this very early stage in the game, in order to be fair, we should maintain the assumption that Noella knows what he's doing, that our knowing all this stuff now explains *some things* about what's happening in the story *but not everything*, and that Noella's probably got, as we like to say, bigger fish to fry.

A car, probably the Buick, breaks into the scene from the top edge of the screen; it's coming down the access road toward Henry's house, traveling slowly but kicking up a considerable amount of dust nonetheless. This would be Royd, Mother, and the newborn baby, returning from Mrs. Smicker's. Henry pops out from under the big oak, running; he's obviously heard and/or seen them coming, and he's running home to meet them. We make a quick descent and follow along just above and behind him. He runs up to the backdoor and opens it. He goes into the house. He leaves the door open; we descend further and follow him inside. He goes down the hallway to Mother's room. He peeks in. Royd's in the bathroom. He's standing at the sink washing his hands. Mother's in bed holding a bundle of white towels. She looks up.

"Oh, Henry. Come on over here and have a look at your baby sister, God bless her."

Henry and Royd are standing in the backyard with a lawnmower. The lawnmower is large by today's standards, but there is nothing special, nothing *godly* or *holy* about it at first blush. Royd stands between the mower and the house, his back to the house. Henry stands to Royd's right and in front of the mower. Behind Royd, we can see Mother, in the house, standing in the living room with the baby over her shoulder, watching Henry and Royd. The reflectivity of the glass makes her look semi-transparent, almost spectral and floating. The words:

# LAWNMOWING 101

appear then fade out. The cicadas are pulsing electrically. The whole situation looks hot and strained.

Royd, grimacing, brings the plastic goggles off of his forehead down over his eyes, then he puts his right boot up on the engine of the mower and grabs the cord all in one motion. His face is sweating. He pulls the cord. Nothing happens. We zoom in tight on his face. A silver ball of sweat drops off the tip of his nose. We pull back. He lets the cord back into the mower and pulls it again. Nothing happens. He takes his boot off the mower, puts the goggles back up on his forehead, and wipes his face with his arm. He kneels down, unscrews the gas cap, and looks into the hole.

"Helps to put gas in it. Gas can's in the garage near where the shovel's 're at. Go on, git."

Henry walks toward the chain-link gate at the corner of the backyard and disappears around the side of the house. Royd stands up. It's an odd picture: Royd, standing before the lawn-mower, his hands on his hips, grimacing in the burning sun; Mother and baby, floating spectrally in the living room window behind him, unbeknownst to him; the cicadas, humming their demented harmonies. Several minutes pass like this, and the scene becomes more and more pregnant with the stress and pressure of absence; there's a weird, sad, agonizing sort of vacancy; we can *see* that every thing is very much *there*, on the surface, but just below, we *know*, this world is infinitely hollow.

Hauling the gas can in front of his body with both hands, Henry waddles unstably back into the backyard. He drops the can into the grass next to Royd and steps back. Royd pours gas into the mower and screws the cap back on. He looks at Henry.

"You watchin' this?"

Royd turns around toward the house. He must have felt the pressure of eyes. He sweeps his right arm and hand violently to the right.

"Clear out, goddammit! This ain't no spectator sport!"

Mother's eyes widen. She steps back with the baby and disappears.

Mother's presence in the window has irritated Royd. He thinks Mother has surely got something better to do than surveille his and Henry's efforts to mow the yard. Royd shakes his head.

"Don't *ever* be like 'at."

But like what, *exactly*, does he mean? Don't ever be a watcher? A viewer? A voyeur? Nosy? Meddlesome? Concerned? Interested? Bored? And aren't we, all of us, implicated? *We* are watching from behind a sort of window, or glass, too. Apparently, Royd would have us *all* fuck off; but then, in a very real way, he doesn't exist without us, he cannot *be* without *us*.

Royd puts his boot back up on the engine of the mower, pulls the goggles down over his eyes, leans down, and jerks the cord. This time, the mower starts up. It's impossibly jarringly loud.

Noella slows everything way down; in slow motion now, Henry puts his hands up over his ears.

Royd steps slowly behind the mower ... looks at Henry ... and, grimacing, says something to Henry that Henry (and we) can't understand. It just sounds like long slow walrus barks. Royd raises both hands to his (own) ears and then brings them both down. He does this twice. He wants Henry to stop covering his ears. Henry takes his hands off his ears.

"This ... is ... how ... it's ... done," Royd yells slowly and monstrously at Henry.

Then everything snaps back to normal speed: Royd grabs the handle of the mower and pushes; there's a loud pop, and something—a piece of stick maybe—shoots out of the mower and hits Henry in the forehead; Henry puts his hand to his forehead, and Royd trundles on over the grass with the mower.

W<sup>E ARE IN A FAR CORNER</sup> of the backyard, looking toward the house. It's twilight, almost dark. The words:

# PART THREE
## LET THERE BE LIGHT

appear then fade out. That must be Henry, reclining in the deckchair; Mother and Royd are sitting around a metal table, and all of these people and things sit on a concrete slab that extends a little ways off roughly half of the back of the house, the half that's contiguous with the dining area inside. The slab takes up a quadrant of the backyard; it goes about fifteen or twenty feet into the yard then terminates; the backdoor steps out onto it, and there's a little metal corrugated awning over the door, under or in which there is a light; but on the other side of the door, going under the living room window, it's grass (which we already knew). The remainder of the yard is grass and nothing else, and there's a short chain-link fence around the whole situation.

We have been creeping slowly toward our trio but also keeping our distance by sticking close to the fence. We stop in the corner where the fence meets the house. Henry's just lying there with his hands behind his head, Uncle Avery-style; Mother's concentrating on smoking a cigarette: taking drags, blowing out loose columns of smoke, looking around, rolling ashes off into the ashtray. Royd's looking at a magazine, which appears to be of one of those that consists entirely of pictures of cars that people are trying to sell, the kind of thing you find in those plastic boxes at bus stops and outside grocery stores. It's an odd, stiff scene, like some kind of forced post-prandial r-and-r.

Henry's as-yet-unnamed little sister must already be in bed; although, it wouldn't be *entirely* unreasonable for the worry to cross our minds that she is somehow gone now too, that Emily's disappearance provides narrative precedent for Henry's new sister's disappearance, and we can't rule it out; *but,* since there has been no *other* evidence (beyond Emily's disappearance) to suggest that Henry's little sister is already gone, I think our prevailing expectation is that we will see her again soon.

We creep up closer, until we're some ten feet from Henry. He's grown again—he's represented by a different actor, the third one now. He's taller, older, maybe eleven (making his little sister about four), and so, again, he's disappeared into and rematerialized for us after a multi-year gap. But films and stories have a license to commit and use such gaps, and their commission and use often improves the story and helps move it along. And furthermore, *life* is gappy. Maybe not as gappy as skipping bundles of years here and there, but gappy still. Think about it: memory is gappy; perception is gappy; consciousness is gappy, perhaps especially disabled ones. So, even if you *wanted* to capture *everything,* you couldn't. Gaps *are* necessarily, whether they contain and hide something remarkable or not.

But now we *know* our first multi-year gap contains and hides Emily's disappearance and life as it begins in the Henry household with Royd at the head of the table, both of which are, undoubtedly, significant; but we don't know much about our second multi-year gap: it contains and hides life as it begins in the Henry household with his new baby sister at the table, but beyond that, we have been given no evidence to indicate that there is anything else in there we should be concerned about.

In fact, I understand that the first few years of life for people in a household with a newborn child often end up being "lost years," a blur, practically blacked out; so, *actually*, we may have reason to believe that there's *nothing* particularly remarkable or significant, with respect to our narrative, contained and hidden in this second multi-year gap.

But going back to our first multi-year gap, we *know* that with it, or in it, Noella has intentionally hidden something important, and it follows that he has done so in order to upset us, to pique our curiosity, to get us to continue to read the narrative environment for clues, and to motivate us to try to to figure out what exactly happened back in there. So, whatever is hidden in that first big gap is almost certainly one of the bigger fish Noella has to fry.

And while it's still the case that we know more than Henry does about the "family dyamics" here, I expect, going forward, that Henry and we will be more like partners in this particular investigation, in the investigation into this first gap, because the same important information about Emily, and Royd, has (surely) been hidden from him (Henry) as well, but by different agents and for different reasons: in our case, the information has been hidden from us by Noella in order to generate suspense, intrigue, and a desire to solve the mystery; in Henry's case, the information was *and continues to be* hidden from him by Mother and Royd . . . and Avery . . . probably in order to protect him; but the point is that, either way, both Henry and we have been *and continue to be* (that's the key) deprived of essential information to which we are, ostensibly, ultimately entitled.

We should also be mindful, though, in this connection, of the possiblity that Henry's youth and compromised perceptual and intellectual condition have made any clues that *have been* present in his environment, at least very early on in his life, difficult or even impossible for him to attend to and understand. He may not even know or remember that he had another sister, a twin sister, at this point. [And how would we or anyone else in the story even know if *he knew* he had a sister when he can't or won't talk and when no other access to this thoughts (if any) has been provided?] In any case, what I am sensing here is that all of this is *set-up* for a sort of *Bildungsroman*-type thing, that, in a general but important sense, this is a story about Henry's education, the expansion of his consciousness, and his transition to adulthood.

Henry sits up in the deckchair. He sees something in the distance. We look with him. It's a light . . . a little white light . . . like a flashlight . . . moving through the trees on the other side of the creek. By all appearances, someone is walking around in the trees on the other side of the creek, making his or her way by flashlight. We look back at Henry. He points.

"Light!"

Startled, both Mother and Royd look at Henry.

"What?" Mother says.

"Light!" Henry says, still pointing.

"Holy shit," Royd says, putting down the magazine.

Mother puts her hand over her heart. She turns and looks where he's pointing. She turns back and studies him.

"Did you . . ."

"Light!" he says, still pointing.

She looks across the creek again. Royd looks across the creek. We look across the creek again. We don't see anything this time. We look back at Mother. She looks at Royd. Royd looks endearingly confused. Mother looks at Henry.

"I'm sorry, I don't see a light, honey. I don't see nothin' but a bunch of trees," she laughs. She sniffles. She starts crying. She's laughing and crying. She looks over at Royd. "Do you see a light, Royd?"

They both look again.

They look at each other.

"No, but . . . " He looks at Henry.

"I know," Mother says, wiping her eyes with her fingers. "What are we supposed to do?"

Mother stands up and goes over and sits down on the deck chair next to Henry. "Oh, my baby. My sweet, sweet baby," she says and wraps her arms around him, Henry still looking and pointing across the creek. Now there can be no doubt, this is the first time Mother and Royd have heard Henry speak.

We zoom-in. Henry's eyes are floating over Mother's right shoulder, wide open, fixated, as if he's witnessing something miraculous or terrifying . . . or gone insane . . . but since we can't see the bottom half of his face, we can't see his full expression, so it could be the *illusion* of awe or terror or insanity; it could be just the result of Mother squeezing him.

We begin a slow pan back, back . . . apparently back toward the corner where the house meets the fence . . . Royd looks across the creek again.

Of course, we have no idea who is walking around on the other side of the creek or even *if* someone is walking around on the other side of the creek, actually, but, because we saw the light too, we tend to side with Henry and to think that Mother and Royd have simply missed it; and because it was moving in that characteristically human way, we tend to think that a *person* was carrying the light, and we assume that that's what Henry is thinking too; *although*, just because we have *perceived* the same thing Henry has *perceived* does *not* mean that we *think* the same thing Henry *thinks*: he might simply see a moving light and *not* infer a human agent or an agent of any sort; he might think that the light itself is an alien or a massive insect, or he might think Elmer Fudd is carrying the light.

So we have to go back and give some real credence to the possibility that, perceptually speaking, we, as an audience, as a camera, are not always an objective arbiter here. I mean, what if we're not always independent, objective perceivers, but sometimes subject to *Henry's* perceptual focalizations? Then Noella has us literally *see through Henry's eyes*, and we are subject to whatever perceptual anomalies, such as visual hallucinations, Henry might incur—and Henry is, after all, pretty clearly now, cognitively atypical.

As predicted, our retreat has terminated at the corner where the house meets the fence. Mother is rocking Henry back and forth gently now, sort of humming . . . or maybe crying—it's hard to tell because Noella has directed that the mic follow the camera back such that our visual retreat has been matched by an equivalent aural retreat. Henry is still pointing, but his arm has gotten tired and is now hanging at a forty-five degree angle, flaccidly indicating the slab.

Royd says something like, "All right, that's enough," and picks up his magazine again.

Though it has faded into an abnormal intolerance for expressions of human love, interestingly, Royd's disposition was basically normal and sympathetic there for a few minutes, which highlights the fact that even pathological people can engender true moments of everyday affability. I mean, surely Ted Bundy or Jeffrey Dahmer or BTK (Dennis Rader) could thank a waiter for a cup of coffee or laugh at a good joke and mean it.

We jolt a little bit, as if coming unstuck, then start creeping slowly back up the fence, presumably toward the far corner of the yard, where we started . . . Royd stands up with his magazine and says something to Mother and Henry. Mother separates from Henry, turns around, and watches Royd as he goes into the house and shuts the door.

We stop at the far corner of the backyard, where, indeed, we started; so it's been a full-circle scene for us, which, in this case, I'm not seeing as significant in any way beyond the sort of closure-satisfaction that comes with anularity itself. Mother and Henry stand up. Mother starts toward the backdoor. Henry's still looking across the creek. Mother takes Henry's hand and they go into the house.

The cicadas vibrate synchronously as we stare at the dark silhouettes of the patio furniture, and I'm thinking: it's as if Noella has taken the line from the Bible, "And God said, 'Let there be light': and there was light," and turned it around so that it reads something more like, "There was light, and *Henry* said, 'Light!'" Here, in *this* world: the *light itself* comes first, and the *word* comes second; the light is not generated by God, but (probably) by a human being (or some facsimile thereof) and his (or her) flashlight; and the *word* is not uttered by God, but by Henry, a mentally disabled child. Allegorically speaking, then, it's as if Noella is saying that Jesus is mentally disabled, that all of humanity is mentally disabled, or enfeebled, and that he and we have learned to talk without any help from God, in a world bereft of God.

But this is also—quite obviously—a, or rather, *another* really momentous occasion because, while Henry may have been processing the language communicated to him by others, this marks the first time that *he* has spoken, that *he* has used language to express *his* thoughts and perceptions and to communicate with the outside world; and so we have to think as well that the order and structure of his universe, the *logos*[8] *of his cosmos*, is undergoing some considerable *improvement*.

And, if we assume (which we probably should) that there *is* someone or something of at least *narrative* (if not objective) significance on the other side of the creek, then we'd have to be pretty daft *not* to think that it could very well be *Emily* and that this heretofore unrecognized land across the creek, this *realm beyond* the borders of prior comprehension, will be of major importance to Henry: a brave new world which he will be impelled to visit and explore (however cliché that may sound).

---

[8]The organizing principle most often identified with language, reason, and design.

Henry is walking along the creek below Mother's house. We follow on behind him. From the point of view of Mother's house (and Avery's house), he is walking down and away to the right. It's late afternoon, obviously hot, and the cicadas sound angry and insane; they're screaming and pulsing that mental screaming and pulsing that one imagines deranged or psychotic people hear all the time. It appears Noella is wasting no time getting Henry (and us) across the creek. And, sure enough, the words:

# THE OTHER SIDE

appear then fade out as Henry comes upon an old wood bridge. He pauses. We catch up to him.

Now, before we go on, it bears emphasizing, vis-à-vis temporal structures and gaps (again), that so far in this film, Noella has chosen only a handful of really slow-moving scenes to represent almost ten years of human time; thus, we've been subject to a sort of temporal contradiction, or at least a temporal tension because, on the level of the individual scene, time has dragged on languorously, almost soupily; but on the level of the whole, time has raced by, bundles of years falling invisibly by the wayside. I suspect, however, that this has been by way of introduction and that Noella is trying to get us to a point where we can focus on a more temporally contiguous series of events.

Which triggers another point: except for his physical behavior and his one verbal outburst, Henry has been pretty much a black hole identity-wise: he hasn't talked or explained himself to us or to any other character (obviously); we have been privy to none of his internal monologue (if he has even been *able* to engage in internal monologue in his life yet); and there has been no narrator or character who has functioned to explain to us, at any point, directly or indirectly, what's *really* going on with him, or in him. Whether we see substantial developments in these areas or not, it seems to me that if we were (at least) given that more temporally contiguous, concentrated series of events, then our project to understand and identify and identify *with* Henry, the person, would enjoy a significant and satisfying boost.

Henry starts across the bridge, but just as he does, Noella slows the film speed down—not *way* down this time, but just enough—and he adds a subtle, low, one-note tone, a synthesized soft-fuzzy tone, pitched to harmonize nicely with the cicadas; each effect is barely discernible alone, but together, they charge the scene with a sudden visceral power. Henry floats over the bridge on the thick bouyancy of the combined effects; we zoom-in over his left shoulder and follow his face closely; the background is a blur of green and brown. He looks slowly this way then that, sweating and intense; he appears much older. This is clearly another huge, unprecedented, super-individuating moment for Henry.

It is true, though, that there's also lot of predictable, tread-worn stuff going on here formally-speaking, or narrative structure-wise: you know, the hero crosses from his familiar-safe homeland over an obvious boundary of some sort and into an unfamiliar-dangerous foreign land, where he will undoubtedly be faced with trials and garner information he will need to survive back at home. And I have to confess, it makes me feel sad, almost sick, actually, to think how rare it is that we are told a story that doesn't in some really essential way function by virtue of this basic structure; it feels like we are interminably trapped in this fucking structure.

But then, what *I* have to understand is that we enact, in our lives, countless times every day, mere variations of this structure: we get out of bed and leave the house to go to the store to get the stuff we will need back home in order to live; we leave one room for another to get something we'll need back in the first room; we reach over to get something we'll need back where the rest of our body is; we reach out and communicate to someone else in order to get something or set some chain of events in motion that will in some way generate the production of the things we'll need back home. We can't get away from this structure; it seems to be metaphysically hardwired; so it only makes sense that we'd find it manifested pervasively across all of our narrative arts.

But I hasten to add that this sort of annular structure-function is *not* represented on *every level* of our lives or of the stories we tell and *at all times*: it manifests polyvalently, to be sure, but not *omni*valently and *omni*temporally. I mean, obviously, someone can move from, say, Missouri to California and never once return to Missouri; and Jim Jarmusch's film, *Stranger Than Paradise*, shows characters who, on at least one big important level, take one-way trips from Ohio to Florida (and beyond), never to retrace their steps—and I *love* that about that film, that it highlights that *there is one-way-ness too*.

When Henry sets foot on the other side, the film speeds back up, the tone drops out, and we're back to just cicadas. Noella has used this technique before, back in the lawnmowing scene, but here, there's no humor. Henry heads left and walks back up the creek under the cover of the trees; we follow him closely.

He stops and looks into the woods, and we look with him of course, but this time, he disappears . . . or we are no longer behind him . . . or no, what's happened is that Henry and we have *merged* . . . perceptually . . . or at least visually and aurally. Yes, Henry and we, the camera, are now *one*—which is also a first.

We scan the trees . . . but we don't see anything . . . except trees . . . then, suddenly, like a ghost, Henry *de*-merges from us, or he kind of materializes out of the front of us, walks into the woods a few feet and stops; and thus, no sooner had it begun, it's done, the mergence is over, leaving us to wonder whether there was some reason, beyond the mere coolness of the effect itself, why we were merged with Henry in the first place or at all . . . and nothing really comes to mind . . . except maybe that Noella would have us approach getting closer to Henry in a very, I guess, conservative way . . . I don't know.

Anyway, we stay where we are, behind him. He looks around then comes back, walks past us, sits down in the shade, and looks across the creek toward Mother's and Uncle Avery's. We sit down beside him and look across the creek too, like friends. The scene is a sort of mirror-image of the earlier one where Henry was sitting with Uncle Avery, except now it's Henry and us. The sun is starting to go down, which forces up into the sky that thick, inane Texas orange.

There's a dog, a bloodhound (Uncle Avery must've gotten that dog), sniffing around by the creek, on the other side of the creek, below Uncle Avery's house. The dog runs down the edge of the creek in our direction, his nose to the ground. He stops, looks up, and starts barking at us. Henry gets up and hides behind a tree; we get up and hide behind Henry.

Now we're hiding from a barking dog. This is disconcerting to say the least. The dog is basically shouting at us, madly, incessantly, as loudly as it can. It's threatening and infuriating. If a *person* were to shout at us out in public like this, he'd be considered insane and dangerous; we'd call the police; it's a verbal assault; but when a *dog* does it, it's okay, it's considered to be okay.

Uncle Avery's backdoor cracks open. Uncle Avery sticks his head out. He whistles.

"Luke! Luke!"

The dog barks one more good time at us, like a good "*Fuck you!*" then turns and runs back to Avery's house.

Uncle Avery comes out of the house. He walks over and opens his chain-link gate. Luke runs through the gate. Uncle Avery closes the gate. He and Luke go inside the house.

Now Mother's backdoor opens. It's Mother. She steps out onto the slab. She probably heard Avery calling for Luke. And it must be dinner time. She looks around, presumably for Henry, then goes back in.

Royd comes out and walks to the end of the slab. He puts his hands on his hips. He whistles.

"Henry! Henry!"

The cicadas stop coincidentally, and it's hard not to think that it was the sound of Royd's voice . . . and/or the utterance of Henry's name that stopped them.

Henry and we move steadily backwards through the trees a few paces, then we separate: Henry heads left through the trees, back toward the bridge; we continue backwards but angle away from Henry, deeper into the pines, and faster and faster now . . . Now we're flying backwards in super-fast-motion through the pines . . . everything's a backwards blur . . .

We stop.

We turn around. We're nose-to-nose, as it were, with a big pine tree. We look up. It spires vertiginously above us. We circle around it, still looking up. We start to rise up along its trunk.

Up and up we rise . . . up into and through the branches . . . up, above the other pines. We can see Henry now; he's crossing the bridge. We stop at the top of the tree. There is a breeze—we can hear it, and we're swaying in it. Henry is now running across the grass to his house. Royd sees him and goes back inside; he leaves the door open. Henry comes through the short chain-link gate, closes it, enters the house, and closes the door.

Noella has us sit with this view for a while. He seems to want to impress upon us, once again, the triangular or Trinity-ish nature of the situation; although it has, of course, been modified: the apex, our ostensible holy ghost representative, is now this big pine tree on the other side of the creek instead of the big oak. The full significance of this move is not yet legible (to me anyway), but it does highlight (almost painfully clearly) a *one side (of the creek) versus the other side (of the creek) duality* . . . and maybe a man-made versus nature-made duality as well (i.e., with the two houses on the one side and the forest of pines on the other) . . . and maybe a child versus adult or parent duality too because inherent in all of this rising-up-trees business is the more general notion of *uprising* itself, which could metaphorize and prophecize a forthcoming *rebellion*: Henry v. his parents.

All of this makes good sense given Henry's age—and of course no one needs reminding that rising up the stiff shaft of a big tree and being ejaculated from its tip makes good sense given Henry's age as well—but since Henry appears to be on a slower developmental timeline than most, it will be interesting to see whether it takes him longer to reach these typical developmental milestones.

ROYD AND HENRY and Henry's *still* yet-to-be-named (for us) little sister are sitting at the kitchen table. The table seats six. Henry is sitting in the same spot he was in when he was shoveling Cheerio's into his mouth, his back to the kitchen; Royd's at the head of the table, to Henry's left; Mother's going to sit opposite Henry; and his little sister, who is three or four, is diagonally opposite Henry, on Mother's right and to Royd's diagonal-left. The chair at the other end of the table, to Henry's diagonal-right, and the one on his left are empty. No one sits next to Henry. Though presumably Emily would have sat in the chair to his left. We watch from a stationary position, just above and behind Henry. The word:

# BIRTHDAY

appears then fades out as Mother sets down a large plate piled high with *piping hot pieces of golden fried chicken.*[9]

"We really should call Avery and ask him down here for supper, Royd," Mother says and returns to the kitchen.

Royd's looking for a piece of chicken with his fingers.

"Why's that?"

"Well, he's my brother, Royd, that's why. And it's our birthday."

By which surely Noella means to communicate to us—beyond the overt sexism of Mother having to slave away in the kitchen on her birthday—that Mother and Avery are, like Emily

---

[9]I felt compelled to put this phrase in quotes because I wanted to use *and* disown it at the same time. It's a derivation of a Kentucky Fried Chicken or Popeye's ad. It makes me literally viscerally sick to say it or even read it, so I know it's powerful. The sickness centers around the word "piping."

and Henry, *twins*, which puts an even weirder twist on the already weird fact of Mother and Avery's incest, and it opens up a whole new conceptual thing about *twinship*: no doubt, the two sets will mirror one another in crucial ways going forward.

"Well go ahead and call then." Royd takes a drumstick.

"Don't you eat that before sayin' grace," Mother says.

"Probably passed out drunk already though. Henry, go call your Uncle Avery, see if he wants to come down for some chicken."

Royd's supposition that Avery's passed out drunk bolsters our initial suspicion that Avery is a drinker, and his command to Henry to call his Uncle Avery implies that he thinks Henry is now capable, both verbally and otherwise, of actually placing the call. Then again, could be Royd's just fucking with Henry; could be he knows or suspects that Henry will not be able to perform all the steps required to make the call and is simply setting him up to fail, to enjoy watching him fail, to *shame* him. If the latter, then of course Royd qualifies as the sort of piece of shit that fucks with disabled people in order to make himself feel superior.

Henry gets up from the table, and we back up into the living room to get out of his way then come forward a step to focus on Henry and Mother and the phone, which is sitting on the counter under a cupboard some four or five feet to Royd's right.

"You know how to call, Henry?" Mother asks as she sets down a bowl of green beans in front of Royd. She looks worried.

Henry shakes his head.

"Okay, well it's real easy," she says.

Royd laughs.

"Yeah, all you gotta do is pick it up." He takes a bite of chicken.

"Here you go, honey," Mother says, picks up the receiver, and hands it to Henry. He holds it up to his ear and mouth. He looks at Mother. She smiles.

"Is it ringing?"

He nods (apparently, it's just a two-way phone between Mother's and Avery's, and that's what Royd meant by "all you gotta do is pick it up"). Mother walks in front of us and disappears into the kitchen to our left.

Fifteen, maybe twenty seconds pass. We pan back.

"See, I told you. Drunk. Passed out on the couch with that dog I bet."

Royd says these things spitelessly, matter-of-factly, complacently. He takes a bite of chicken and looks up.

"Henry. You can put the phone down now."

Henry puts down the receiver.

"Now you and Mother come on over here and join Maybelline and I."

Finally named, Maybelline forces a rounded tablespoon of mashed potatoes into her mouth. She's cute, in that generic way almost all little kids are cute; her defining characteristic is her wavy brown hair. She looks like Shirley Temple.

Henry and Mother sit down. We return to our spot above and behind Henry.

"Somebody wanna say grace?" Mother says.

"God is great. God is good. Let us thank Him for our food. A-men. All right, listen. I don't know what it is. Maybe, *Maybe*"—Royd points his drumstick at Maybe suggestively— "it's all the festivity, but I been thinkin' it's high time we took a vacation, all together, like a reg'lar family. That is what families do, ain't it? And we are a family, so . . ." Royd takes a bite of chicken.

"We ain't got the money for no family vacation, Royd."

"Don't have to be no big deal, Mother," he says, chewing. He sets the drumstick down then picks up his fork. "Maybe just drive out to Carlsbad Cavern for a couple days. Interstate twenty. Straight shot. Y'all want to go Carlsbad Cavern?"

Royd looks at Maybelline. He eats a bite of potatoes.

"I wanna go," Henry says, forming a full, albeit simple, sentence this time; but Royd does not acknowledge it or Henry; he continues to look at Maybelline.

Maybelline takes the spoon out of her mouth.

"Ahng goh."

Royd drops his fork onto his plate with a clank and wipes his mouth with his napkin.

"Well that settles it then don't it Mother? If Maybe[10] wants to go to Carlsbad Cavern, we're goin' to Carlsbad Cavern. Leave Friday, first thing in the mornin.'"

Royd smiles and goes back to eating. We zoom-in on his face. Contentedly, he stares as he chews through eyes half-closed, as if he's dreaming a happy dream; but our concern, of course, is that his dream will be everyone else's nightmare.

We pan back to our original spot behind Henry and are, unfortunately, left to watch and listen to the four of them eat for some time. There's no more talking, only the super-amplified sounds of utensils hitting plates and chewing and slurping. The

---

[10] Maybe is, of course, short for Maybelline, and that it means *mere possibility* and connotes *uncertainty, ambiguity,* and *indeterminacy* is clearly intended by Noella to be significant: it functions, rather blatantly, as the proposition that, in this film, and perhaps in life, we know very little if anything with *absolute certainty.*

scene is, through these moments, decidedly David Lynchian in the way it anguishes over the grotesque details of human ingestion. Recall the family-dinner scene from *Eraserhead* and the cream-corn-slurping sequence from *Fire Walk with Me*: both are repulsive and nightmarish. This scene, though, is not so much a nightmare as it is just unendurably off-putting.

This scene, this *whole* scene also bears a striking resemblance to the one in *Slingblade* where Doyle, the mother's asshole boyfriend, tries to apologize to Karl, a mentally disabled lawnmower repairman; Frank, an eleven year-old boy; and Frank's mother, Doyle's girlfriend, for being so "assholish" the night before and announces, optimistically, that they're all going to be spending a lot more time together. In fact, it suddenly dawns on me (and I'm a little embarrassed I didn't notice this sooner) that this *whole film* bears a striking resemblance to *Slingblade*; it's so striking, in fact, I think we have to assume that Noella is intentionally referencing *Slingblade* and setting up express intertextual resonations with it on both macro- and micro-levels. I mean, we're in the rural south, we've got the asshole boyfriend or step-dad, we've got a young boy who's being victimized, we've got mental disability, we've got lawnmowers . . . and, looking ahead, in *Slingblade*—if we've seen *Slingblade*— we know that Karl kills Doyle with a lawnmower blade.

R OYD'S DRIVING, Mother's in the passenger seat, and Henry and Maybe are sitting in the back: Henry, behind Royd; Maybe, behind Mother. We're sitting in the back as well, above and behind Henry's left shoulder, in that space between the rear windshield and back deck. There's country music playing over the radio at a pretty good volume. It's Hank Williams' super-breezy and easy-going "Jambalaya on the Bayou." The words:

# ROAD TRIP

appear then fade out. Since our characters are privy to the music, this is not a *true* musical soundtrack moment, but it *is* a musical soundtrack moment *in effect*, a sort of *pseudo-soundtrack*, and, because it's the first of its kind and because it suddenly forces us to try to assimilate this artificially happy environment with the predominately solemn and somber environments that have come before, it feels starkly inapposite and unsettling.

We pan over to Maybe: she's asleep (somehow). We turn to Mother, who's singing along with the song. We pull back to our spot above and behind Henry: Henry's now moving the whole top half of his body forward and backward, subtly but autistically, in time with the music, and Royd's head is tilted to the left, sort of half-lying on his left shoulder. It's a subtle expression but one that some of us will recognize as *strained tolerance,* or maybe *thinly veiled intolerance.* He looks in the rearview mirror; we see his eyes and his eyebrows, and we feel like he's looking at us, but he's looking at Henry, of course.

"All right, that's enough," he says, leans forward, and switches off the radio.

"What? Why Royd? That's a good song," Mother says, looking over at him.

He looks at her; she looks away.

"I told you y'all could listen to the radio, Mother; I didn't say you could wear me down to where I could hardly see straight, okay, because that's what was happenin'."

He looks at the road then back at her.

"Do you want to die, Mother? Do you? Answer me."

"No."

"And do you want your kids to die?"

"No."

"Okay. Well. That's what was fixin' to happen. All of this with your yah-yah singin' and his . . . rockin' back and forth like a retard . . . You see what I'm sayin'? You 'bout got us all killed, okay. Okay?"

"Okay Royd, I'm sorry."

"Besides, Maybe's tryin' to sleep."

Royd and Mother look straight ahead now; Henry looks out his window. Everyone's quiet.

It might've been callow and unsophisticated, but basically what Royd's done here is *gaslighted* Mother (and maybe Henry too); or, it was an *instance* of gaslighting, rather, because gaslighting is *systematic*, or repeated, sabotage of another's sanity or epistemological or moral ground (sometimes, ultimately, to the point of the victim's complete psycho-emotional disintegration). Gaslighting is a favorite tool of psychopaths and sociopaths, who use it, wittingly or unwittingly, to wear down and control their victims. It can be a devastating form of psychological abuse.

In this case, Royd commits the transgression of peremptorily shutting down a perfectly wholesome and innocent good time: we all know that enjoying music together in the car is a natural and important diversion for people when they're on a long road trip, and Royd has just impetuously killed off that diversion. Somewhere down deep, subconsciously, Royd (probably) knows it was wrong of him to do that, but his automatic reaction is not to take responsibility for his transgression, but to unload responsibility onto Mother (and Henry): citing driver distraction and the ostensibly life-threatening situation that entails (an intimidating and effective advertence), he blames *them* for "making him" do what he did, *and* he manages to elicit an apology from Mother to boot: he gets *her* to apologize for *his transgression*; *she* takes responsibility, takes the fall, pays the price, does the time (as it were) for *his crime*. However crudely and unconsciously Royd's done it, and however contemptible, you have to admit, there's a certain (albeit perverted) genius to gaslighting.

We might also be right to suspect that, deep down, Royd is *jealous* of Mother and Henry and of the good time they're having *without him*, that *any* good time of which he is aware and from which he is excluded (or, perhaps, is not the source) makes him feel so viscerally sick and out of control, he's literally *compelled* to put an end to it. I once knew a man who, every time he went to a restaurant and heard people at other tables laughing, would get violently angry; so much so, he would turn and glare and glower at them in a way designed to get their attention and communicate his disapproval and contempt; if that didn't work, he might even get up and ask them to stop, to stop laughing, to stop having a good time (without him).[11]

---

[11] True story.

Henry's and Mother's characters and conditions are somewhat illuminated as well. Henry's rocking back-and-forth to the music does suggest that he might fall somewhere on the autism spectrum. And Mother's humming and singing suggests that she's got a fun-loving side, and when you add this to how much she apparently cares for Henry—recall the scene on the slab in the backyard when Henry spoke for the first time and she was so overcome by emotion—you get what appears to be a good person. On the other hand, we should wonder what sort of character flaw gets her mixed up with a guy like Royd in the first place. Perhaps she struggles with some deep shame (*incest*) which would cause her to think poorly of herself and make her a fitting counterpart to Royd: she'd be the pleaser type; he, the supercilious-autocratic type.

As the sequence of events in the film does (as we predicted) get more temporally contiguous, the characters start to fill out and become more real, or realistic; and as they do, related questions about their individual and collective realities start coming up, questions about how things, in fact, go for these people, on a day-to-day basis. For instance, if they're driving on a Friday, doing Carlsbad on Saturday, and driving back on Sunday, then is this because they are constricted timewise by Royd's work and Henry's school? What does Royd do for work? How does the family get or have money? Where does Henry go to school? Does Henry even go to school? Does Maybe go to school yet? If not, will she go to school? Is school even in session? What time of year is it? Fall? It looks like Texas in the Fall, maybe October. And does the fact that Maybe was delivered at Mrs. Smicker's mean Henry and Emily were delivered at Mrs. Smicker's too? If all three kids were delivered at Mrs. Smicker's as opposed to the hospital, then maybe none of them has been registered as even *existing* by any state or county or municipal recording authority. Does the same go for the adults?

If none of these people are registered as existing, then the school system would never miss them; they'd, none of them, be or have been subject to state and local truancy regulations; they'd, none of them, have been "properly" educated and socialized; and if this is right, then these people can operate in their own really narrow, insular little reality, largely sealed off from the outside world, and they can function pursuant to their own unique, solipsistic "logic." It's a "surreal reality," a claustrophobically *trapped* reality; and, in this way, it's a lot like the nightmare in which the family in *Eraserhead* is imprisoned.[12] But, this trip to Carlsbad stresses the seal and exposes the family and their perversions to the outside world . . . and the outside world, to them.

We are looking out the side window. Noella speeds up the film, both visually and audially. The brown scenery rips by incoherently. We retreat, as if suddenly sick, deeper into the space between the rear window and rear deck and focus our attention inside the car. Movements are swift and minute: Royd's and Mother's and Henry's heads snap this way and that; an arm raises and lowers; and the hum of the car on the highway has become a high-pitched whir, punctuated by the occasional "swiph" of a passing car. The light changes quickly; hours evaporate into seconds. A piercing whistle starts at twilight; Henry's

---

[12]If a story is in some sense the dream or nightmare of the writer, then you have to wonder about guys like Noella and Lynch. The scenarios they depict—at least here, in *Lawnmower of a Jealous God*, and in *Eraserhead*—are so autistically insular, one might wonder if they, Noella and Lynch, are, themselves, somewhere on the autistic spectrum, perhaps Aspergérian—a sense or feeling of, or just an overall concern with *trappedness* is reported by many Aspergérians.

hands shoot up over his ears, and Noella gradually slows down the film as we descend into darkness. The piercing whistle metamorphoses into Maybe crying. She must have been crying for a long time. Mother glances at Royd.

"Godammit," he says, not looking at her. "I *told* you. We left too late. When we go back on Sunday, we leave *exactly* when I say."

There's a cut, and we pull into a place called Big Spring's Lamplighter Motel. It's a two-level job where all the doors open onto the outside. We're in Big Spring, Texas, still two-to-three hours out of Carlsbad.

There's another cut. We're in the motel room. It's dark, but we can see by the glow of the TV. The room is entirely typical: there are two beds, a TV on a squat long chest of drawers, a little table and two chairs by the window; and there's a mirror, sink, and bathroom down the other end. We are in the bathroom area, in front of the sink, looking out at the scene.

Maybe then Henry are in the bed closest to us; Royd then Mother, in the one closest to the door. Maybe's on her side, facing the wall, asleep. Henry is lying on his back, watching TV, a western, blankets pulled up to his chin, his head bent at a sharp angle against the pillow and headboard. Royd is sitting up, in a white t-shirt, blankets up to his waist, watching the western. We walk along the feet of the beds toward the little table and chairs by the window. We sit down in the chair farthest from the door. Mother is under the covers, facing us, asleep.

We watch the western. It's black and white. Two cowboys, an older one and a younger one, are crouched behind some bushes, talking. The older one says how they're going to rob the stagecoach when it comes by; the younger one says he understands, but he's worried they might get killed or caught; so the older one straightens up and says something like, "If yer gonna cry about it, you can just go on back home to yer momma right now": this is *man's* business, and he's *serious* about robbing this stagecoach.

*But look at his fucking little cowboy hat.* How could anyone be serious with him wearing that fucking little cowboy hat? It's so tiny and cute, and the way he's got it cocked slightly to the right on his head just so . . . It's a fucking little party hat and he's the huffy little birthday boy. And I have to wonder (again) if it's just me or is Noella also clued in to this whole cowboy gender dysphoria thing and sometimes trying to highlight it for our consideration. It's like the traditional woman within every cowboy leaks through his exterior in the form of effete sunhats and high-heeled pointy-toed boots. The gun is for shooting anyone who laughs at them . . . fade to black.

THE SCREEN STAYS DARK and there is no sound for some time, perhaps a minute, after which Noella slowly but surely dials up the sounds of our sleepers breathing. One of them moves under the sheets, mewls[13]—it sounds like one of the kids, like Henry—then rakes at the surface of his skin with his fingernails.

Fuzzily, we fade-in on what looks suspiciously like a close-up of male genitalia; the picture snaps into focus, and that is, indeed, what it is: dark pubic hair and a dick and balls lying on a hairy left thigh, obviously Royd's. We zoom-out abruptly (we're still sitting in the chair by the window, as if that's where we slept). Royd is sleeping on his side, in bed with *Maybe* now, and Henry is on his back, under the covers, in bed with Mother: Royd and Henry have switched places in the night.

And with this, suddenly, any and all prior implications and intimations of incest and pedophilia jolt starkly to the fore, and it looks like Noella has delivered us into the darkest territory here, that he's crossed a line, and in so doing, has delivered *Lawnmower* into the company of films like *The Woodsman, The Lovely Bones, Twin Peaks* and *Fire Walk with Me*;[14] but if he has, then he has done so, again, without providing any *direct* evidence that anything nefarious has *actually* occurred because Royd's waking up naked in the bed with Maybe is, of course, not *proof* that an atrocity has *in fact* taken place.

---

[13] Another word I find viscerally cringeworthy, but no other word contemplates the phenomenon: whimper, whine, moan, pule—no word but "mewl" refers to this particular act and sound, unfortunately.

[14] But don't we need to confront these issues? Aren't film and literature and art appropriate venues in which to do so? In addition to courts of law? I don't know; I'm asking you.

Henry scratches at his left shoulder then down on his left arm. He scratches his right arm. Mother moves under the covers. We focus on her. She moves again, mewls, then scratches at her right shoulder. She rolls over onto her back. She scratches at her left shoulder. We zoom-in on her face. Her eyes pop open to the sound of some horns and violins doing that shaky-scary one-note thing, and the words:

# BED BUGS!

appear (in red) then fade out with the violins (the whole thing of which causes me to laugh out loud).

She throws off the covers, and jumps out of bed. We stand up and move over into the corner, out of the way (I'm still laughing). She lifts up the sheets and rifles through them. There are little black dots everywhere.

"Bed bugs! Get up! Come on! Get up!"

Henry and Maybe get out of bed. They have red bites in lines all over their shoulders and arms. Maybe's face bunches up, silently at first, then she emits a high-pitched whine, inhales as deeply as she can, and, finally, bursts out crying. Henry looks at Maybe then at Mother.

"All right, you two get in the shower, right now! Go on. Don't be shy. Get washed up, and we'll get some ointment. Okay, go on, git!"

Henry goes over and gets Maybe, and they go into the shower room.

"Royd. Royd! Get up!"

Royd was awake, just staring blankly at the side of the opposite bed. He looks up at Mother with only his eyeballs.

The shower comes on.

"Where are your *clothes*, Royd? *Why* are you . . .?"

Royd props himself halfway upright on his left elbow.

"Well can you at least get up and go get us some daing oint-ment! *Now*, Royd. We got bed bugs."

"Yeah, yeah." He sits up, his elbows on his knees now. "Just lemme . . ." He looks around absently.

"*Here, Royd*. Your clothes are right *here*, in the corner." She looks at him and points emphatically to a pile of clothes and boots on the floor against the wall between the front door and the long dresser.

"All right. All *right*," he snaps suddenly, raising his voice through his teeth, then he stands up, walks around the bed, takes her firmly by the shoulders (his dick waggling below), puts his face up close to hers, looks her in the eyes, and says, "*Now shut the fuck up.*"

W̲ᴇ'ʀᴇ ʙᴀᴄᴋ ɪɴ ᴛʜᴇ ᴄᴀʀ: everyone's in the same seat; we're in our spot behind Henry, and we're driving on to Carlsbad Cavern, presumably. Everyone stares mutely out his/her respective window; outside, it's flat and gray and dead. The words:

# CARLSBAD CAVERN

appear then fade out. At any given moment, one of our foursome is scratching at her shoulder or arm. Noella gives us plenty of time now to think about what's been happening and to take stock. And we do; we think:

—that the simultaneous occurence of the bed bugs and Royd's bare nakedness is no mere coincidence;[15]

— that while bed bugs are not known to carry disease, *in this case they do*—they are the medium by which the disease at issue is transmitted from one of our family members to the next;

— that since transmission of the disease occurs intrafamilialy and the bugs at issue are *bed*[16] bugs, the disease is incest-based and sexually transmitted;

— that Mother's spurring Henry and Maybe into the shower to, as it were, wash off the disease, serves, ironically, to actually

[15] It's fitting now to imagine the bugs emerging *from* Royd, crawling out in lines, like ants, from all of his exposed orifii, across the bed, and all over and *into* Maybe and everybody else; although, I don't want to suggest that Royd somehow is the *original* source of these bugs or the fountainhead of their family disease, but just that he is currently the most *active*, most symptomatic carrier and that he *represents* the original source of their disease . . . because the actual origin of the disease goes *way* back, indefinitely far back.
[16] The bugs are "du lit," as the French say, or "of the bed," meaning *a consequence of sex.*

propagate the disease because she is initiating, however unwittingly, practices that encourage incestuous sexual experimentation;

— that incest is the key to *both* Royd's and Avery's identities, or characters, and that a, or even *the* critical distinction between the two of them will be the *different approaches* each takes to its commission;

— that Royd's violent reaction to being called-out for being naked and in the wrong bed is in direct proportion to the violent shame he feels deep inside for his incestuous-pedophilic thoughts and deeds (and for the incestuous pedophilia he, himself, probably suffered as a child);

— that it was inevitable that, instead of normalizing things for the Henry household, Royd would make things infinitely more perverse because Royd, it's sufficiently clear now, is a predator with a nose for easy prey;

— that, probably unbeknownst to Uncle Avery and Mother (or Mother just turned "a blind eye"), Royd did, indeed, victimize and abuse Emily, and that's why she's gone; and,

— that Maybe is his next victim.

So there's a kind of tragic, ruined feeling in the car . . . but, inapposite as it is, there's also something ironic and funny going on (at least to us because no one else in the car is laughing): it's the constant scratching. I mean, the fact that the painful silence is relieved by a symptom of the very disease everyone is determined to stay painfully silent *about* is ironic and funny . . . and tragic.

There's an abrupt cut and we jolt whiplashingly to a halt in a parking space way out in the middle of nowhere in the empty parking lot of what we assume is Carlsbad Cavern, the ridiculous choice of parking space recalling Clark's (Chevy Chase's)

idiotic parking job at Wally World in *National Lampoon's Vacation* (1983); the jolting clumsiness with which Noella effects this transition is also funny, in a goofy, slap-sticky kind of way. It's as if Noella felt the need to apply the salve of humor across these otherwise miserable scenes, as if he wanted to say that, even in the worst of times ... perhaps even *by virtue* of the worst of times, funny shit still happens. Royd rips the keys out of the ignition.

"Come on, let's go," he says, gets out of the car, and slams the door. The rest of us just sit there.

We cut to our foursome walking in a loose line through the empty parking lot: Royd's some ten yards in front of Henry, and Mother and Maybe are a good fifteen-to-twenty yards behind Henry and steadily, it seems, losing ground; but, surprisingly, *we* are not enmeshed with them, as we have become so accustomed, but are suddenly detached, walking two rows over and seeing them from the side and from a distance, which, on the one hand, provides us a less claustrophobic place from which to view our subjects, which is sort of a relief, but it also arouses in us a sense of uncertainty, a feeling probably not too unlike the discomfiting sense of abandonment a dependent or a codependent person feels when separated from her group, however cruel they may be.

Speaking of abandonment, Maybe logs the occasional high-register vocalization, or plaintive chirp, and Mother keeps stopping and looking back and telling Maybe to quit dragging her feet and complaining about being left behind and to *just come on, honey, and catch up.*

As if we could stand it no longer, we cut across the parking lot and come up behind Maybe. Noella clearly has us sympathizing and identifying with Maybe at this point. Maybe stops and we stop behind her. Mother stops.

"Come on, honey. *Come on.*"

Maybe starts crying.

"Oh for gooodness' sake."

Mother comes back and picks up Maybe, who's too big now for Mother to carry, and they go on after Royd and Henry like that. We follow on behind them.

Royd and Henry stop and wait for us in front of a yellow-brick one-story building with gold-trimmed glass double-doors. It's the ticket office. As we approach, Royd opens the door on the right and goes in. Henry waits for us to get all the way there. Mother puts down Maybe with a grunt.

"All right, Henry. Go on in," she says, stretching her back.

Henry opens the same door; Mother catches it; Henry goes through, then Maybe, then Mother. The door closes and we're left just looking at it, or at the two gold door handles to be precise, as if we are unable to open a door ourselves, which is funny (again), and sad: we've been left outside, like the family dog, and no one's even noticed.

The door opens, and we are forced aside, out of the way. There goes Royd, then Henry, then Maybe, then Mother. What, are we *leaving*?

No, no. Wait ... Everything looks different. This is not where we were a second ago. We are on *the other side*, the *cavern side* of the ticket office now. There's a sign with an arrow that says "To Carlsbad Cavern," and there's the path ... and now we can see that, because the front and back doors to the ticket office are identical, Noella has been able to cut us seamlessly from front to back without us being the wiser. We turn and hurry off after the group.

We should notice, though, that there was (ostensibly) an interaction with another human being back there, inside at the ticket window, to which we were not privy (because we fell into the gap Noella laid for us at the front door) and that there have been other opportunities on this trip for us to meet people and observe how Royd et al. interact with strangers (for example, at the bed bug motel registration desk or at any gas station or store: interactions in which I, for one, am keenly interested) but from which Noella has excluded us. What then, you may ask, is the meaning of this?

Well, the easy answer—and we discussed this before—is that the interactions that exist in these gaps are simply too trivial to commit time and money and film to, but we might also think that, for Noella, the exclusion of these sorts of interactions is a metaphorical way of saying that *for this family, there are—at least in effect - no other people*, that "the family compound" is not only a physical place back in rural East Texas, but also a portable psychological configuration, or construction, a *stronghold* they take with them wherever they go, which protects them . . . which protects them from other people and their prying eyes and their judgments and their laws, and which protects them from having to acknowledge other people as *real*—because it automatically consigns them to oblivion.

We walk again in a loose line: Royd, Henry, Mother, Maybe, then us—down a dull gray concrete path, down through lustreless yellow-gray hardscrabble terrain, pressed down under a pewterized sky. There's not another soul in sight; it is as if we are the last, the only people on earth. Bereftness and abandonment are *manifest* in this no-mans-wasteland between the ordinary surface world and the extraordinary subterranean one we're about to enter; this is the transitional space that will lead us to *another, our second*, "other world" (because we'd have to be pretty oblivious not to notice the similarities between this scene and the one back home where Henry and we crossed over the bridge and into the forest world on the other side).

And while "crossing over to the other side" does not *necessarily* entail a trip to the unconscious (it could be a trip to a more objectively metaphysical "place," like heaven, death, hell, purgatory, the dark side, etc.), caves and forests are (along with water, darkness, flying) pretty common archetypes of the unconscious, and descending into caves and entering forests often represent the act of entering the unconscious (among other (*obvious*) things); add to this the fact that we're dealing with a central human *subject*, Henry, and his intimate psychological-emotional dealings with his immediate family, and such an interpretation begins to look like a pretty safe bet.

In any case, visits to each, the forest and the cave, should ultimately yield up for Henry (and I mentioned this before too) important information which he can use when he gets back . . . *if* he gets back, though, because there is always a danger that he won't. But it's unclear what not returning from a trip to the unconscious entails. Insanity maybe? I don't know.

You and I can't feel the chill, of course, but we can see it in our family as they hurry along rigidly, hands dug deep into pockets, skipping here and there against the sharp morning breeze. Except Maybe. Maybe somehow manages to meander lackadasically, obliviously, and she quickly falls behind again, and so do we.

It seems Noella's and, by extension, our concern for Maybe's well-being has us shadowing and, as it were, protecting her for the moment, while Henry's masculo-primal desire to explore the cave has him currently shadowing Royd (in spite of everything); and Royd, it would appear, is still aloof and indignant and sulking about what happened back at the motel, which to some of us will look like the window-dressing of a guilty mind. Before too long, Mother turns around, comes back, and picks Maybe up.

Royd and Henry have stopped up ahead in the distance. They are at the edge of something, looking down. Royd goes ahead and descends gradually into whatever it is until he disappears. Henry watches him, then turns and motions for us to come on, then looks down at Royd again, then back at us . . . but he waits. It's strange to see Henry showing so much enthusiasm, so much emotion: he's clearly jacked-up about going into the cave, but he also seems to be in a certain amount of pain, probably some not insubstantial amount of which is being caused by waiting for Mother and Maybe, and us (it seems). We pass Mother and Maybe and hurry on to join him.

Noella's got us so intimately intertwined with this family by now that we half-expect Henry to acknowledge us as we reach him, and we zoom-in on and search Henry's face when we do, but he does not acknowledge us; he continues to look past us, anxiously waiting for Mother and Maybe. So we look past him, and down, and see that we're standing at the top and back of a sunken amphitheater, just beyond and below which sits the massive black hole that is the mouth of the cave. It's an arresting sight: so huge and dark; it's like it's breathing . . . and we are going to go down in it.

Oddly, though, it looks as if this amphitheater has no stage. There are some twenty or so curvilinear rows of stone seating, and there are three sets of steps: two sets running down each side, and one running down the middle; but instead of terminating at a stage, as expected, the set that runs down the middle is intercepted by the set that runs down the left side, is merged with it, then forced down to the right until it terminates at a small landing, which is all the way at the bottom right-hand side of the theater, directly below the right-hand set of steps. My first thought was that it's not so much an amphitheater but a place for meditation, but now I think it's possible that the landing below serves as a small stage or at least a place where speakers, maybe park ranger types, make announcements and dispense information to people before they enter the cave.

Royd has been meandering around on the landing but now steps off of it, starts left down a path, and disappears again. As he does, I experience what can only be called a *gestalt-shift* because suddenly it's plain as day that *the mouth of the cave is the stage*, that the amphitheater is oriented around and designed to direct attention toward the mouth of the cave, and that I was looking at them as two separate things when I should've been seeing them as one. Suddenly, it looks like the Hatch Shell[17] outdoor theater on the Charles River esplanade in Boston, in a general sort of way.

But while it's obvious now that this is the intent, I still can't quite figure out what nature of performance could take place here because from the amphitheater, you can't see anything but *the hood* of the stage, or what *would be* or serve *as* the hood of the stage, and, if there *is* a stage, it is below the horizon of the theater, invisible. But perhaps the point is not vision but audition: maybe music sounds particularly heavenly played from inside the mouth of the cave, and the idea is not to see but to hear . . . to listen and maybe close one's eyes, or keep them open and contemplate humankind's place in nature or whatever. Shit, I don't

---

[17] I thought it was called the "Half Shell"—I think understandably—for years until a grad school friend of mine, who was from Boston, set me straight.

know. What I do know is that, for a relatively educated person, I am feeling pretty stupid right now for not knowing anything about Carlsbad Cavern, its amphitheater, or even caves in general. Though, of course, it should not surprise us that our family has come here entirely unarmed educationally speaking.

Mother and Maybe finally arrive, but we only know this by the audio track because Noella keeps us focussed on the scene below; so, behind us, Mother says, "Whew. Look at that, Maybe. It's a theater or somethin.'"

Henry bolts off down the steps in front of us. We follow Henry directly this time—Noella has us firmly reattached to him; Mother and Maybe will fall behind again undoubtedly.

And sure enough, when we reach the bottom of the amphitheater, Mother shouts, "Henry! Wait!"

Henry and we look up. Mother and Maybe are still at the top of the amphitheater. Mother has put Maybe down but is picking her up again now.

We turn around, step up onto the landing, go over to the railing, and look down. There's a quick cut, after which we see Royd, frozen mid-stride as he walks down a ridiculously tortuous path toward a small black hole at the chasm's nadir, but the scene is destablized and vertiginated as soon as it is presented because Noella immediately pulls the old Hitchcockian Dolly Zoom effect on us: we appear to be zooming in on *and* receding from Royd simultaneously. Henry and we pull back abruptly and, as it were, shake off the dizzying effect, but we keep looking down; Noella then un-freezes the frame, and Royd continues down the twisted path toward the black hole below.

By giving us, his family, the silent treatment and by physically distancing himself from us, not only is Royd (probably) prefiguring the day he *totally* abandons us, but he's also trying to gaslight us once again, especially Mother: by separating off and sulking, he wants her to come to doubt that there was anything suspicious about his behavior back at the motel and to apologize to him for thinking that there was: a tall order, no doubt, but the sucessful gaslighter *always* gets his victim to apologize, to pay the price, to do the time for a crime that he, the gaslighter himself, has committed. And his favorite victim, his most faithful partner in crime is, of course, none other than the *blind pleaser*. A more sophisticated target will see what the gaslighter is up to and understand his attempts to gaslight as just more evidence of his culpability and of his sociopathy or psychopathy.

The black hole below is like a second, smaller mouth, deeper inside the larger one we saw from the back of the amphitheater, so, in this way, it's reminiscent of a fish or a *whale* (because we're so biblically inclined) gullet. In fact, the overall narrative architecture of this place is becoming increasingly anatomical and digestive: the amphitheater is the stomach; the landing, the duodenal sphincter; the tightly-tortuous path, the duodenum itself, or small intestine (the Lombard Street of the human digestive system); and the small mouth below, the ileocaecal sphincter, leading to the large instestine, colon, rectum, anus, etc. It's just weird.

"Whew," Mother says, coming up behind us again; we turn around, and Henry, as if on cue, takes off left, blows past Mother and Maybe, and starts running down the path to the black hole. We stay where we are. "Whoa! Whoa there, mister! You stop right there and wait for me and your sister, you hear?"

Henry stops and turns around, wincing.

"Thank you. Now just gimme one second to catch my breath," she says, steps up onto the landing, carries Maybe over to the railing next to us and, keeping an arm around her, sets her on it. "Ooh, what's down there?" she says to Maybe, and she and we look down.

There's a quick cut, and again Noella freezes-frame and pulls the Dolly Zoom effect on Royd (again) just before he enters the black hole.

"Woo!" Mother says and lifts Maybe up off the rail, back into her arms. We back up, off the landing, toward Henry a few paces, and stop. Mother looks over at Henry. "That scared me," she laughs. "Was that Royd all the way down there?"

"I don't want to go in the hole. I don't want to go in the hole, Mommy," Maybe says, laying her head on Mother's shoulder.

"Oh no, I'm sorry, honey," Mother says, appraising her. "Did Mommy scare you? I'm sorry. It'll be okay. It'll be . . ."

"No Mommy! No!" Maybe says, raising her head up off Mother's shoulder and studying the right side of her face. "I don't wanna go! I don't *wanna* go now!"

"What? No, honey. It's okay. Mommy's right here. Everything's okay. There's nothin' to worry about."

Mother turns away from Maybe and looks at Henry apologetically, but Maybe is still looking at Mother, her expression modulating swiftly from serious and upset to just plain demonic; then her right arm swings back and she punches Mother in the eye; and to make matters worse, instead of recoiling her hand, she leaves it in Mother's eye and claws at it, as if trying to scratch it out.

Mother screams, grabs Maybe under both arms, and sits her down forcefully on the step to the landing. Maybe starts crying and screaming hysterically.

"Jesus Christ!" Mother says. "What're you tryin' to fuckin' blind me? Shit! *Shit!*" She paces back and forth. She stops. "Yeah, you know . . . fine then. Okay? You don't have to go in the hole.

You don't have to go in the fuckin' hole, *okay*? *Jesus*." Mother turns to Henry. "Well go on, then. Hurry up. Catch-up with Royd.[18] We'll just meet you back at the . . . ticket office . . . or the car . . . or *whatever*."

Henry just stands there.

"Well go on, then. Git!"

Henry turns and runs off down the path; we are right behind him.

Obviously, something real and unvarnished has burst forth from Mother here, which is a first for her character . . . no, that's not true: she did show some initiative in the bed bug situation; but still, notice: these sorts of forthright expressions and sacreligious expletives seem to manifest *only* in, or more precisely, *after* the damage of really extreme situations has been done, and even then, they only address the immediate surface aggravations, not the underlying causes of the situations: *after* the integrity of her eyeball is at stake and she is in serious physical pain, she merely smooths things over by relenting to Maybe's desire *not* to go into the hole and to Henry's desire *to* go into the hole; and *after* Royd has disrobed in the middle of the night, climbed into bed with Maybe, and her whole family wakes up covered in bed bug bites, she merely identifies the need for showers and ointment and locates Royd's clothes so he can put them back on. She seems to be in the Sisyphean business of repeatedly setting a runaway train back on track only to have it . . . well, you see where I'm going with this.

Noella, then, is so far painting Mother as the sort of character who suffers from a critical lack of insight and foresight; who lacks the capacity for *proactive* reflection and for obviative

---

[18]Notice again how she calls him "Royd," not "daddy."

and preemptive *control*; who very often merely *reacts to*, and ultimately pretty much *acquiesces to* the desires, reflections, decisions, and actions of others; who seems to exist in a mode of perpetual deference; who is, indeed, as I've said, a *blind pleaser*.

It's a *type*, I think, in lit and in life; and it's an *adaptation*, unconsciously developed by a subject in order to *survive* the abuses or at least hardships delivered upon her in her childhood.[19] Her program for survival is to be obedient, amenable, agreeable, sweet, non-confrontational, non-reflective (even *contra*-reflective), self-abnegating, oblivious, naïve, viscous, a path of least resistance, Pollyanna, and for all this, then also (she can only hope) beyond reproach, beyond responsibility, beyond the angry eyes of guilt or blame or shame, out of harm's way; but if we know any better, then we know that she is, in herself, delusional, and to others, an illusion; that this pleasing presentation is inauthentic and artificial for *at heart* she is not "just the sweetest person in the world"; at heart, she is *no one*, a nullity, a cipher, a zero, absent, empty, evacuated, and for all this, then also an *abandoner*: she has abandoned herself and in the same stroke abandoned those whom she purports to love; and all of this, in the end, means Mother is just a kind of "yes-man": a facilitator, a propagator, an accomplice, an enabler of whatever covert naughtinesses are afoot.

The irony here then of course is that it is *Mother* who is blind, and it's Maybe who is trying to make her see, who is—biblically speaking—trying to remove the log or beam or plank

---

[19] It does seem that the general mechanisms of biological evolution are taken up again as the general mechanisms of social-personal evolution: in both, we are subject to the implementation of adaptations which are tailored in response to conditions present in our environments and which promote our survival therein.

or whatever it is from her eye so she can see that everything is *not* okay, that it's not okay to follow Royd into the hole, that maybe it's not okay to follow Royd *at all*, that she can't be a mother and guide and protect and advise her children or presume to be able to remove specks, motes, or splinters from *their* eyes until she pulls her head out of her *own* benighted ass and faces up to what's really going on, with her, with Royd, with Avery, with her whole family.

Maybe is, or represents raw emotion, intuition, instinct, and we can look at her behavior in Freudian terms: because she is so young, she has not yet developed the capacity to repress, via personality structures like the ego and superego, these bolder dispositions and to construct socially acceptable behavioral artifices in their stead; and, as a result, the cave (as it were) of her [personal] unconscious[20] has not yet been dug and opened for business, and she is not yet properly bicameral, in this sense, for it is the repeated act of repression that digs the hole. It also seems apropos or, indeed, even compulsory to add, while we're on this metaphor of the cave, that, because Maybe is so young, the "cave" of her sexual being is not yet open for business either—*clearly*. So, perhaps her tantrum is the product of the *terror* that accompanies the intuition that her psychological innocence is in jeopardy *and* her sexual innocence is in immi-

---

[20]There are many conceptions of the unconscious: Jung's "personal unconscious" is a slight specification of Freud's "unconscious"—both notions contemplate the containment of an individual's repressed memories, instincts, and desires, but Jung's notion emphasises repressed memories, to some end; there's Jung's idea of the "collective unconscious," which is a sort of an ancestral common memory, complete with universal archetypes; there's the idea of perceptual and reflective unconsciousnesses, wherein perceptual and reflective signals are registered by the organism despite flying below the radar of awareness; and so on and so forth.

nent danger, that soon these "caves" may be forced open and inhabited . . . by Royd.[21]

If this is right, then, back on our biblical interpretation, Royd is, or represents, Satan, the King of Hell, such that now it's just totally apropos that he's going down into a cave because, in addition to being a metaphor for the unconscious and sex or sexuality, a cave is also an insanely common (and now em-barrassingly obvious—I really should've thought of it before) metaphor for the underworld, Hades, Hell; and it just makes perfect sense that *Hell* is exactly where he's taking his family.

---

[21] I apologize for these repulsive images. To write such things revolts me to no end. But these are, I think, the implications of the story, and, however odious, I feel it my duty, at the moment, to explicate them to the best of my ability.

Henry proceeds in fits and starts; he runs, then sort of skips to a stop, then darts ahead a few steps. Then he stops and looks down, down the twisted intestinal path toward the black hole below. The words:

# DESCENT,
# DISINTEGRATION,
# DELIVERANCE

appear then fade out. We hear now—or Noella brings to our attention—the hush of a light breeze, pushing up out of the cave; it is impossible to tell whether it is real or a well-executed sound effect, but, in either case, it is constant, a sort of perpetual exhalation, and, in that, it is the subterranean counterpart to God's massive exhalation at the beginning of the film.

Henry darts off again, but now he's just straight running. We take off after him, and, very much in the spirit of *The Blair Witch Project*, our passage is marked by the discombobulating unsteadiness of someone running with a hand-held camera.

We catch up to Henry just as he reaches the black hole, where Noella has us merge seamlessly with him—so Henry and we are now *one* again, or for the second time—and with this mergence, Noella drops the jarring hand-held camera effect for one where it's as if we are riding in a railway- or mining-car . . . yes, we're riding in a mining-car now, our two hands on the container edge in front of us, travelling at a moderate speed, down the tortuous path, silently at first, but the sounds of the wheels grinding and screeching over the tracks gradually fades-in as we begin to take notice on either side of an increasing number of ancient alien formations emerging from the stone in light as we descend that is less and less from above and more and more from below, from small, variously placed, variously colored artificial lamps, illuminating here and then there a piebald menagerie of twisted needle-toothed beasts and creatures, like a giant sickly green angler fish . . . a jaundiced laughing Buddha . . . a towering blue multi-monster-faced totem pole . . . a forest of bursting red dicks . . . a gaping orange spike-toothed vagina . . . a pink clown face gobbed with cauliflower blooms like cancer all over it when suddenly the grade and speed of the car dramatically increase, a chorus of ecstatic screams erupts and we corkscrew down through a tunnel of blurred streaked lights round and round and round and round until finally the lights and tunnel are gone and we are off the rails just falling and screaming through total darkness . . . fade to silence.

Wow. Well, needless to say, with this, the plane of reality on which Henry has existed thus far in the film is pretty much totally foreseaken for a figurative and fantastic one; it's a radical, material departure for Henry, which alerts us, in no uncertain way, to . . . well . . . not only the central importance of the scene to the interpretation or interpret*ations* of the film as a whole, but also to the potential instability of Henry's personal experience; I mean, if one minute he can be running down the path into Carlsbad Cavern and the next be on some kind of thrill-ride through a tunnel of terrors, the climax of which has him shooting out into deep space screaming, well then I don't know what else to conclude except that he is at least sometimes capable of going completely fucking insane.

But now here we sit in *dark silence* again: a state we will no doubt recall being in at the beginning of the film, after we were spit out of God's mouth and fell unconscious to earth, but it (the dark silence) is different this time because this time we are with Henry—we *are* Henry (for all practical purposes)—and because this time the dark silence is the result of a *second, deeper fall*, not from the sky to the surface of the earth, of course, but from the surface of the earth to the *center* of the earth, the whole cinematic production of which—with its pantheon of archetypes and metonyms, like bursting dicks and toothed vaginas and mining-cars and screaming and monsters and faces and fish and gods and darkness and subterraneity—supports, or is at least consistent with our assumption that our descent into the earth can imply *all* of the following: descent into the unconscious, descent into madness, descent into hell, descent into a grave (or death), a quest for something of great value, vaginal penetration, and, finally, ejaculation, whose concomitant state of being is, of course, ecstatic, orgasmic self-disintegration, or what the French call *la petite mort*.

Screen's still dark, but we can hear Henry's and, ostensibly, our light breathing: in … out … in … out, like we're asleep. Then we hear what sounds like barking, way off in the distance, and then we're running, and our breathing intensifies; the screen's still dark, but we can hear that we're running, through the grass, for a while, then over something hard … and maybe hollow—a bridge, probably the wood bridge over the creek down from Mother's—then on dirt and through brush, probably under the pines on the other side of the creek, the barking getting louder all the time. When we reach the barking, a faint image presses up through the darkness and floats transparently on the surface of it: it's a young girl in a white sun dress, about Henry's age, sitting on a branch in a big pine tree with Luke barking up at her incessantly from below. This has to be Emily. There's no one else it could be. The image and the barking fade. The screen goes dark again.

"I'm usually real good with dogs, Henry," a girl, Emily, says through the darkness. "I'm usually real good with *all* animals 'cause, I mean, well I wouldn't 'a' got very far if I wasn't now would I?" She laughs quickly, nervously. "But *this* dog . . . well I know he's Uncle Avery's and his name is Luke 'cause *finally* Uncle Avery whistled and called out his name and made him come, which, when he did, that's when I jumped down and run—but Luke's got it out for me somethin' fierce, Henry, and Uncle Avery don't keep him penned up, even at night, so he can chase me around whenever he wants to, and I cain't do nothin' about it, cain't go nowheres, cain't git no food or thangs; I cain't git nothin' done, not around here anyway . . . *and then my flashlight broke*. Can you imagine? I knew I shoulda had a extra, and I got a bag of stuff I coulda put it in and everything, but they're hard to find, Henry; you'd think you could find one easy, but you cain't . . . or I been unlucky; but anyway, I dropped this 'un when I was runnin' from Luke, and it done broke on me, so I had to sit for a long time last night in the dark up in that tree, which was hard to climb too 'cause it didn't have no branches down low, but I'm also a good climber now . . . *but you gotta do something about that dog, Henry; you gotta do something about Luke*; I cain't come back 'til you do; so you just do it, and don't worry about how I'll know, Henry, *'cause I'll know when you done it*. I *know* stuff like 'at, Henry, 'cause I reckon you and me is connected. So once you done it, I'll know and come back; and when I come back, I'll have me another flashlight, and I'll give you a sign with it, and then *you'll know* you can come over and find me. Okay Henry? Okay? Henry . . . okay . . . ," she says over and over as Noella fades her out and fades in the sounds of kissing, of wet mouths coming together and apart and together, along with the elevated, desperate breathing of . . . it sounds like adults now . . . and clothed bodies, arms and legs, struggling with each other on a hard surface, an occasional flash of amber light revealing nothing as the whole affaire becomes more and more heated and more and more difficult for us to endure, time no doubt protracted not only by the confounding and repellent, incestuous, almost child-pornographic nature of what is being insinuated here, but also by our participation, our complicity in it—*I mean, we're still Henry*—so it is with considerable relief when finally our attention is drawn through all of this to a noise, like a sharp electronic chirp; it's distant at first, and singular: there seems to be just one source, but the sources and sounds grow steadily, exponentially in number, proximity, and volume; soon, there are not just many, but thousands of them chirping and screaming all around us. We open our eyes: we are lying on our side, looking at a faceless wall of stone.

We stand up into a moving cloud of bats. We duck down to try to get below it. We look around; we are in a massive underground room; there is no one else; we have strayed from the path but can see the path's lights and make our way back over to it; we duck under the rail and run, to the right, then we stop, turn around, and run the other way, the same direction as the bats, toward an opening and a rectangular red light.

The rectangular red light is an "Exit" sign; the black current of bats flows beneath it and through the rounded opening in the rock; we run through the opening and stop behind the wall on the other side. The path leads up to a tiny spot of gray light, must be hundreds of feet above. The bats are flying en masse up to the spot and, apparently, out—this is the way out. We run.

But we're back to seeing via the hand-held camera again (we have been since we got up off the floor of the cave a minute ago), and now we, or rather some able-bodied camera person— maybe even the actor playing Henry, himself—is bumbling and huffing and puffing with it up the arduous path, his labored breathing (it does sound like a young boy) being a big part of the audio track at this point, along with his footsteps and the bats; and you can tell, *whoever* has the camera, that he is looking where *he* is going, *not* where the camera is pointing, that the camera just mindlessly bouncing along in his right hand somewhere next to his head.

All of this, this ascent, goes on and on, turn after turn, (seemingly) without pause or rest, which, of course, conveys (to us, the audience) the undertaking and (presumed) accomplishment of some kind of seriously Herculean feat, or task, which is almost as exhausting to watch as it must have been (or may have been) to execute. But the idea, Noella's idea seems to be that this superhuman level of exertion is consistent with Henry's youth and energy, and with his heightened levels of fear and excitement, that Henry, in this situation, would be able to ascend such a path and reach the top in one, long, continuous effort. And in any case, what does it matter if it's realistic or not?

The light changes gradually as we climb: everything, more and more, is cast in a coat of dull silver-gray; the number of bats gradually increases as well: the rushing sound of their bodies flowing through the cavern, which was at first sublime, is now fully present in our awareness, and the chirps and screams bouncing and echoing off the walls has gone from loud to almost deafening. It's pretty clear as well that Noella has dropped in a phaser on one or both of the these two audio tracks: the flow of bat bodies and/or the chirps and shrieks, but, in any case, the overall sensation is of wind and/or water, flowing from one side to the other: everything around us is whooshing and swirling in a really disorienting way—where all of this, I suppose, is in order to mark or distinguish, dramatically, the transition out of cave-reality and back up into surface-reality: we got the mining car on the way in and the washing machine (effect) on the way out.

As we approach (finally) the opening, we find ourselves running more and more with, or more like *inside* the swarm of bats; they're condensing all around us in order to get through the hole, a classic bottleneck situation. Noella drops the washing machine effect now for really high volume, close proximity chirps and flaps; we can hear the bats actually hitting us now as we run. We run through the bat-thick opening.

On the other side, the bats disperse quickly, and there is much more light and space. We pause. Pneumatically, visually, aurally, physically, we can "breathe" again. We recognize this section of path: we have just passed back through the gullet (where we merged with Henry on the way down), and we know, we can see that the larger opening above, emptying out into sky as it does, is the last.

We take off running again, but this time not as frantically or desperately; it's more like a jog, our footsteps, less frequent; our breathing, less labored. The path is still steep, but the straight-aways lengthen and flatten out; the massive horde of bats is still screaming overhead, but there's so much more room now, and with all of us on our way out, there's a real sense of decompression and impending freedom.

When we reach the last straightaway, just at the base of the amphitheater, we walk. There is a tall stone wall to our right, preventing us from seeing the amphitheater, but it quickly decreases in height as we approach the landing. When we're just in front of the landing, we look up to our right and see: the amphitheater is filled with hundreds of people now. We stop and, as we turn to face them, we vacate Henry for a position just in front of and below him, where we see, directly above and behind his face and head, a tremendous, dense flush or gust of bats blow up out of the chasm with a kind of echoing crack, turn as one, and scatter into the dusky sky; the audience gasps then erupts in applause, which continues unabated as Henry stands, freeze-framed now (by Noella), basking, as it were, in adulation, and we start going in circles around his head, looking at him, at his face, frozen in a bleary sort of ecstasy. Then we start to rise, up, up, straight up, until the applause is gone, Henry is gone, and—but for the occasional bat—we are up in the darkening sky alone. We hang there in the sky like this, pointed west at the horizon, watching the sunlight fade down and the starlights fade up, then we wheel around to the east and fly.[22] Fade to black.

Screen's still dark, but, after a few seconds, it sounds like we're back inside the Buick, driving down the road. We can hear the engine and the tires, the occasional movement or sniffle. The car slows down . . . the turn signal clicks on . . . the car stops. It makes a turn then speeds on for a minute. It slows down again, almost to a stop, makes a turn, this time onto a gravel road, and our eye opens.

We are, indeed, back in our spot in the Buick, on the deck beneath the rear windshield, just behind and to the left of Henry's head. It's still totally dark out, but, we can see by the headlights, we are on the access road leading to the house. The crunching of the gravel and the jostling from the uneven road wake up

---

[22] Thanks again to drone technology, no doubt.

Mother. She draws a deep breath and extricates herself from the crease between the seat and the door. Henry, we can see, is awake. Maybe's asleep.

"Get up," Royd says. "We're home."

"I'm up, Royd," Mother says.

We bear left, illuminating the house somewhat.

"What the fuck?" Royd says, leaning forward.

"*Royd, please.*" Mother says.

"Henry. *Henry.* I thought I told you put those 'coon guards on them garbage cans before we lef'."

"I, I did," Henry says. "I *did.*"

"Bull*shit* you did. What the fuck is all that then!"

Just ahead, in the headlights, in front of the garage, there's garbage, strewn all over the place, and there are two garbage cans lying open on ther sides.

Royd shakes his head.

"It's just one goddamn thing after another with you, isn't it, Henry?" He pulls the car up in front of the house and puts it in park. He looks at Henry in the rearview mirror. "Okay, I don't give a shit what time of the mornin' it is, you're gonna get out there and clean that shit up, right now. You hear me?"

"Yes," Henry whispers.

"What was that?"

Henry looks up at Royd in the rearview mirror.

"Yes," he says matter-of-factly.

AS OPPOSED TO *plot*-wise—which we'll get to in a second but with the somewhat revised understanding that plot discussions, or discussions about *why* what happened happened and the *meaning* or *meanings* thereof, are *actually* subject to a certain *inexhaustability*, and thus it was sort of silly for us to worry *at all* that the "big reveal" early on in the film might spoil everything—it should serve us well at this point to make sure we understand, generally speaking, *what* just happened, that is to say, *story*-wise, or *narrative facts*-wise, and *what* just happened, generally speaking, is this:

Henry, on his descent into the cave, went into some kind of fugue state, wandered off the path, passed out behind an outcropping in one of the Cavern's massive "rooms," *for hours* it seems (because they arrived at the Cavern in the morning, and Henry emerged from the Cavern at dusk), had an encounter (of some sort) with his missing twin sister, Emily, during which she: (i) yammeringly[23] informed him that she had come back to see him but had had trouble with Luke, (ii) basically instructed him to *kill* Luke, and (iii) made out with him—then he ran up and out of the Cavern with the bats, at some point over the course of which we have to assume that Royd, Mother, and probably Carlsbad Cavern people too started looking for Henry so that when he reappeared at the base of the amphitheater (during what we now know was a scheduled bat-viewing), he was spotted, gathered up, and debriefed (to whatever extent possible); after that, they (our family), we can only assume, got back in the Buick (Royd, furious; Mother, inconsolable), drove all

---

[23] Yammering on as she does when telling Henry her Luke story is consistent with Aspergerian speech in many situations. It's often the case that Apspergerians are either yammering on about something that interests them (and no one else), or very much shut up in silence and non- or low-responsiveness.

night (some eight hours), and got home at around three or four o'clock in the morning only to find the area in front of their house bestrewn with domestic garbage.

So correct me if I'm wrong, but I think that pretty much captures it story-wise. But now *plot-wise* we want to ask: What does it all *mean*? *Why* is all this in here? What is the point, purpose, or function of all this? And we get a whole bunch of responses, or possible answers, some (but of course not all) of which I can lay out for you here, in roughly chronological (to the story) order.

"Descent, Disintegration, Deliverance"—the idea here is, I think, that before Henry *descends* into the cave, he is one person; that as he descends, that "original" person *disintegrates* or is deconstructed; and that through the introduction to, and knowledge (however partial[24]) gained from Emily *and* through the accomplishment of the (Herculean) *task* of ascending back out of the cave, he is . . . or at least starts the process of reconstruction or *deliverance in earnest*, or, to put it simply: he starts to *grow up* in some *material* way. And if you go with the Christian notion of "deliverance," you mean that he is being *delivered* out of the darkness of falsity and/or evil and into the light of truth and/or good . . . with regard to some significant aspect or aspects of his life-situation.

---

[24]For instance, Henry *knows* that the encounter with this girl is momentous and historic for him, but even if he has a vague intuition, he does *not know*—yet—*exactly or explicitly* who she is or what she wants, ultimately: she does *not* give her name or explain to him that she is, *in fact*, his twin sister, Emily; and he has *no idea* what the amorous act, the kissing, is all about: it is, for Henry, the utterly unitiated, just the tip of that infinitely more complex iceberg. And, of course, the dramatic irony here is that *we know* all this stuff and Henry doesn't.

We might also acknowledge a resonance (or intertext) with the 1972 John Boorman film *Deliverance* (based on the James Dickey novel by the same name), in which a kind of chubby man-boy, Bobby (sublimely played by Ned Beatty), is *delivered* into the truth of manhood, which, ironically, involves murder and some heavy-duty lying, which is to say that in order for him to *survive*, into *true* manhood and *at all*, he will have to commit or be party to the commission of murder, and he will have to lie, deftly, to the police, about said murder. Both of these interpretations make *Lawnmower* (as I may have mentioned once before) a kind of *Bildungsroman*:[25] a "novel" dealing with a young person's psycho-emotional, spiritual, etc., education as he passes into adulthood or manhood. But now, whether adulthood turns out to be a paradoxical (and perhaps mad or insane) place where it is true or good or best to murder and lie is another, further question.

We'd be remiss if we neglected to add that when we start talking about a person or an identity: an "I," or a self, *distintegrating*, or de-*construct*-ing, and then re-*construct*-ing, the implication, or at least the suggestion, more generally, is that the self is a *construct*: it is something that is built and can be dismantled and rebuilt, that it is, in other words, revisable, changeable, impermanent, plastic, ephemeral, transient, non-essential, and the like, and that the common idea that the self is some sort of redoubtable monolith of permanent essence is an illusion. And we'd ... well, those of us in the know would have to be pretty blind *not* to see here a material similarity between deconstructive thought, or Deconstructionism, and Buddhism,

---

[25] German word, means *building story*—usually involving a male, sexist as it is.

particularly Buddhism's notion of *anatman*, or the doctrine of *non-self*.

We've already mentioned that this scene seems to represent a second, deeper fall, such that what we have here is a sort of "second falling," and with that notion, I can't help but think of "the second coming," or rather a *revised* notion of "the second coming," you know, where here comes Henry, this really weird, perverted second Jesus; or, even better, here comes *Emily*, this really weird, perverted, *female* second Jesus because, after all, *she's* the one who, in this story, has just promised to come back a second time, once Luke, the dog, is disposed of. But so again, Noella is blending ideas found in Deconstructionism and Buddhism with ideas from Christianity: it's all mixed up and, in this way, also very postmodern.

In any case, the structural similarities or parallels with the beginning of the film are clear, including the moments of "dark silence" that Noella has us, the audience, experience prior to the commencement of the action, and I can't help but liken those dark silences to moments of meditation, where, in keeping with what we were just saying above, meditation (diligently practiced) can be a vehicle for *change*, both physical, i.e., in the actual physical circuitry of the material brain; and mental, i.e., in the sorts of thoughts one has and behaviors one exhibits or undertakes. We . . . who we are is not set in stone.

That Henry is conveyed into the depths by a mining car is a ham-fisted but nevertheless effective (and sort of fun) metaphor, trope, figure, sign, whatever, that Henry is *mining* for something of value. Of course, he doesn't know what that something-of-value is; he's just following his nose, as it were, but we know that the "ore" here is consititutive of, is some composite of: (1) backwards-looking stuff: lost unconscious epistemological material, or memories, having to do with his long-lost sister, Emily; and (2) forward-looking stuff: unconscious, instinctual sexual material, which, surely, will play a big part in his transition into manhood. It is important, though, to see that the backward- and forward-looking stuff are in a sort of dialogue or dialectical relationship, where the memories and the sexual knowledge that comes with them will, very likely, feed or fuel or motivate Henry's future behavior, his particular aims and pursuits. My guess is that, when we resume the action back at home, Henry will exhibit new focus.

As we descend into the cave, images of the unconscious are obvious, with the sexual ones: the bursting penises and toothed vaginas, and the diseased one: the cancer-faced clown—sticking out the most, at least to me; to me, they indicate Henry's desire for and fear of sex, his fear of disease (be it associated with sex or not), and his fear (and, perhaps, desire[26]) for death. Our ejaculation after deep penetration is . . . well, just that.

And Noella's decision to have us *see as* Henry, *to be* Henry for most of the scenes in this series is a right and effective one because it helps us feel closer to him, to better or further identify with him, a main character who otherwise speaks very little and to whose interior voice (if any) we do not have access.

Those images that distinguish our descent are also frightening (or they're *supposed* to be); they're surefire indicators that we are, among other things, on a trip to, or at least through Hell; and with that, it would be hard *not* to draw a parallel between our story and Dante's *Inferno*, right? Where Hell is a place for

---

[26]There could be a Freudian thanatic element here, a sort of let-me-just-get-this-shit (life)-over-with-already kind of feeling. It's not exactly suicidal; it's far short of suicidal. As Freud suggested, such a feeling could be a part (however occasional) of all of us . . .

those who reject the way of the spirit for one of the appetites and violence. It's pretty clear by now that Royd will be quite at home in Hell, but our hope, I'm sure, is that Henry is just passing through as a part of his educational journey: so he can learn to recognize and identify evil when he sees it (going forward), and so that he can reject it on his quest to be, and to defend good. But given Noella's apparent fondness for ambiguity, it's doubtful things will be so black and white; more likely, paradoxically, Henry will somehow do both: defend the good and right *and* take up violent and appetitive behaviors . . . and speaking of appetitive behaviors, let's turn to incest.

Incest repels most people, but it does so with an equal amount of attraction or draw; this, our *repulsed fascination* with incest, has pretty clear analogues in the compulsions many of us have to gape at car accidents, road kill, or other forms of tragedy and death, including horror movies. We squint our eyes or look through our fingers at shit that scares the bejesus out of us—but we look all the same.

Why? Well, there's certainly the *thrill* . . . and the *catharsis* of our worst and most outrageous fears . . . a kind of *exorcism* of those demonic fears and possibilities maybe. And of course incest has the added draw of being about *sex*, and if it's not also rape or pedophilia, then it's not nearly as bad as torturing and murdering someone, right? It'd be a lesser crime than killing someone, right? I mean, as long as it's not also pedophilia or rape, the worst thing about it (beyond it's just being taboo) seems to be the ostensible biological-genealogical insult or violation (the intuition of which explains maybe *why* it's taboo); but this only applies if a baby is produced, right? I mean: no incest-baby, no biological-genealogical harm, right? I don't know; I'm asking you.

Anyway, Emily and Henry's "moment" down there in the cave resonates with and, I think, confirms, or at least corroborates, or supports, other, or rather *all of the other* possible sites of incest in the film because the cave, I think, is also the subconscious of the *film*, of the narrative *itself*, and any activity therein presents us with a paradigm, an *archetype* for our family's behavior across this narrative world. Indeed, recall how, while Emily and Henry are kissing on the cavern floor, Noella has us hear the sounds *adults* would make, kissing on the cavern floor. So, this archetype functions atemporally, as if all the incest events of the narrative/film take place without regard to time: past, present, and future—or cotemporally, as if all the incest events of the narrative/film take place at the same time.

Either way, the point is, or at least the *theory* is that this ubiquitous familial-psychological archetype, *incest*, programs or, like a disease (a miasma), spreads out into and affects, invisibly and insidiously, unconsciously, every key player in our narrative, in our family, such that . . . well, we already *know* that Mother and Avery had an incestuous relationship, but if we think that there was incest between Royd and Emily[27] and Royd and Maybe, then there almost certainly was or will be; the enormous and critical difference being, of course, that any incest between Royd and Emily and Royd and Maybe would also have to be—necessarily, because of the involvement of an adult and a child—rape and pedophilia;[28] and any incest between Mother and Avery could *not*, of course, have involved

---

[27]Though, in this case, of course, the incest would not be biological, but only [il]legal—Royd not being Emily's biological father.

[28]This, again, I know, is horrible stuff, horrible subject matter, and I apologize; but, again, it may also be stuff that we ought deal with, come face-to-face with . . .

pedophilia—because the two participants, as twins, would always be the same age—and, given the film's portrayals of Avery and Mother (thus far), any incest between the two of them very likely did not involve rape either . . . at least not by Avery of Mother; in fact, it's an interesting question here actually because, given our theory and Emily's sexual aggressiveness in the cave just now, we might be justified in thinking that if there was any rape between Mother and Avery, then, contrary to our (albeit empirically justified) prejudice the other way, it was by Mother of Avery. Is that possible? I mean, assuming she didn't physically restrain him or otherwise blackmail him or something, could she have *coerced* him, even *raped him* by mere or sheer sexual aggression? What if he's mentally disabled and she's not? I don't know; again, I'm asking you.

Whatever you decide, one thing, or rather two things we can probably all agree on are that (1) *Lawnmower* is, among other things, a "descent story," and (2) there are *a lot* of descent stories. The Ancient Greeks call this business of descent "katabasis," meaning, appropriately enough, *to go down* ("kata"—down; "basis"—to go), and they, of course, use the term to describe situations, common enough in their myths and stories, when a central figure goes down into the underworld for one reason or another; but I guess one thing the term doesn't capture or contemplate is the oft- (*but not always*) undertaken *return trip*, where, as we have said, the central character returns not empty-handed or with nothing to show for it, but *with* something, be it knowledge or some accomplishment.

I can't help but think that katabasis in myth and story just echoes or is isomorphic with or is maybe even caused by the experience of katabasis in our everyday lives, especially when we broaden or generalize or liberalize our idea of "down" (and

I think we should) to include not just trips literally *down* to somewhere, but also (as we discussed earlier) trips *across* or just *over to* somewhere and back: simple departure and return; and where, moreover, these don't even have to be just *physical* trips: we depart from and return to *mental* places too, all the time, and when we return, *something* has changed by virtue of the experience of the trip and the time it took to take it.

In any case, Jesus goes down, or departs, and returns; humans (in Christianity) are said to have fallen only to go back up in the end (if all goes well); Zarathustra, Odysseus, Aeneas, Dante: they all go down and come back up. Who else? Orpheus. Orpheus goes down to the underworld, Death, to get his lover, Euridice, but fucks up and looks back, which obliterates her, but he still returns with something . . . some knowledge, like, *Fuck, I really shouldn't have looked back: I really should trust and heed the wisdom of the gods and not look back next time!*

And, like Orpheus, Henry goes down and hooks up with his "lover," Emily, seemingly in order to bring her back to the surface world so she can be with him; but, unlike Orpheus, Henry's lover is *his sister*, and, unlike Orpheus, it looks like he's managed *not* to fuck it up because he doesn't look back on the way out or commit any other sort of no-no; rather, he completes the Herculean task of running out of the cave with the bats with flying (as it were) colors. *Although*, of course, lest we forget, in order to clear the way for Emily's *second* or *true* return, he *will* have to complete the additional Herculean task of killing or otherwise doing away with Luke. So, I should think it's safe to say, to predict, that we will see Emily again in due course up on our surface-level reality, but where the questions then will be: Does she exist only epistemologically for Henry, that is, only in his mind, or is she really, metaphysically there for anyone to see? Or does it matter?

Going back to the bats, though. Probably the first thing that comes to mind when we think about bats is vampires, and vampires mean blood-sucking, preying on others, nocturnality . . . *evil*, in a word; indeed, some call the bat "the bird of the devil" (though a bat, of course, is not a bird, but a mammal). And this interpretation makes pretty straight-forward sense in our story, does it not? Royd is the devil; the cave, his primary (metaphysical) residence; and the bats, the denizens of his lair. It's true, too, that vampire bats drink the blood of cows and horses, and of the occasional human (though technically they do not suck, but lap the blood from surface of the host's skin after tearing it), which, there's no sense in denying, is predatory and parasitic and just pretty fucking horrifying behavior; so, it's no wonder bats, or at least vampire bats have come to represent evil. But most bats just eat insects or fruit.

What a lot of people don't know is that bats *also* represent death & rebirth and super-powers of perception. Bats often indicate the "death," or end, of something and the "birth," or beginning, of something else (vis-à-vis whatever the relevant subject matter is, be it a person, a town, a country, a planet, whatever)— where I guess the analogical reasoning is that bats are "reborn" from the "belly" of the earth at the end, or "death," of each day; *and*, bats often represent the ability (usually in a human) to perceive in a *way* that most other humans cannot, and to perceive *things* that most other humans cannot—where the analogue, of course, is echolocation: a unique perceptual ability to locate objects in space via reflected sound attributable to bats and dolphins but not to most other animals, at least not to the same degree.[29] And it should come as little surprise that our Henry character rather snugly accomodates these two more benign interpretations: in him, the boy is starting to die away as the man is being born, and Henry is also showing signs of having a superpower of perception, one that allows him to see in a way that others cannot and to see things (namely the light, Emily) that others cannot.

So, the metaphor of the bats here goes both ways (as it were) simultaneously: viewed with one eye through the Royd-lens, bats are or mean or represent evil; viewed with the other eye through the Henry-lens, they represent growth, change, unique perceptual powers, things we commonly think of as good. This sort of ambiguity, I understand, can be disconcerting; still, I feel obligated to point out that bats aren't the only metaphor to bat (as it were) for both teams, the good and the evil.

Snakes, for example (and surely there are others), with their predatory sneakiness, fangs, and poison, are, as we know, frequently recruited by the forces of evil; but, their sort of overall "penis-ness" can imply fertility and birth, which we usually associate with good; and, of course, their sloughing-off-of-old-skin-for-new clearly implies birth, rebirth, self-transformation, and self-healing, all of which we habitually associate with good. So, it looks like we have no choice but to conclude that such metaphors are *deictic*, their interpretations not fixed, but dictated by context and perspective, or point of view.

A natural next question—and you can see how this plot or, at least, plot-related stuff can just go on and on and on—would be: Well then what about good and evil themselves? Are they

---

[29] Because humans and probably other animals can echolocate to *some* degree; I mean, I can hear that a car is coming from behind me on my right without turning around to look, etc.

deictic? Or, more precisely, is whether some *thing* or *act* good or evil wholly determined by context and perspective? But, in the interest of getting out of this cave and back into the cinematic action, I'll spare you.

So, on our way up and out of the cave, I count six (I may have missed some) optimistic signs: (i) the bats, which we've already said represent (for Henry) rebirth and a super-power of perception; (ii) the "washing machine effect," which suggests cleansing and restoration; (iii) the up-and-out, or liberating, trajectory of Henry's *physical* movement, which corresponds to the up-and-out, or liberating, trajectory of Henry's *mental-spiritual* movement; (iv) the completion of the seemingly endless run up and out of the cave with the bats, which equates to the successful achievement of a kind of Herculean task; (v) the rousing (albeit miscontrued) round of applause from the large and approving audience; and (vi) our, the camera's and the audience's, release out of Henry, up into the sky because it's not insane to think, at this point, that *we, the audience,* have come to be, or at least have come to act as, or stand in as, Henry's spirit, his mind, his newborn reflective capacity, his capacity for conscious thought, his internal voice.

And, finally, the garbage scene. First, the garbage: we are lead to believe—and *perfectly reasonably*—that racoons are responsible for the garbage being all over the place in front of the house, but given Emily's story about being chased into the tree by Luke, etc., and Henry's seeing a light across the creek (a number of episodes back), *and* just how narratively and metaphorically fitting it would be if *Emily* were the one to "expose all the family's garbage" (i.e., all their *dirty little secrets*), doesn't it make *at least* as much sense that *she* did it, rummaging for food, as the racoons?

Granted, she could *not* have been down in Carlsbad Cavern, physically, *and* physically back at home *at the same time*, but I think Noella made it pretty clear that she was *all in Henry's head* down in Carlsbad—I mean, he was clearly in some kind of seriously altered mental state when he was down there with Emily, right? And if she *was* all in Henry's head in down in Carslbad, then, of course, *she could have been* physically back at home at the same time, and that is, indeed, exactly what is implied by her story: that while Henry and family have been on their trip to Carlsbad, she has been back at home, has been chased into a tree by Luke, has left the area, and sent Henry a sort of telepathic transmission or dream-message or something, apprising him of all of this and requistioning him to get rid of Luke.

*Now*, this does *not* mean that this is, *in fact*, what has happened, that Emily *was*, in fact, physically back at home, etc., because *everything* she does and says could be the product of Henry's imagination; but she *could've been* . . . she *could've been* physically back at home.

What's more, *without* this uncertainty, or ambiguity, about who or what spilled the garbage, the scene is not nearly as meaningful and compelling or beguiling, and its inclusion in the film as a whole, not nearly as sensible. Perhaps this is a case where the story is transitioning from something more straightforward to something more fantastic, and this scene captures a moment where our more straightforward logical expectations, that the racoons did it, and our more fantastic narrative expectations, that Emily did it, collide . . .

Second: the Joyce-ian Yes. At the end of *Ulysses*, as Molly Bloom's long internal monologue rises to conclusion, Molly expresses, in spite of everything, a longish series of yeses that culminates in a final, resounding, capitalized Yes. It is a Nietzschean Yes, and, like the brackets, or arms, of absolute value, it functions to affirm *everything* within its embrace. Henry's Yes at the end of this section is just this sort of Yes. It's the Yes of *being*, speaking through Nietzsche speaking through Joyce speaking through Molly speaking through Noella speaking through Emily speaking through Henry speaking *to* us, so we know that, Yes, Henry is going to step up to it now, whatever it is, Yes.

Screen's dark, but we can hear the TV going. The narrator, a woman, is talking about dogs, dogs that run obstacle courses (we note: Henry is a sort of dog running an obstacle course). The word:

# PICKLES!

appears then fades out. Pickles, the narrator tells us, is the best in the business, the fastest, most accurate, most focused, most adroit competitor on the circuit today, and the gold medal winner two years running of the World Dog Obstacle Course Championships in Honolulu, the Super Bowl of dog obstacle course competitions. There's barking, the image snaps on abruptly: it's Pickles.

Unexpectedly (I guess because I had no idea what to expect) and disappointingly, Pickles is an unattractive, smallish, black tousled mop of a thing. His little barking fit, it's obvious, has been induced by his owner (who's dangling a doggy treat at Pickles just off camera) and inserted here by the director for us to misconstrue as an affirmative response to, and confirmation of all the glowing things the narrator has been saying about him, a sort of "Yeah, that's right! I'm the best!" type boast, but where it's been pre-interpreted and presented to us in that really simple happy dog kind of way that's hard to criticize. The whole thing makes me existentially sick.

We break free from our forced up-close-and-personal, face-to-face encounter with Pickles and the TV and zoom out until we take up a position at the back of the living room, at the border of the living room and the dining room. Henry is lying on the couch against the wall to our right; Royd is sitting in the Lazy Boy to our left, and Maybe is standing directly in front of the TV, jumping up and down.

She turns to Royd, points at the TV, and says, "I want Pickles, Daddy! I want Pickles!"

We look at Royd as he looks blankly at Maybe . . . for a good five seconds too, which feels like a long time and is kind of funny because suddenly Royd is *every parent*, caught in the "I want a puppy" trap; but again, Noella puts us in that weird position of having a nice, sympathetic moment with an unsympathetic, evil character. Then, as if a mere blink of an eye could result in time-travel (yet another—I've stopped counting—gap in time), we cut and jolt unceremoniously into the next scene, in which Royd, Maybe, Henry, and this dog (which looks suspiciously exactly like Pickles from the TV just now) come bolting through the front door, the dog leading the way (we're still standing in the same place but have turned forty-five degrees to our right so we're looking down the hallway). Mother, prompted by the sudden commotion, says, "What the . . ." from the kitchen behind us.

We track the dog: he races down the hallway toward us then breaks off into the living room, where he stops, extends his forelegs out in front of him into the classic dog "ready position," and barks psychotically at us (i.e., the camera person), trying to get us to play or do something, but we don't respond;

so he waggles up to us, barks sharply, and jumps . . . he jumps up and down, barking at us at the apex of every jump. He stops jumping and looks up at us, but still: nothing. He drops down into the ready position again. He darts from side to side, from ready postion to ready position, looking up at us expectantly each time: still nothing. Then, in what appears to be an act of confused desperation, he turns around in circles a few times and fires off toward Mother in the kitchen, but as soon as his paws hit the linoleum, he (of course) skitters out of control and slides into a chair (Henry's chair) at the dining room table and there is a great commotion as the dog scrambles and worms frantically to extricate himself from the chair and right himself but only skitters and slips and falls some more and . . . he's pissing . . . he's pissing now. Now he's pissing and skittering and slipping and falling all over the kitchen in piss, tracking and whipping piss around all over everything.

"All right, no! No!" Mother hollers at the dog then looks past us, at Royd, who must be in the living room behind us. "What the heck is going on here, Royd? Whose dog is this? Huh?" I guess Mother was out of the house or otherwise not privy to Royd and Maybe's decision to get a dog today. "Well somebody put the thing in the backyard. Now! And get me a towel."

It's not uncommon to see, in the middle of a film or narrative like this, a lighter episode or an episode designed to serve largely as comic relief follow hot on the heels of a heavier, more dramatic episode, and that's what Pickles, both the dog and the episode, are doing here: they're largely post-high-drama comic relief. Which is not to say that there's nothing else here; there is: there's Noella's and our insidious sympathy with Royd, again; there's the continued equation of Henry with dogs; there's Royd's ongoing patronizing of Maybe (to some ignominious end, we're sure); contrary to Emily's mandate down in Carlsbad, there's the *addition* of a dog to the situation instead of the subtraction of one; there's the literal and metaphorical presence in Pickles of a chaotic free radical run amok "inside the house," or *inner sanctum*; there's Mother's persistent inability to prevent the development of objectionable or untoward, unseemly situations . . . There's *a lot* going here, a lot being sustained and perpetuated, but none of it, it seems to me, is as important as tension diffusion and comic relief. As said, it's not an original sort of writerly or directorial move, but it *is* a timely, thoughtful, considerate, audience-sensitive one; it shows Noella's got his viewers' best interest in mind: it shows that *he* knows that, right now, his viewers need a little break.

I T'S NIGHTTIME. Royd is sitting in the Lazy Boy; Henry is lying on the couch; Pickles is lying on the rug in front of the TV, and *The Dukes of Hazzard* is coming on: it's a sort of Rockwellian portrait of the good life in the American south in the late twentieth century, except it's pretty obviously meant to be satirical and condemnatory. The words:

# THE CALL

appear then fade out as Waylon Jennings[30] sings the Dukes' theme song: "Just the good ol' boys, never meanin' no harm . . . " and Bo and Luke Duke: (i) "yee-haw" their way down rural "Georgia"[31] backroads in "The General Lee,"[32] (ii) fly through the air and jump over shit in same, (iii) slide (Luke does) across the hood of same in order to expedite getting in same, (iv) shoot an outhouse with explosive arrows,[33] (v) ogle and grope their own buxom, red-bikini-clad cousin, Daisy; (vi) get admonished at the breakfast table by their Uncle Jesse, (vii) easily foil the

---

[30] Jennings is also the series' narrator.

[31] It's clearly not Georgia, but California.

[32] Their red, confederate-flag-bedecked stock car.

[33] The outhouse, of course, explodes, constituting what the producers, directors, and everyone else involved in the production of the show obviously knew would be, for the audience, a really provocative and pretty much one-of-a-kind TV intro moment because the audience had no choice but to wonder: *Why the fuck would they do that? What if there was someone in there? If there was—justified or not—wouldn't this have to be one of the most horrible and disgusting representations of killing someone, ever?* And, as I understand it, the producers made fans wait until season 1, episode 6 to find out that the boys were only using the outhouse for *target practice*, that it was *unoccupied*, and that Luke had shot one of his "dynamite arrows" *by mistake. But still, wouldn't it have rained down piss and shit like nobody's business?*

moronic local law enforcement guys, Cletus and the inimitable Roscoe P. Coltrane, and, of course, (viii) confound the double-dealing county commissioner, Boss Hogg.[34] The whole thing of which is so brutally and painfully stupid, it would be difficult, I think, not to see it as the centerpiece of an indictment against the Henry-type household, the South, the United States, the 1970s . . . against all of us, all of humanity, even because . . . well think of it this way: if the Nazis reflect negatively on all of us because a bunch of people, just like us, substantially similar to us, took up and embraced a *totally evil* thing, then *The Dukes of Hazzard* reflects negatively on all of us because a bunch of people, just like us, substantially similar to us, took up and embraced a *perniciously stupid* thing, right?

I mean, this is, of course, assuming that:

(1) all people are *indeed* substantially similar—but they are: all people are beings that fall under the category *human being,* the organizing concept of which requires that all its constituents be just that: substantially similar;

(2) a bunch of people did *indeed* take up and embrace the *The Dukes of Hazzard*—but they most certainly did: it was an extremely popular show; and,

(3) *The Dukes of Hazzard* is *indeed* a perniciously stupid thing—but I don't see how it couldn't be: *The Dukes of Hazzard* seems as demonstrably perniciously stupid as the Nazis were demonstrably totally evil—but I understand that in just asking you to look and see for yourself how perniciously stupid *The Dukes* is, you might not see anything perniciously stupid at all, but something harmless and funny and the like.

---

[34] Who eats three raw livers for breakfast every morning.

So probably the best, most dispositive way to show that *The Dukes* is truly perniciously stupid is to come up with a list of criteria, which we can all or most of us agree on, for what makes something perniciously stupid, or, even better, for what makes a *TV show* perniciously stupid, and then show how nicely *The Dukes* matches up. Now, I'm not going to go into any real detail here, but a good list of criteria could go something like this:

> A TV show is perniciously stupid if it is written, directed, and acted in a manner befitting someone who has suffered some material cognitive insult and if it endorses, approves, sanctions, or promotes sexism, misogyny, racism, violence, destruction of property, and/or ignorance, including but not limited to educational ignorance, social ignorance, cultural ignorance, logical ignorance, and so on.

And it's not hard to see, if you know anything at all about *The Dukes*, that the show squares up pretty precisely with this (albeit admittedly *ad hoc*) list—at least that's my humble opinion.

This is *not* to say, however, that I think we ought to prohibit or censor in any way such shows, but perhaps only that we should clearly rate and label them with a "PS" for *perniciously stupid*. I realize that with some cross-section of the public this will backfire, generating even more interest in such shows; still, it would provide notice of content and allow people to make an informed decision.

Another non-dispositive but, I think, really interesting way to see if you think *The Dukes* is perniciously stupid is to take *the shame and embarrassment test*. Like their close relative, *guilt*, shame and embarrassment provide sure-fire indications, subjective psycho-emotional indications that we perceive something to reflect negatively upon us and that we are taking on or shouldering, to some notable extent, responsibility for its badness or stupidity. When I accidentally fart in public and people hear it and know it was me, I shoulder responsibility for the foolish act and am embarrassed; if I were to drive drunk and kill someone with my car, I would shoulder responsibility for the bad act and feel shame. Both of these examples pick out the simplest type of case: one where *I* am the agent in question, and I am ashamed or embarrassed by something I did because I am *directly* responsible for doing it.

But sometimes I feel ashamed or embarrassed by something bad or stupid some *other* person or persons did, that is, I shoulder some responsibility for something I am *not* directly responsible for. In such a case, my shame or embarrassment is *indirect*, or *vicarious*, where the theory is that I feel ashamed or embarrassed because, as a human being, I am substantially similar to, and belong to the same type of animal as the one that actually did the shameful or embarrassing thing, which is basically just saying that I am ashamed or embarrassed *by association*. For instance, *even when it's someone else who farts aloud in public,* I still feel a *real pang* of embarrassment because he or she, the actual agent, has suddenly exposed the facts that it really could have been any one of us, that we human beings are animals that fart like this, and that I, too, am one of those animals.

Likewise, *even though I have absolutely nothing to do with him or his supporters,* I feel ashamed and embarrassed when Donald Trump speaks (or Tweets) to, or on behalf of the United States *and people support him* because that shows that we—including me of course—are an animal that can and does support *dangerous morons*; and *even though I utterly condemn them and what they did,* I feel shame when I think about the Nazis and the many people who took up and embraced them because that shows that we—including me—are an animal that can and does commit and support the commission of mass murder; and *even though I had nothing to do with its production*, I feel embarrassed when I see scenes from *The Dukes of Hazzard* and think about how many scads of people loved and probably still love the show because that means that we—including me—are an animal that can and does love perniciously stupid shit.

So the question is: *Do you?* Do *you* feel ashamed or embarrassed by *The Dukes of Hazzard*? Because if you do . . . well you know the rest of it.

We cut to a fairly close-up shot of a telephone, but we can still hear the TV going in the background. It's the phone on the counter in the kitchen, near the dining room table. We are given time to study it, the phone, and as we do, Noella fades down to zero all audio tracks, including the TV, forcing us to focus on the phone in an audial vacuum. The phone is a big, plastic, beige, obtuse-looking thing. We hear the sound of someone taking a deep in-breath, then the phone rings explosively.

"Good Lord!" Mother says as her left hand and arm reach into the screen (from our left), pick up the handset (she's been standing in the kitchen this whole time[35]), and pull it off screen, where (invisible to us because we're still looking at the fat base of the phone and the now taught curly-cue cord) she says,

"Hello . . . Hi, Avery . . . Good. How are you? . . . Well that's good . . . No, what's on your mind? . . . Mm hm . . . Mm hm . . . Yeah . . . Yeah that's . . . that sounds like a great idea, Avery . . . Mm Hm . . . Yeah, I think it will . . . Mm hm . . . Okay then. I'll send him up first thing in the morning . . . Mm hm. God be with

---

[35] Like Mother is the archetypal *mother*: an invisible ever-presence, unperceived but nonetheless always there, in the domicile of consciousness.

you. Bye-bye." Mother sets the receiver down in the cradle and we cut.

It's daytime now, morning presumably—and it does look like morning: the light is morning light, Fall morning light to be exact: it's more sideways and thin. We are floating along just above and behind Henry's left shoulder as he walks down to Uncle Avery's across the grassy open space between his house and Mother's. Noella amplifies the light crunch of Henry's shoes in the grass.[36] There are no cicadas (they are not active during the cooler months), which is nice, a relief, because without them, everything feels decidedly less agitated and insane.

But there's something moving in the distance, down by the creek. It's a dog. Its head pops up. It's Luke. He's spotted Henry, and us. He barks and comes running toward us. Henry picks up the pace; we pick up the pace. Luke adjusts the angle of his approach and increases his speed. Henry starts running; we follow suit, joggling along behind him with the camera. Henry is running hard for Uncle Avery's now, trying, presumably, to get through the open gate and behind the chain-link fence that goes around his backyard, but he doesn't make it.

Luke overtakes him just outside the gate, tackles him really (he's a big dog), then straddles him and licks wildly at his face and hands; Henry squirms and shrieks—it's hard to tell if he's laughing or crying. Suddenly, unfortunately, Luke's hips contract over Henry's right upper thigh and buttock in that unmistakable involuntary way . . . they do it again—Luke's overstimulated; he looks worried, helpless—they do it a third time, a fourth, a fifth . . . he's dry-humping Henry ardently and in earnest now.

---

[36]Probably another clue that Henry is on the spectrum: sensory supersensitivity is often reported by those on the spectrum.

This is, of course, hard to take on a couple levels: I mean, nobody, or at least most people don't want to see a dog hump anything, much less a human—the implications of bestiality are just too deep to tolerate; but it's also disconcerting, when we see something like this, to wonder if maybe love and affection in animals, all animals, including humans, almost always automatically leads to sex, that love and affection are but the instruments, the tools, of a deeper, instinctual, evolutionary motive to copulate and propagate the species, whatever species that may be.

"Goddammit, Luke! Stop that! Luke! No!" Avery yells.

We pan back quickly. Avery's backdoor slams shut behind him as he hurries down to the scene, but despite his admonitions and impending arrival, Luke continues to hump Henry, his (Luke's) expression evolved now to one of singular determination, of dogged commitment to seeing this thing through. Avery swings his right boot into Luke's chest; Luke yowls and sulks away, still humping, auto-humping the air.

"Party's over, Luke!" Avery says. "Now go on! Git!"

Luke slinks solicitously back toward Avery, whining, his pelvis still contracting involuntarily. Avery makes to boot him again and says, "I said git the *fuck* outta here!"

Luke runs away sideways some ten or fifteen yards, stops, and drops sulkily into the grass.

"*Jesus*," Avery says then turns back to Henry.

Henry is in a tight ball on the ground, on his knees now, in the fetal position, rocking backward and forward, like the simple essence of humping has been transferred from Luke to him; Avery stands over him in his blue gas station suit, looking down at him, his fists resolutely on his hips, like Superman.

"All right, come on now, Henry. It's over. You can get up now."

Henry doesn't move or respond. Avery kneels down beside him and puts his hand on Henry's back.

"Hey . . . Luke wasn't tryin' to hurt you, son. He just a dumb dog. He don't know what he's doin'." He laughs.

Henry still doesn't respond.

"All right," Avery says, taking Henry by the upper arms, "come on, let's get up. Here we go."

Avery gets Henry stood up.

"Okay now? All good?"

Henry nods weakly.

"Okay, but now look, Henry. When that kinda thing happens, you got to show the animal who's boss, like I did. Kick, yell, punch . . . whatever you got to do. Hey, anything 'cept just take it like a sissy, know what I mean?" Avery laughs.

Henry nods weakly again then sniffles.

"All right, well, come on then. We got work to do," Avery says, puts his arm around Henry's shoulders, and leads him through the gate into the backyard.

We float over the fence on the long arm of a small crane or boom and set up, not behind Henry, but facing him and Uncle Avery, who has let go of Henry and put his fists back on his hips.

"All right." he says, "as you know, I had spoken with your mother last night, and we reckoned you'd be inter'sted in mowin' my yard. For money. Now. You can use my mower. You don't have to brang your 'n' up here. I got one. So whenever I want you to mow, some ever two weeks or so dependin' on the season, I call your mother and set it up, then I'll set the mower out here in the backyard and you can come up here and mow it. Understand?"

"Yes sir."

"Now, can you count?"

"Count?"

Uncle Avery looks off toward the creek, squints, then looks back at Henry.

"Yeah, you know. Count. One, two, three, four. You got to be able to count money if you're gonna be in the lawnmowin' business, Henry. So you don't get ripped off."

Henry just stands there looking at the grass.

"All right. Don't worry 'bout it. Whenever you come up and mow, I'll show you how to count the money."

W E ARE IN A DARK ROOM, watching, from a few feet away, a boy, an actor we've never seen before, sleep; but it's no mystery, not this time, who this actor represents because—and we all recognize this immediately—this scene is a deliberate, albeit modified, reiteration of the scene that initiates Part Two: Labor. The words:

# PART FOUR
# INSULATION WORK

appear for a few seconds then fade out. Indeed, the employment of the word "work" here is also a *modified reiteration*: of the earlier-enlisted word "labor." The word "insulation," on the other hand, is entirely new; but still, its use here should not come as a *complete* surprise because, in *discourse-time*, which is also *audience-experience-time*, barely five minutes have passed[37] since we were watching an episode in which our family's perverse secrets were radiating out all over the place, and so it just makes good sense *now*, discourse- and audience-experience-wise, that Noella would have our family—probably especially Royd—doing some remedial "insulation work"—to try to keep whatever was in, *in*; and whatever was out, *out*, from now on.

Henry is sleeping on his back, his head set squarely in the center of the pillow, his body entirely under the covers, which

---

[37] In *story-time*, or *character-experience-time*, three to four years have passed. For more of this sort of stuff, see Gerard Genette's sometimes stultifying but truly seminal narratological work, *Narrative Discourse*.

are pulled up nicely under his chin and everywhere else uni-
formly undisturbed, as if he's been made-up with the bed . . .
or dead. The arrangement is decidedly artificial and funereal.
Slowly, we move in closer until we're right up on him, right
up in his face. He's around fifteen-sixteen now, so we have just
vaulted over another multi-year gap. We watch him sleep close
up like this for quite some time. He . . . everything is perfectly
still and silent, except for the light in-out hiss of his breath.

"Get up," Royd's voice irrupts into the darkness as if he's
been standing right behind us all the time, or even as if we *are*
Royd right now because Henry's eyes snap open, he turns his
head and looks directly into the camera, directly at us, implicat-
ing us as the source of the voice, which marks a(nother) first:
Noella has put us in postitions of sympathy vis-à-vis Royd, but
never, until now, has he made us *consubstantial* with him . . . in
the same way he's made us consubstantial with Henry.

Needless to say, it's a provocative move . . . and pretty dis-
quieting. It's almost offensive, to be wholly identified with or
*as* Royd like this, but I feel certain that Noella's putting us in
Royd's shoes *can't be* to imply that we are, *all of us, somehow,*
pedophiles too; no, that would be absurd and just plain stupid
really because it's so outrageously false. We have to assume that
Noella is not fool enough to make such a patently erroneous
accusation as this . . . of his *whole audience*, both actual and potential, which is to say, *all of humankind*. So why does he do this
to us?

Well, on the one hand, it's a good way to generate tension
and suspense, to take hold of us, emotionally, and make us
squirm in our seats a little bit, right? Because we don't want to
identify with Royd or see things from his point of view: he's an
asshole, and he's evil, and what if he does something illicit? On

the other hand, Royd *does* have a perspective in this world, like it or not, and maybe Noella feels like he needs to explore it with us, in earnest (though hopefully within the bounds of decency), in order to do his due dilligence (as it were); and, it suddenly occurs to me, it would be entirely consistent with this hypothesis if it were to turn out that "insulation work" is, quite literally, what Royd does for a living. There are shades of Faulkner here; specifically, *As I Lay Dying*, where every character, *however despicable*, is allotted a number of chapters in which his or her perspective is explored—come to think of it, there are shades of Faulkner cast all over this film.

"Get up, put your blue jeans and a long-sleeve shirt on, and meet me in the kitchen," we say.

Henry stares past us emptily. He blinks a few times.

"Right now," we say.

Henry pulls the covers down, slides his legs over, lets them drop off the side of the bed, and tips upright.

We turn. A larger, older Maybe is asleep in the other bed (she must be about eight now). We walk toward the door and into darkness.

When we fade back in, we're positioned just over Royd's left shoulder (i.e., de-merged from him) as he sits at the kitchen table, eating a bowl of Cheerios (with milk and a spoon). Customarily, of course, we have been positioned just over *Henry's* left shoulder, so it would, indeed, appear as if we are attached to, and focalised through Royd for the moment, perhaps for this whole episode, or chapter.

Royd (looking older now too, but the same actor) goes at the Cheerios lustily: he slurps; he chews with his mouth open; he drives the back of his spoon down hard against the bottom of the bowl, producing a loud, nerve-jarring, metal-to-porcelein *dink!* each time he goes back for another bite; and each time he puts the spoon into his mouth, he hits it against his back molars in such a way as to create this intra-oral, metal-to-teeth sound that no description or imitation could sufficiently capture, but which is, I can assure you, utterly spine-tingling. This could be a very long and painful episode, one over the course of which we *really* come to know and hate Royd *intimately*. He has, however, left the milk and cereal on the table for Henry, and he's set a bowl and spoon at Henry's place.

Henry emerges, almost materializes out of the darkened hallway.

"Come on sit down. Breakfast's ready," Royd says.

Henry sits down. It's going to take a minute for us to get used to this new, older, teenaged Henry. He's taller, of course, but not *tall* by any means, and he's thin: wiry, not robust, build-wise. His skin and hair are browner than the previous Henry's, though his hair is cut in the same way it's always been, basically a bowl ... it's a little shorter now actually. And he's not un-hansome, although he wears a kind of detached, motionless, *e*-motionless facial expression, like a mask, which is consistent with both being on the spectrum and being inured to life in Hell.

Henry takes the Cheerios and pours a bowl full. He pours in milk. He picks up his spoon and eats like a normal person. He eats quietly and inoffensively.

Royd drops his spoon into his bowl, sits back in his chair, and looks at Henry.

"You know what blowin' insulation is?"

Henry was about to put a spoonful of Cheerios in his mouth, but he stops, puts the spoon down, and stares at a spot in the middle of the table, out beyond his bowl.

"No sir."

"Well, you know it's my job, *right*?"

"Yes . . . yes sir."

"Well look. A man's got to have him a trade, okay, and this one's mine. It's important 'cause it helps people keep their houses cool down here, 'cause it's so hot, you understand?"

"Yes sir," Henry says.

"Not to mention it puts food on your plate."

Henry starts to eat again.

"So what I do is put insulation into the walls and attics of people's houses, so when they turn their air-conditioners on in the summer, all that cool air doesn't just disappear out of the house."

Royd pauses, maybe to give Henry a chance to say something, but he doesn't.

"Here, look," Royd says, sitting forward. "*Look.*" Henry stops eating and looks obliquely over at Royd, who has formed, over top of his bowl, a kind of crude box with his hands, but where the fingertips of his two hands stay about an inch-and-a-half apart from each other, as if he's holding a large invisible potato. "It's like a ice chest, see?" They both look at Royd's hands now, and we, too, have moved around the table to our left to see Royd and his hands better. "The stuff they put in the walls of the ice chest is insulation, okay. It's the stuff that keeps whatever's inside cool."

Royd looks up at Henry for confirmation and sees that Henry's interest in his hands, or in the box he's formed with his hands, has increased, so Royd looks back at the box too, considers it, torques it a little bit.

"So you see what I'm sayin'? The insulation is . . . " Royd stops and looks at Henry again: Henry's still staring intently and abstractly at the box, still very much in its thrall. Royd looks back at the box for a few seconds.

Then all at once he turns his hands into claws, flashes them at Henry's face, and shouts, "Henry!"

Henry shudders and jumps in his chair, his face open in a silent scream, then he shrinks and turns away; we swing quickly back over behind Royd. Henry looks retracted, sheepish, ashamed.

"Jesus Christ, Henry," Royd laughs. "Jeez Louise." He shakes his head. He looks at his watch. "All right, come on now," he says, pushes his chair back, and stands up. "Finish up, let's go."

We are reminded here that real, material growth, change, edification, evolution, transformation, etcetera, take *time*, that, while important and substantial metamorphoses are *definitively initiated* at watershed moments like the one we had back at the end of the "Descent, Disintegration, Deliverance," they *develop by degrees* and are not *fully realized* until somewhere way down the temporal stream. This is not to say that Henry has not come along at all since that watershed moment; he has: his good table manners, for example, which are evidently really important to Noella, indicate progress; and not only that, they point up a distinct but discreet realm in which Henry can diverge from and perhaps even safely (subtly) contradict Royd. *But*, it's also painfully clear that Henry is still very much terrified and cowed by Royd.

And he was *absolutely petrified* by Royd's monster-in-the-box trick just now; so much so, it's easy to picture Noella telling Henry (the actor) to get, you know, *completely lost in the box, man, just totally autistically mesmerized by it*, but then intentionally *not* telling him that the box is going to explode into a monster in the end—that's how genuinely visibly scared shitless Henry looked. But there's nothing mysterious about the monster-in-the-box metaphor here, or anywhere: it stands for *hidden evil* (it's hard to see how it couldn't); it obviously applies to Royd; we'll see if it applies to Henry; and, indeed, why should we be surprised to find ourselves thinking that it applies to Mother, Avery, Emily, Maybe, and everybody else in the world (us included obviously) because maybe we all cultivate hidden monsters . . . of at least one sort or another.

But so *beyond* this well-worn, even worn-out (but not necessarily untrue) stuff, what else? Is there anything else we can say about the box and, more specifically, about Henry's captivation with it? Well, it's easy to see that a "box," generalized as *an enclosed space*, is the greater conceptual category of particular consitutent things, like caskets and caverns . . . and *wombs*. And with that, with *wombs*, I suddenly realize that I failed to make the cavern-womb connection back there in "Descent, Disintegration, Deliverance" because—*clearly*—Emily and Henry curled up together in the cave is a modified reiteration of their time together in Mother's womb; and it makes sense that Henry would be captivated by something (the box) that reminds him, consciously, of Carlsbad and Emily, and, subconsciously, of Emily and the womb.

And finally, if we think Henry falls somewhere on the autism spectrum, then it also stands to some reason that he would be drawn to enclosed spaces (like caves) and thus, also, by extension, to things that *represent* enclosed spaces (like Royd's hand-box) because people on the spectrum struggle with sensory over-stimulation, and enclosed spaces provide them a lot of relief in that regard. It's important to note, however, that people on the spectrum *have to be in control* of these enclosed spaces, primarily over their ability to get *out* of them, to not be *trapped* by or in them; otherwise, they go nuts.

Temple Grandin's self-huggie machine comes to mind immediately: the self-huggie machine is a contraption which Grandin, a famous Apsergerian, designed and built herself: you crawl into it, on your hands and knees, and pull a lever that draws in the padded but firm sides of the contraption around your body for a "hug," the intensity of which you control by how hard or softly you pull the lever. Grandin's revolutionary invention for herding cows through tight spaces in a way that doesn't cause them to feel trapped and to panic also comes to mind and shows her, an autistic person's remarkable, visionary insight into the importance of *comfort and control* for animal consciousness (and we are all animals of course). So the idea here would be that, in staring at Royd's hand-box, maybe Henry, too, is enjoying Aspergerian visions and insights into ways he might someday gain comfort and control in his life.

We cut to Henry and Royd in the Buick: Royd's driving; Henry's in the front passenger seat; we're in the backseat, behind Royd. We drive in silence down a dark green road (I say "dark green road" because the vegetation along the sides of the road is so remarkably thick and tall and dark green). We drive to a corrugated metal barn and park in front it, to the right of a glass door. Affixed to the front of the barn is a large hand-painted wooden sign that says "East-Tex Insulation" in big red letters; there's a phone number, and there's a cartoon-type picture or scene painted on there, as well, of a smiling white man in blue overalls and a blue cap shooting a series or stream of pink balls out of a fat beige hose at the yellow sun; one of the balls (the first one shot out of the hose) is (already) partially eclipsing the sun; and the pink balls are evidently being fed into the hose by a reddish-pink rectangular machine, which comes up to about the worker's waist and completely obscures his right leg. His left leg is out in front of him a little bit, under his hands and the up-angled hose, fireman-style, for support.

"Wait here," Royd says, switches off the car, pulls the keys out of the ignition, and we cut.

We pick up as we're coming through the front door of the building, wholly merged with Royd again now: seeing with his eyes a narrow, dimly-lit hallway, at the end of which there is light angling out of a partially open door; and hearing with his ears the Bee Gee's tune "Stayin' Alive," coming (evidently) from the room behind that door. And because all ordinary walks are magically transformed into groovy struts by "Stayin' Alive," we groovily strut down the hall . . . which is totally ridiculous . . . and yet another example of *having a good time* with (or as) Royd.

At the end of the hall, we stop, and, in a directorily affected way (the way one will recognize from horror movies), we push open the door very slowly, revealing, by degrees, a fluorescently lit, windowless white room . . . with, on the back wall, a wooden sign that says Wall of Keys, under which hangs an array of what look like car keys . . . a large metal desk, with a binder on it, on the corner, open and facing the door . . . a pen, on the desk next to the binder . . . a swivel-chair behind the desk, twisted just so, so that its last inhabitant could get up and out . . . and there it is, over on the other side of the desk, near the wall, a grey, medium-sized, dual-speaker, radio/cassette jambox.

In keeping with Royd's musical anhedonia, the first thing we do is walk over and turn off the jambox, which, of course, terminates "Stayin' Alive" and categorically and unceremoniously disproves its principal (and probably only intelligible) claim.

Then we go back to the wall by the door, to a grey punch clock we didn't see, find our punchcard from the array to clock's left, punch it in the slot just below the clock, replace the card, and turn our attention to the binder on the desk, which we can see now is open to a sheet of paper on which the date, FRIDAY, JULY 8, 1983, is handwritten in pen at the top in blue block letters. We turn the page. The next page says MONDAY, JULY 11, 1983, at the top. Down the left side of the page, also handwritten in blue pen, is a loose column of names: Anders, Belton, Gorman, Jones, Wall, Wuthrich—and to the right of each name, there is another name and an address. To the right of Belton is the name Caldwell and an address: 12 FM 254, Craig, which we stare at for a second.

We initial above Belton then go over to the Wall of Keys, remove a set, hang our keys in its place, and go. Immediately to the left of the door to the room, or, I guess, office we were just in is another door, which I didn't notice before; we go through it and out into a really large, cavernous warehouse and garage: there are hundreds of bags of what must be insulation shelved along the far wall; there's a truck up on a service lift in the middle; there's automobile maintenance and repair equipment along the back wall; and lined up along the near wall are a bunch of what must be insulation blowing machines and hoses: they are the things that Blue Overalls Guy, from the sign outside, is using to shoot insulation balls at the sun.

And suddenly it makes sense, metaphorically and hermeneutically speaking: Blue Overalls Guy is Royd; he's Royd disguised as a good-natured cartoon character, who is, you know, *funny*—and we've seen a number of times now how Royd can be funny—but what he's really doing or, rather, *also* doing is, of course, blotting out the light of the world (the "sun") and blotting out, or annihilating, Henry (the "son").

We walk down the left side of the warehouse-garage, out the back door, and into a parking lot, where there are a number of white vans and pick-up trucks, all of which say East Tex Insulation on the side with the phone number. We go up to one of the trucks (the one that matches the set of keys we picked off the Wall of Keys presumably) and look in the truck-bed: there are a bunch of bags of insulation, a blower, and a couple of hoses. The truck appears to have been pre-loaded. We get in the truck and start the engine.

We cut to Royd and Henry inside the truck, driving. We are no longer merged with Royd (which is an actual *physical* relief), but sit between him and Henry. Royd is turning the wheel to the right, onto a gravel access road, and we can see now, just ahead, surrounded by a bunch of oaks, an old, all white colonial-type house: two-story, doric columns, ample front porch. We pull up in front of the house, facing it at a slight angle, and Royd puts the truck in park. The air outside, over top of the hood, is shimmering with yellow bands of gas and heat that distort the house into bleary waves.

"Wait here, and don't . . . *do anything*," Royd says then opens the door. A seething chorus of cicadas floods into the cab. Royd gets out and we follow.

This time, though, notice: Royd's left the car and a/c running for Henry—which was very thoughtful of him: a move, no doubt, designed by Noella (who *is* good with these sorts of subtleties) to, once again, further his campaign to complicate and problematize and destablize any absolute, or all-or-nothing, assignments of good and evil we might be making, consciously or unconsciously, about Royd or anyone or anything else in this world for that matter.

We follow Royd up the steps and onto the porch and stand behind him to his left. There's a screen door then a regular door. We ring the bell. After a few moments, a little old lady cracks open the regular door.

"Yes," she says through the crack. "Who is it?"

"Good morning, ma'am," Royd says in the super-rehearsed manner of a service- or salesman. "My name is Royd Belton. I'm from East Tex Insulation, and I have a work order for insulation this morning for a Mrs. Caldwell at twelve FM two fifty-four in Craig. Does that ring a bell?"

"What? Oh. Yes, of course," she says, still peaking through the crack, her left eye and nose and cheek all darkened and distorted by the screen. "My son, Randy, he was here last week, and he was up in the attic, lookin' for this and that and God knows what, and when he come down he said there wasn't no insulation up there, that it's just wood and wind and whatnot, and to call you . . . well *he* called you because he said if he didn't, then all the cool air from the air conditionin' down here would just keep leakin' out from up there, and my 'lectric bill'd keep, well, goin' through the roof, which I guess it is, and I'd keep bein' hot, which I am."

"Yes, ma'am, Mrs. Caldwell. It is Mrs. Caldwell, isn't it?"

"It is," she says, continuing to eye-ball us fishily through the crack and screen.

"Okay. Well, that's why I, or *we*"—Royd points backwards with his right thumb toward the truck—"me and my assistant, are here, and we can definitely help you with that. So, would it be all right if we pull the truck up a little closer and come in and take a look?"

She pokes her head through the door a little farther to see the truck then retreats again and says, "I know it looks like I ain't got no manners, talkin' at you through the door like this, but you understand, after the whole thing with my son and the 'lectric bill, which he pays for—he's over in Longview now, but he pays all my bills, bless his heart—but I don't want to hear about it from him no more, you know what I mean? So I'm just tryin' to keep the cool in." She stares flounder-eyed at us for a few long seconds, then we cut.

Now we are, all of us, including Mrs. Caldwell (who is, indeed, quite petite), up on the second floor landing of the house, just at the top of the stairs, standing around a wooden ladder that drops straight down out of a trap door in the ceiling, down to the red carpeted floor. This puts us in *another* situation where Royd's about to lead us into the dark mouth of some enclosed mystery space that represents (among other things) the unconscious, lost memories, old secrets, madness[38]; only this time, we're not going *down* into this space, into a capacious cave, but *up* into it, into a cramped, claustrophobic attic; this time the mystery space promises to be hot and uncomfortable, not cool and pleasant; this time we'll be working, not vacationing; and this time, we're not going to *explore* the space and *free* any entities existing therein, but *seal* it up and *trap* (via the "insulation" and the "trap" door) whatever might be in there. And if you happen to be thinking right now that what we have on our

---

[38] Recall Bertha Mason, the madwoman in the attic of Rochester's Thornfield Hall in *Jane Eyre*, and Mrs. Allardyce from the 1976 film *Burnt Offerings*—to name just two. And, by the way, I saw *Burnt Offerings* when I was nine, while spending the night at a friend's house—my parents would've never allowed me/us to stay up late enough to see such a thing; I was too young and too innocent to see it, and it has haunted me pretty well ever since.

hands here is yet another instance of *modified reiteration*, you'd be right.

"Well go on then," Royd says to Henry. "We got to git up in there and assess the situation." Royd looks at Mrs. Caldwell, who smiles inanely as Henry starts up the ladder. Royd climbs up next; we follow.

The attic space is in your typical A-shape, elongated but compact, so you can't stand up all the way in it, and there's bric-a-brac strewn all over: a couple of old suitcases, some bar stools, a coffee table, lamp, etcetera; there's the heater/air-conditioner unit: a large silver metal machine, humming; and it's true, there's no insulation: it's all bare wood beams and boards. Down both ends, air vents, with wire mesh covering them, open onto the outside. We're all squatting around the open trap door, facing one another. Royd directs himself and his voice down through the trap.

"There a light up in here, Mrs. Caldwell?"

"Light?"

"Yeah, yes ma'am, a light, a light switch?"

"Light switch?"

"Yes."

"Well I ain't never been up there."

"Right," Royd nods. "Okay. Don't worry about it then."

"Want me to call Randy?"

"No. No thank you."

"Randy was just up in there, so Randy'll . . ."

"No, no," Royd interrupts. "That's okay, Mrs. Caldwell. Nevermind. We'll find it. And we can see anyway, so . . ."

"You sure? 'Cause . . . well I don't want to call him, but I can. He's at work, but I can call him."

"*Jesus*," Royd whispers to himself then aims his voice back down the hole. "No. No need to call Randy. Don't call Randy. Thank you."

"Okay."

Royd looks around.

"All right. First thing we gotta do is get all this shit down outta here," he says, indicating the bric-a-brac.

"You boys want some water or somethin'? Tea?"

"*No.* Thank you. Mrs. Caldwell. Nothin' for us right now. That'll be all." Royd shakes his head.

"You sure? I can make some tea . . ."

Royd does not answer this time; he just stares blankly into the space in front of him.

"I'll make some tea."

Royd looks down through the trap door, watching Mrs. Caldwell walk away presumably, then he turns to Henry.

"All right. Pop quiz. What just happened?"

Henry looks off, away from Royd.

"Hey. Come on now. Look at me." Henry looks obliquely at Royd. "What'd I do? I just did somethin' to, you know, *de-fuse* the situation, to *neutralize*, if you will, what you might call a *difficult* customer . . . *Well say somethin', goddammit.*"

"Nothin'," Henry blurts. "You didn't do nothin'."

Royd eyes Henry peevishly.

"So what are you sayin', Henry? Are you saying I didn't *do* nothing, or I *did* somethin', which was nothin'?"

"You did. You did somethin' which was nothin', Royd."

"Hm. Mm hm. And what was that, exactly?"

"You, you didn't *say* nothin', you didn't *say* nothin' when, when the lady asked if we want tea."

"Okay. Then what? Then what happened?"

"She, she stopped talkin', and, and she went away."

Royd stares at Henry; Henry continues to look only indirectly at Royd, like a dog that's waiting to get beat . . . or somebody with Asperger's. They're both sweating profusely; their faces are rolling with sweat, and the fronts of their shirts are already soaked through. Royd turns and looks down the length of the attic.

"After we get all this shit outta here, we're gonna have to hoist the blower up, up in here with us. Ain't no way around it. Blower's loud, and we're gonna need to be in eye-contact at all times, so I can tell you when to feed it and shut it off." Royd looks back at Henry. "Hey. This is *man's* work. You cain't mow yards for a livin' like some fuckin' Mexican," he says, and suddenly I feel like I can see *through* the scene, like it's a palimpsest to *Noella's* dad, in real life, informing the young Albarb that he *cannot make movies for a living* and that he needs to *get a real job and become a doctor or a lawyer* or something.

We cut to the truck outside where Royd and Henry are struggling to get the blower out of the flatbed, but it's clear after a few seconds that Noella has switched directorial gears for the moment, from longer single-shot scenes to short clipped montage, so we're suddenly getting that, you know, quick, efficient, pretty much cubist rendering of aspect after aspect of Royd and Henry's labor: as they're struggling to drag the blower across the flatbed, Royd stops and points at something for Henry to do; then they're both straining all stooped over to drop the blower from the back of the flatbed onto the ground; then they're struggling on either side of the blower to heft it up the front porch steps; then they're doing the same up the steps inside the house; then they're throwing a rope over a rafter in the attic and tying it to the top of the blower; then the blower's swinging corpsily from a rope as Henry steadies it and an invisible Royd hoists it up into the attic[39]; then they're carrying bag after bag of insulation over their shoulders into the house; then Henry's feeding bags of insulation up to Royd in the attic as Mrs. Caldwell, with tea cup and saucer, stands there watching; etcetera etcetera, and all in pretty short order; *but,* Noella *has* made sure that both Royd and Henry look sweatier and sweatier and worse for the wear every step of the way—especially Henry.

There's no true- or pseudo-soundtrack here, over this montage, only the hard sounds of what Royd and Henry are doing . . . and the cicadas whenever we're outside.[40] The idea, no doubt, is not only to give us a sense of what it's like to be an insulation blower in East Texas, but also it's pretty clearly, and more importantly, about Royd's/a "dad's" attempt to show Henry/a "son" what he does for work, to show him how to blow insulation, with the idea that blowing insulation might one day (soon) be a way for Henry to make a (real) living. I grant you, it's hard, if not impossible, to imagine this sort of take-your-kid-to-work-day being Royd's idea, but you *can* imagine it being Mother's and how Royd might ultimately capitulate to her saying stuff to

---

[39] Which is unsettling and only *almost* funny because the blower is reminiscent of R2D2, and *why would you lynch a droid, right?* But since the two assailants are obviously white, and the long and sick history of racist lynching in Texas biases us with the concern that the blower might be black, any headway into humor the scene might make is, as it should be, summarily derailed.

[40] Although, I have to confess to supplying—albeit involuntarily—my own soundtrack: Loverboy's "Working for the Weekend" has, somewhere over the course of this exercise, insidiously wormed its way into my mind, along with ghastly visions of Royd and Henry laughing and pulling each other's pants down and throwing insulation balls at each other in jest, which ends with Royd threatening to ram an insulation ball down Henry's throat—all of which is, no doubt, a really unfortunate, bad-habit-like mental artifact of having grown up on so many nauseating montage sequences in 1980s film.

him like, "He don't have to be your partner, Royd; just show him how to do it."

But all the narrative/metaphorical signs point to No Way: the fact that the job takes place through and behind a "trap" door tells me that *this* dad's, or step-dad's, or *faux*-dad's, line of work is just that, *a trap*, a dead end for Henry; and, if we were right back there (and I think we were) when we said Henry's motivational trajectory now is to explore and open and emancipate entities, secrets, memories, etcetera, in the attics and caves of his unconscious, then it only makes sense that he will *not* take to lifelong work "trapping" such things inside those attics and caves and "insulating" against their escape.

The montage ends with a longer, semi-close-up shot of Henry, up in the attic, with gloves and safety goggles on, pouring softballs of pink insulation out of a bag into the hopper on top of the blower and closing the lid. Royd, now with gloves and goggles on as well, is all the way down the far end of the attic, kneeling with the hose, pointing it into the corner. The image is blatantly phallic: Royd, grappling with his massive, deformed penis, preparing to urinate (or masturbate) into the corner. He gets (it) set and looks back down the attic, past us (the camera), and says, "All right, Henry. Go ahead, turn it on."

We pan quickly over to Henry, who's standing in front of the trap door next to the blower (we're situated about halfway between Royd and Henry now), and we zoom in on him a bit. He reaches down behind the blower with his left hand, hits the switch, and, *instantly*, everything is caught in *slow motion* and seized by an explosive onslaught of low, slow, relentless, machinic roaring so loud and violent that Henry founders against the blower and both our visual and audio tracks break up and distort . . . there is the fear, as Henry embraces the fulminating machine, that he is going to continue to lose his balance and fall through the trap door with it . . . but he doesn't . . . slowly, he pushes himself up off of the blower with both hands and begins to spin away from it . . . and, we can see through his goggles as he turns, his eyes are open, and his mouth is open, and the expression on his face is strangely void or inane . . . but as he continues to spin, it becomes clear that he is still off balance, that he's turning on a bias . . . his right arm and hand, in the shape of an arc, sweep from left to right in front of him as his left hand flattens back against the face of the blower in a desperate attempt to stabilize . . . then his eyes close sleepily, and, slowly, languidly, he commences to fall backwards, painstakingly down, down, through the trap door, gently pulling the blower down with him. Fade to black and silence.

Okay, I want to stop here a second because . . . yes, this is the third time, in the attic just now, that Noella has used slow motion in the film: the first was when Royd was showing Henry how to mow the lawn; the second, when Henry was crossing the bridge to the other side of the creek for the first time—and I want to say that each time he's used it, he's done so really efficaciously, that is, something awesome and sublime and otherwise hidden has been revealed. Which tells me that slow motion is, or at least can be a tool of perception on par with the microscope and the telescope.[41]

Just now, in the attic, without slow motion, Henry's reaction to the blower and his subsequent spin and fall would have come off as loud and terrible and funny (in a slapstick-ish kind of way)—which, mind you, would not have been bad; but in

---

[41] If the microscope and the telescope directly manipulate *space* to render the invisible, visible, then slow motion directly manipulates *time* to render the invisible, visible.

*slow motion*, the loudness and terror and humor are not lost; they are complicated and deepened by the revelation that *also* inhering in this sequence of movements is a thing of frightening *beauty*; so, allow me to risk repetition for detail and describe the scene again. In response to the sudden, world-eating din of the transcendently expressionless machine, Henry slowly, clumsily-gracefully, desperately falls against the machine and embraces it, not entirely unlike an inept teenager, fawning and falling all over a wholly unsympathetic love interest; then, histrionically, he rejects her for rejecting him by doing a perfect push-up off of her, or away from her. Then, from roughly ballet's third position: left arm outstretched, right arm and hand arced in front of his chest—like Baryshnikov in safety goggles, he dips his head back ever so slightly, ever so balletically and sweeps his right arm and hand from left to right across his chest in a gesture of lordly beneficence, all while turning and flattening his left palm against his love's vacant face and the roar of her fury thrums on; then, finally, the instability of the spin gets the better of him, and, like flubbing the landing on a triple-axle or -Lutz or whatever it is, he falls, dreamily, nightmarishly, beautifully backwards, down the hole, pulling his love down with him by her face. Fade to black and silence.

There is nothing: no image, no sound, for some time, maybe ten seconds . . . then, gradually, Noella fades up the audio: someone's talking . . . a couple of people are talking . . . a man and a woman . . . it's Royd and Mrs. Caldwell, the whole thing of which strongly suggests to me that Noella has merged us with Henry again for the moment, that we are regaining consciousness with him, first aurally, and then, probably in a moment or two, visually as well.

"But don't you think we should call a ambulance . . . or a doctor? Oh, I really think we should call a ambulance or a doctor right away," Mrs. Caldwell says.

"No, no," Royd says. "He . . . It wasn't that far a fall. He's gonna come around here in a second."

"But what if he doesn't? What if that thing fell on him?"

"No, it's . . ."

"Or what if he hit his head? I'm sure he hit his head. Is he even breathing?"

"Yeah, he's breathin."

"I don't think so. Look. His chest ain't movin."

"Henry. *Henry*," Royd says. We hear him get down on his knees and come closer. "Henry!" he barks.

We inhale sharply, our eye snaps open to a close-up of Royd's face, glaring down at us, and we cut.

I HAVE TO SAY, this film is really starting to win me over; I mean because look it: we now have *a tale of two machines*: the lawnmower and the insulation blower: it was the best of machines; it was the worst of machines—which, to me, is compelling, and I'm going to talk about it, but more importantly for the moment, what this implies, this tale of two machines, is that we've got ourselves *yet another modified reiteration*: the current *blower*-scene is a *modified reiteration* of the older *mower*-scene; and it's a good thing too because I have been thinking about this whole *modified reiteration* thing, and I have come to the conclusion that what they're doing, all these *modified reiterations*, is giving the film a robust sense of *internal and external coherence and development*.

Because, first of all, when stories reach *back* into *themselves*, internally, *intra*-textually, and take up again, but in *new* ways, past scenes, moments, elements, etc., they drop *threads* from present scenes down to past scenes, moments, or elements and *draw them up into the present* for re-*member*-ing, reassessment, and reinterpretation, which is to say, aspects of the story's past are taken up, again, anew, into the present of the story, and revised, as the story projects, trajects, develops, *evolves* into the future, and this sort of *systemic-dynamic-creative repetition* generates in us, I think, the sense that the narrative is not only continuous, consistent, coherent, and intelligible, but also motivated, future-directed, and developing . . . that it's *going* somewhere.

I don't know if I'm explaining this very well, but since it all pretty much counts as continental philosophical fare, it might help to know that it will tend to come on all fuzzy at first, soak in osmotically over time, then hit you all at once one day as this massive revelation; it also might help to know that, even later, sometime after the "revelation," you may well come to think of such stuff as sort of bathetic, or, that is, as the sort of mealy-mouthed and ultimately either totally self-evident or totally unintelligible bullshit you're kind of embarrassed you got so *wowed* by in the first place. All right, that's not entirely fair because some really sublime and important truths are *so close* to us, so mundane, so parochial, so *everyday* that they're difficult to see and describe in clear, pointed language, so we have to resort to oblique, poetic-type language and to *butt-squeezing* words, or key terms, with *italics* to try to *coax* as much *meaning* out of them as *possible*, which is kind of *cool*, but also kind of *annoying*.

But anyway, the same goes for when stories reach *out* into *other* stories, externally, *inter*-textually, and appropriate and transfigure scenes, moments, elements, etc., from them, except that, in this case, the story is not only furthering the development of itself, it's also cohering with and furthering the development of a certain group, or community, or family of related stories, ones that share a certain (to borrow a by-now utterly overused Wittgensteinian coinage) *family resemblance*. The threads here, instead of dropping down internally and connecting to past scenes, moments, etc., of the story *itself*, cast out externally from the story, attach to *other* stories, and draw it, the story at issue, into a web of relationships with those other stories, the result of which, after a number of threads are cast, is a sort of genealogical map, or family tree, of related stories. *Slingblade, Eraserhead*, and *As I Lay Dying* immediately come to mind as three big, conspicuous, external, or *inter*textual, reference stories here.

It just makes sense then too, doesn't it, that as the (or *any*) story progresses it, by sheer virtue of its ever-growing past, or history, lends itself more and more to moments of *intratextuality*, like the blower-mower *intra*text we have before us now because, it's clear, at the beginning of the story, Noella and we (the audience) have no other way to *orient* ourselves than by referring *inter*textually to *other* stories of which *Lawnmower of a Jealous God* is a relative: we might think or say, for instance, "Okay, I've seen this sort of thing before; it reminds me of *Slingblade*," and so on; *but*, as we roll along, as more and more elements and moments and scenes etcetera are gathered together under one narrative roof (as it were), we get, more and more, something with a unique (relatively speaking) history, or past of its *own*, a past to which our narrative memories are naturally attuned and which enables us, eventually, to think or say stuff like:

"Okay, this whole thing with the *blower* is totally reminiscent of, and kind of the same as that scene with the *mower* a while back, right? I mean, both involve Royd and Henry, where Royd is trying to show Henry how to do something, some kind of work, either blowing or mowing; both involve loud machines; both involve adult women watching them and Royd's rejection of those women; in both, Henry gets hurt: he incurs or may have incurred some sort of head injury; and both scenes are delivered to us in slow motion, which highlights their importance, both jointly and severally, and exposes for our scrutiny all their otherwise imperceptible details. But then there are also all these differences too . . . ," you might add. And they are:

— Mowing takes place *outside*, outside the confines of the house, out in the open, in a free and totally exposed, unconcealed environment; blowing takes place *inside*, inside the house, within the secret confines of the attic no less, in a very much hidden and concealed environment.

— Mowing is a *movement*-based activity: you can't mow if you don't move, *a lot*; blowing requires movement, but not nearly as much: you can blow a goodly section of attic and move very little (you just aim the hose).

— Royd makes mistakes at mowing, like forgetting to put gas in the mower; he is good at, more proficient at, a real pro at blowing.

— The sort of head injury implicated in the mowing scene is funny, a moment of relative levity (recall the little piece of stick that shot out from beneath the mower and struck Henry in the forehead); the one in the blowing scene is deadly serious.

— *Lawnmower* is a big part of the title of the film; *Insulation blower* is no part of the title of the film; therefore, lawnmowing is very likely more important and will play a bigger role than insulation blowing in this story. Now, I realize that we haven't seen much lawnmowing yet, and none out of Henry himself, but I feel certain that we will; in fact, I'll go out on a limb and say that I would be very surprised if lawnmowing, if *Henry* lawnmowing is not the main subject of the next episode.

— Mowing is work that *beautifies* the outside for all or anyone to see and enjoy (in principle), so it's like *art*, at least in these respects; blowing, while certainly practical and important, is work that seals up the inside and is ugly, hidden, and noxious, and thus (probably) not like art at all.

— Thinking metaphorically now, and possibly foreshadowing-ly, and definitely wishful-thinking-ly, mowing does the following, *generally speaking*: *it uses violent means to cut something down to size and thus enhance overall beauty and promote future growth*, but we can see how, if mowing is equated with Henry and blowing is equated with Royd (and I think it's safe to say that they are), that Henry, himself, at some point, might use violent means to cut something (Royd) down to size and thus enhance overall beauty and promote future growth; and indeed, further substantiating this sort of hopeful forecast are the facts that, just a few moments ago, we saw the blower (aka Royd) swinging by a noose from the attic, and we saw Henry *take down* the blower (aka Royd) as he fell out of the attic. Blowing, on the other hand, and again, *generally speaking*, does this: *it uses violent means*[42] *to secure an enclosed, or hidden, space*, and it's easy to see that what Royd's doing with the insulation is preparing and securing his secret den of iniquity, that the blower *machine* represents the relentless engine of his monstrous pedophilic desire, and that the *hose* represents his massive cock—noting, of course, here, that there is no "hose" (or cock) in mowing.[43]

We should note, too (although it's probably clear pretty much a priori), that *intra*textual (internal) modified reiteration and *inter*textual (external) modified reiteration are *not* mutually exclusive by any means: a scene or something in a scene can do both simultaneously. For example, Henry's *falling* out of the attic just now *modified-ly reiterates* ... or perhaps it's more grammatically efficacious (and conceptually equivalent

---

[42] In Re: blowing's violent means: the rotating augurs in the hopper that reduce the insulation balls to shreds for blowing would make mincemeat out of any part of you too, *toute suite*, and the volume at which it does anything is, as you already know, world-eating.

[43] *Massive Cock: Blessing or Curse?* I had a roommate in college who had a massive cock. I didn't know he had a massive cock until one day I opened the door to our room and saw him dancing completely naked in front of the mirror, admiring his very own massive cock as it swung and twirled around, well, *massively*, from his mid-section. I said, "Sorry," pulled the door closed, and walked away. Neither of us ever said a word to the other about the incident (for indeed, what could we have possibly said?), but I've always thought since then that *Wow, you know, maybe it helps him get sex, or it helps be more impressive during sex, but if that's the sort of thing you're compelled to do when you have a massive cock, then I want nothing to do with it. What a dick!*

enough) to say *creatively reiterates*[44] not only the two prior big *falls* in the film: our *fall* out of the heavens at the beginning, and Henry's *fall* through Carlsbad Cavern a while back, but also to the *fall of man, the fall of the Roman Empire, The Fall of the House of Usher, Falling Down* (the 1993 film), and surely others.[45] [46]

And now, since this is *falling's* third conspicuous appearance in the film, I think it's safe to say that it's achieved *thematic* status. Perhaps Noella's read his *Being & Time*, and all these *lit-*

---

[44]I have also used the term *creatively maintenizes*, as in both *maintains* something of the old thing *and* creatively does *maintenance* on some broken or discardable or currently irrelevant aspect or part of the old thing with some new, just as functional, or perhaps even *more* functional aspect or part. The German word "aufheben" captures the sense of a lot this; it means: *to, all at the same time, keep or preserve some aspect(s) of something, to cancel or get rid of some aspect(s) of that thing, and (thus) to change and (ostensibly) raise up that thing to a higher plane.* Though, of course, with the "raise up" bit, we're off into issues of *dialectics: positive (teleological) dialectics*—where we think some *progress* is being made, that the thing in question is *improving* toward some goal via these changes; or *negative (non-teleological) dialectics*—where we think the thing is making *no real or ultimate progress* via these changes; or *both*—because goals are attained and then lost, or the interpretation of their attainment turns from favorable to unfavorable over time (a hermeneutic issue).

[45]Where, despite my list, there's *no* requirement that the word "fall" appear in the title or description.

[46]Only if you are so inclined—*modified reiterations* can also be *consciously* or *unconsciously* generated; there is no requirement that they be conscious. It's easy to imagine, for example, that Noella consciously took up and modified aspects of the *fall of man* here but that he had no idea he was reiterating and modifying aspects of *The Fall of the House of Usher*. Also, the difference between the *reiterator* and *reiteratee* can be measured by *degrees of similarity*, such that, for example, mere copies of something would be assigned a really high degree of similarity, say 95°, because the reiterator is way more the *same* than *different* than the reiteratee; and references that are so oblique as to be virtually undetectable would be assigned a really low degree of similarity, say 5°, because the reiterator is way more *different* than the *same* as the reiteratee.

*eral* acts of falling represent a deeper metaphysical, or ontological, condition of Being: *Falling*—which most of us are in all the time, you know, *falling* cluelessly through life, *but also* from which it's metaphysically possible for us to wake up and catch ourselves, to *resolve* to stop *falling*, and to change and become *authentic* because, I mean, again, all three falls end, for Henry and us, in the dark silence of meditation, and we have already talked about how meditation can help you change.

The screen is still dark, but (not surprisingly) we hear cicadas, hundreds of thousands of them it seems, their metal-throated drone swelling and throbbing and grinding that one note down to swales of deathly silence, all-too-brief, like mixed-blessings or false-promises because the massive cacauphonic chorus inevitably reconvenes. Then someone starts up a lawn-mower and the two sounds, the mower's and the cicadas', blend to form a kind of concussive harmony, their individual violences notwithstanding.

Our eye opens: we are on the ground, at Henry's feet, looking up at him. He's posed, statuesque, against a clear blue sky, gazing meditatively, like a war hero or something, out to some distant horizon. His right hand resting casually on the mower's handle bar, his plastic goggles placed proudly (somehow) up on his forehead, he is bathed in deep golden sunlight. Clearly, we are meant to understand that he has *arrived*, that with this, Henry's will and fate are in sync.

Against the space of blue sky between the top of Henry's head and the edge of the screen, the French words:

# COMME IL FAUT

—which mean *as it should be*—appear then fade out. We were right, then, of course, a moment ago, when, in the last episode, we predicted that mowing would be the main subject of this, the next, episode. But how difficult *really* could it have been to make that prediction when title of the film is *Lawnmower* of a Jealous God, not *Insulation Blower* of a Jealous God or *Leaf Blower* of a Jealous God or whatever? I mean, maybe it's pretty good that we were able to predict that it would be *the very next episode* that lawnmowing would rise to prominence; but still, the film is more than halfway over now, so lawnmowing had to take center stage at some point very soon, that is, *toute suite*; *and*, it just makes sense too, doesn't it, that it would do so right after the scene where an alternate career path fails to launch.

We rise up beside Henry, up to eye-level, and we can see now, to his right and behind him, Mother and it must be Maybelline (now eight or so, recall, and played by a different but still Shirley Temple-ish actress), standing in the living-room window (again . . . ), looking out at him, watching him, and, beside them, Pickles is bouncing up and down in and out of the window frame, barking. Then we swing in a smooth arc around behind Henry's head until we are just over his right shoulder, between him and the house (ostensibly blocking his onlookers' view), and we can see now that he is gazing out over the field behind his house to the creek and beyond. Perhaps Noella wants us to think that Henry is thinking about Emily here, that he is imagining that she is watching him and is thus going to do something to try to impress her, to show off for her. It recalls that archetypal high school movie scene where the football player makes eyes with the cheerleader then saunters out onto the field and scores a touchdown on the very next play.

Henry brings the goggles down over his eyes, grabs the handle, and starts off across the lawn. We follow on behind him. Henry and we turn at the fence, pass back to other side, and turn again; then, as he continues to mow, we look toward the house: Mother, Maybe, and Pickles are gone from the window. We stop, but Henry, we can hear, mows on. We turn and look after him (as if we expected him to stop too) then back again at the empty window . . . the sight of which we absorb for some time . . . until we start to descend, to sink, slowly, straight down; down, down, until finally we settle into the fresh-cut grass, where, to the soporific drone of the mower receding, we close our eye on the empty window and, ostensibly, go to sleep. Fade to black and silence.

T HE TELEPHONE RINGS and we open our eye: we're lying on
the couch, watching TV—it's *The Facts of Life*—and we are
Henry, we are merged with Henry again. The words:

# TOOLS OF THE TRADE

appear then fade out. Of course, "tools of the trade" is a phrase
commonly used to refer to the things someone has to have in
order to do his or her job, but probably most people don't know
that the expression has a root in bankruptcy law, where things
deemed to be *tools of the trade* are exempt from attachment by
creditors in the event of bankruptcy, which is to say, for example, that a bankruptcy court is not going to order a carpenter-
by-trade to sell off his five-thousand dollar box of tools to pay
off his credit card debt: those tools and the carpenter's ability to
use them to continue to work and earn a living in the manner
to which he is accustomed are protected under the law; lest you
think, however, that letting someone keep his tools and continue to work is some kind of pure gesture of sovreign beneficence, or a kind of legal-gubernatorial *gift*, understand: the
bankruptcy law *also* allows the State not only to garnish some
percentage of a bankrupt person's, or *debtor's*, wages in order to
pay his debts and to pay whatever attorney and court fees have
been assessed him, but also, from what I understand, to continue to assess and collect taxes for any post-bankruptcy-filing
income; *so*, the State would clearly very much rather a debtor
continue to *work* and function in the economy than become a
drag on it by claiming unemployment, maybe backsliding into
a life of crime, going to jail on the tax-payer's dime, and so forth;
but—*I know*—it's not like *Henry* is going to file for bankruptcy

or claim unemployment or be in a position to engage any of these instruments and apparati of American enfranchisement: he's off the grid; he probably doesn't even have a social security number, so almost certainly all that "tools of the trade" means here is that, in this scene, Henry and we are going to see assembled before us the tools of the landscaping trade—the heart of the heart of which, we already know, is the lawnmower.[47] We get up, walk into the kitchen, pick up the receiver, and put it to our right ear . . . but we don't say anything.

"Hello. Anybody there?" Uncle Avery says through the receiver.

"Hello," we say.

"Oh. Henry. You know it's customary to say 'hello' when you pick up the phone, son . . . so I know you're on the line. Know what I mean?"

"Yes sir."

"Okay, well where's your mother at anyway?"

"Asleep."

"Asleep? It's ten o'clock in the morning."

We don't say anything.

"Henry."

"Yes sir."

"Well just come on up and mow then . . . Okay?"

"Okay."

Uncle Avery hangs up, and we cut.

---

[47] In addition to talking about *universal ontology*, or things that we think are *universally fundamental*, we can also talk about *relative ontology*: things that we think are fundamental *relative to* some individual or some more limited perspective, or point of view; so, in this scene, we could also say that we expect to be introduced to some work-related physical-ontological particulars, or material objects, that will be new and fundamental, or essential, *for* Henry—because this is, after all, very much *his* world, isn't it?

Still merged with Henry, we come through the chain-link gate at Uncle Avery's, close it behind us, and turn toward the house; but then, all at once, Noella drops us into slow-motion, cues up the unmistakable intro to Manfred Mann's version of "Blinded by the Light" (1976)[48]—only keyboards and hi-hat to start, if you recall—and invites us to behold a big shiny red lawn-mower, posed formidably but flirtatiously in the overgrown grass behind the house—the music, the slow-motion effect, and the pose imbuing it with a kind of romantic consciousness and casting it and us in the roles of lovers in the thrall of a love-at-first-sight-type moment, which, of course, is totally absurd and, perforce, causes me to laugh out loud; but, as the song progresses and we are drawn, slowly but inevitably, like the proverbial moth to flame, toward the machine, the humor quickly *evolves*, which is *not* to say that it disappears, but that the purity of its initial appearance becomes *complicated*, thickened, deepened by, in this case, a kind of *poignant purposiveness*, which, *combined* with the humor, is so affectively motivating and inspiring that weird, paradoxical tears spontaneously well up behind my eyes, whose importunity is even harder to check now

---

[48]This is our second *true* musical soundtrack moment of the film. The first *true* musical soundtrack moment of the film was the synthesizer tone Noella dropped in to harmonize with the cicadas as Henry crossed the wood bridge for the first time back in "The Other Side." Still, "Blinded by the Light" marks the first *full tune* Noella has dropped *artificially* into the film. The other full tunes: "Jambalaya on the Bayou" and "Stayin' Alive" were actually produced as *natural*, integral parts of their respective scenic environments, which is to say that they were played *in-scene* by a car radio and a portable radio, respectively, and the characters were privy to their performance. In *true* soundtrack moments, only the audience is privy to a given tune or audio track (so far as I know because, helpfully or not, I coined this distinction). "Blinded by the Light" was written by Bruce Springsteen and was on his fist album, *Greetings from Asbury Park, NJ.*

that our gait has coolly synced-up with the music and we have adopted a sort of viscous strut ... so it's very difficult ... it requires a real sort of ... *facial effort* to hold back these unusual tears, and when the vocals kick in—leading with the titular "Blinded by the Light"—another hot flush of occult meaning blows up behind my eyes, which I immediately hold open as wide as I can, to keep them dry, as we turn our head gradually to the left now, toward the house, where, by steadily increasing degrees, are revealed Uncle Avery and Luke, standing in the big back window, looking out at us: Uncle Avery, smiling and nodding, slowly, dementedly, apparently goading us on to the mower; Luke, standing to his left, his jowls languidly flapping up ... and down ... barking, barking at us from behind the glass, but totally mutely because all we hear is the song: "... the adolescent pumps ... the boulder on my shoulder, feelin' kinda older ..."—and suddenly we're off the rails: we, the sequence, *everything*, by some process of exponential accumulation, are ejaculated into *the divine uncanny*, and there's nothing I can do as we turn our attention back to the mower, as we approach it, as we stop before it, as we slowly extend our left hand, like Adam in *The Creation of Adam*,[49] toward its black handle and the song says for the second time, "*The calliope crashed to the*"[50]

---

[49] Michaelangelo, Sistine Chapel, 1512.

[50] It is uncommon for me to cry during a film, and the fact that I have done so here is surely a testament to the power of this film or at least to the power of this sequence, with all of its aspects and accoutrements. Although, to be clear, I wouldn't exactly say I was *crying*. Some emotion or combination of emotions got the better of me, sure ... and *a tear fell*, but that's not exactly *crying* is it. "Crying" is a gerund, an *-ing* word, which implies some sort of *ongoing act or activity*, and *one tear* does *not* the *ongoing act or activity of crying make*.

"Henry!" Uncle Avery says, intstantly obliterating the whole gestalt; I mean, it's a real needle-across-vinyl-, amandi-interruptus-type moment, and we cut, we sever from Henry to a position to his right, between him and the mower, where we see a fatter, older-looking Uncle Avery[51] and Luke, in real time, coming out the backdoor of the house.

We track Luke as he bolts over to Henry, then we zoom in as Luke punches his snout into Henry's crotch, roots around in it a bit, then starts licking the front of Henry's pants.

"Goddammit!" we hear Uncle Avery say, then we hear the sound of Uncle Avery's boot striking Luke's chest-cavity, and Luke flies out of the frame with a whimper, leaving us looking at the crotch of Henry's pants, inside which there appears to be some movement . . . then we zoom back out to our position between Henry and the mower and a shot of Uncle Avery in his blue gas station suit, standing to Henry's left.

"Go on, git!" he says to a now off-screen Luke, pointing somewhere, away. "You heard me. *Git.* That's right. Frickin' party's over, Luke." He turns to Henry then looks at the ground, shaking his head and laughing a little bit. "'Course I ain't got *no* idea where he got the notion to . . . except he's just a dumb dog, just a . . . What's the Bible say again? *Beast of the field* 'cause that there was definitely the sorta thing separates man from beast, know what I mean, 'cause you don't see no *person* says 'hello' by . . . "—he rolls his right hand around in a circle a few times—"doing *that.* But I reckon there's a lesson we can learn from all this." Avery looks over at Henry, squinting. "Any idea what the lesson here is, Henry?"

---

[51] Though it's the same actor as before.

Henry stares straight ahead for a moment, then he turns around and looks at Luke ... then at the mower ... then at the house ... then at Uncle Avery ... then he stares straight ahead again.

"Well, you cain't just look around at shit and expect it give you the answer, Henry," Uncle Avery says gently but insistently. "You got to use your head, son. You got to *think*. And I reckon when you think about it, you realize, since Luke's just a animal, just a *beast*, then we ought to forgi ... *Nuh uh, Luke*. No!" he says, looking past Henry and pointing again. "You *stay*. *Stay* down there."

Uncle Avery exhales, puts his fists on his hips, and looks back at Henry. "I was gonna say *forgive* him, but now I'm thinkin' *just show him who's the damn boss*." He laughs. He shakes his head. "But *hey*," he says, straightening up. "Forget all that shit, Henry, and feast your eyes"—he opens his palms Christly toward the mower—"on *this*."

Henry and we look at the mower with Uncle Avery.

"*Behold, the Mothson 1216*." He smiles. "Powerful. Robust. Cuts like a hot knife through dogshit. It's the best there is, Henry." He puts his fists on his hips. "The Superman of mowers. I mean ..." He opens his palms Christly toward the mower again. "Just *look at it*. Jet-black engine, candy-apple red chassis ... and hey, ain't nobody git to hem and haw about *did I want the blue one or the green one*, like it was a goddamn purse or a pair of shoes or somethin', Henry, 'cause they ain't got no other colors on these things; this is *it*.

"But probably the *main* thing here, Henry—somethin' I know you ain't *never* experienced before, is ..." He takes a step and points at the throttle bar.[52] "You see this thing here? This bar?" He looks back at Henry. Henry nods. "When you squeeze it, frickin' miracle of all miracles, *mower goes on its own.* It's what you call *self-propelled.* But now I know what you're thinkin': you're thinking, if it's self-propelled, then I ain't got to do nothin' but stand back and watch, but that ain't right. That ain't what *self-propelled* means, Henry. It don't mean like some kinda robot. You still got to *steer* the thing; it's just you ain't got to *push* it no more, okay . . . so, you know, it's simular to a car, where you press the gas pedal with your foot and steer with the wheel, but here you just squeeze the bar with your hand, to give her gas and make her go, and steer with the handle. See what I'm drivin' at, Henry?"

Henry nods.

"Yes, yes sir."

"Good. Now, speaking of drivin'—follow me." Uncle Avery turns and heads for the chain link gate at the corner of the house, not the one Henry came through a moment ago but the one that leads down the side of the garage to the parking area around front. Henry follows; and we, behind him. Avery flips the latch on the gate but stops, turns to Henry, and says, "You ever driven a car?"

"No, no sir, but, but I seen it, on TV, on Dukes of Hazzard." Henry looks at the gate when he talks. "I watched 'em do it, real close, and I, I could. I could do it," Henry adds emphatically.

"That's good, Henry. I'm sure you . . . well come on then, follow me." Avery goes through the gate. "Close that behind you, would you?" Henry and we come through the gate and Henry closes it behind us.

---

[52] Also known as the "bail bar."

Avery walks along the narrow path between the fence and the garage, squeezes past the metal garbage cans, and, since there's no gate down this end, just disappears to the right around the corner of the garage. Henry and we squeeze past the cans and turn the corner as well. There's an old gray pickup truck and a couple of other cars sitting in the parking area in front of the house; we look to our right: the garage door is open and there's a car up on a mechanic's rack in there—but we follow Avery over to a gold- or mustard-colored El Camino with two thick black racing stripes running down either side of the hood. Avery stops alongside the vehicle, puts his fists on his hips, and appears to contemplate it. Henry comes up beside him, puts his fists on his hips, and looks at the car as well; we stay back a few feet so we can see both them and the car.

"Now this here's a 1972 Chevy El Camina," Uncle Avery says. "Definitely the finest of the fleet. It's got a V-8, three hundred twenty-five horses, and . . . well, you can bet your ass she's mint 'cause yours truly fixed her up thataway. I always been good at fixin' shit up, Henry, *specially* cars, so whenever Joe, Torres, over at Joe's Garage up in Henderson, got wind of my 'bilities, which I don't know how he did, but he got holt of me and started hookin' his overage down here for me to fix up and jes' paying me cash under the table, which was good 'cause, well, let's just say it saves us both a shitload of money and trouble. *And*," he says, glancing over at the garage, "Joe supplies me with all the parts I need too. So it's a daing good deal, and a daing good livin' . . . but jus' for *me*, though, Henry, right?" He puts his right hand over his heart. "'Cause ever' man"—he points at Henry—"got his *own* thing. But it shore don't hurt none when he can git that leg up now does it?" He laughs. "And that's what I'm talkin' about here.

"Anyway, long time ago, somebody dropped this here beauty off at Joe's with, it turned out was mice livin' up under the hood, nestin' and chewin' up all the wires and whatnot, which for one thing told me she'd been settin' idle some time 'cause them critters don't jes' come up and habituate in a vehicle that's gettin' started every mornin' if you know what I mean, but Joe hooked her down here, and I got her all fixed up, and we was gonna hook her back up there for pick-up, but then Joe said the owner wasn't comin' by or callin' or answerin' the phone or nothing, so finally he said why don't I jes' keep her and Merry Christmas to me, and I said, 'Don't mind if I do, thank you very much.'" He laughs.

"Now, I *did* have the problem of the plates and the *in*surance 'cause I ain't got no license; but hey, I like it like that, Henry. I don't need no goddamn g-man lookin' me up for *nothin'*, and I reckon you'll be of simular mind about that sort of thing too, whenever you come to think of it. *I know*, Royd's got *him* a license and all that shit, but that's 'cause he works for *the man*, he's *sold out* to the man. But there ain't no need to do that 'cause I got ways around all that shit, Henry. I got a die in there"— he nods toward the garage—"that'll stamp out a Texas plate in two shakes, and, and any five-year-old can make a goddamn registration sticker for Christ's sake. *So*, all's you got to worry about is drivin' safe and not attracting the attention of the *po*lice. But that ain't no trouble 'round these parts 'cause there ain't no *po*lice nowhere 'round here anyhow." Avery laughs and walks toward the back of the vehicle. Henry and we follow.

"So, as you can see, she's kind of a half car, half truck, what with this flatbed and all. Good for haulin' shit, obviously." There's a broom, a rake, several boxes of Hefty trash bags, and a weed-wacker lying in the flat-bed. "And I reckon you know what most of this shit is. But *this* . . ."—he reaches into the flatbed and takes out the weed-wacker—"this *here* is a Mothson 7250 Edgemaster." He hefts it a couple times. "Super light weight." He twists it around, inspects it. "It's got both wacker and edger settin's on the head of course." He snaps the head back and forth between wacker and edger settings then takes the thing properly by the handles and moves it to and fro in front of him as if wacking weeds. "You ever used one of these before, Henry?"

"No, no sir."

"Well, no time like the present," Avery says, handing the weed-wacker to Henry. "Come on."

Henry takes the weed-wacker, and Uncle Avery heads back the way they came, back around the garage, back to the back yard. Henry and we follow.

As Henry closes the gate behind us, Avery lets Luke out the other gate (the one we came through at the beginning of the episode), and Luke bolts off down toward the creek, barking.

Uncle Avery then walks past the mower and over to the wrought-iron table (which sits on the concrete slab behind part of his house, just like at Mother's). There's a thin, white, rectangular cardboard box, like a garment box, sitting on the table. Avery puts his hand on the back of one of the chairs and watches us walk over. Henry's still wielding the weed-wacker.

"Here," Avery says, taking the weed-wacker from him. "We'll get to that in a minute." Avery takes the weed-wacker, leans it against the table behind him to his right, and puts his hand back on the back of the chair. "Well go on then," he says, nodding at the box, "open it. It's for you."

Henry reaches for the box and pulls it slowly across the table towards him. He looks up at Uncle Avery.

"Go on," Avery says.

Henry lifts off the top of the box, and we zoom in: inside there's what appears to be a brand new blue gas station suit and, on top of that, a car key.[53]

"Now I woulda had all this stuff for you on your actual birthday," Uncle Avery says, then we cut back to our position behind and to the right of Henry, "but I had to wait for the 1216 to come in, then I got all caught up with shit for Joe, so I hope you understand. Anyway, sixteen's a big 'un, Henry, so happy birthday, buddy. I hope this gives you that leg up we was talkin' about."

As Henry stares into the box, it begins to give off a blue glow, which intensifies until his face is totally, beatifically illuminated. A dog, Luke, barks in the distance, down by the creek . . . another, smaller one—obviously Pickles—joins in, and we cut.

Now, at this stage in the game, you should really be getting pretty expert at identifying *certain things* on your own, without my prompting, but let's go back to the beginning of this episode and ask nonetheless: What do we see? And I mean deep-structurally, or even metaphysically, speaking? If you said, "A terrifically conspicuous internal modified reiteration of both the 'Lawnmowing 101' scene (from early in the film) and the 'Comme Il Faut' scene (the one just before this one)," then you'd be dead-on, you'd get an 'A,' because you would have noticed that all of the major elements, or parts, in *this* scene: Henry, mower, back yard, back of the house, big back window, splintered-spectres-of-close-relatives-or-pets-in-the-back-window, etc. are *generally* the same as, but *specifically* different from those elements, or parts, in the *earlier* two scenes, and this observation would then set you up for the further in-

---

[53] The second key associated with Avery.

ferences that every relevant part of one of the scenes has a respective *counterpart* in the other two scenes, and that the three scenes together constitute an evolving, expanding little family.

But even if you didn't *consciously* notice or infer all this stuff, never fear: we also process internal modified reiterations and their synthesizing effects *unconsciously*: we just *feel* the narrative tying itself together with them as it (the narrative) becomes for us something both familiar *and* new. And, naturally, *external* modified reiterations work the same way, which, in this case, conscious or unconscious, consist of stuff like that common, or stock, scene where two soon-to-be-lovers make eyes at one another across a crowded room,[54] and of specific scenes or situations from a bunch of films, like *Castaway* (2000), where Chuck Noland (Tom Hanks) has a sort of homosocial relationship with a volleyball he calls "Wilson" (for obvious reasons), and, even better, *Christine* (1983),[55] where this nerdy guy, Arnie, falls in love with his 1958 Plymouth Fury; and "she," with him.

Of course, the representation of amorous "relationships" between people and inanimate physical objects is funny, and it's funny (to risk telling you something you already know) because of the sudden inapposite *animism* of the otherwise inanimate object and because of the object's and the human character's "mutual" *category mistake*: that they are suitable objects of affection for each other; but they (the "relationships") are also really sad and pathetic and pitiful, aren't they, because, in them, *true* consummation, reciprocation, communication, communion, etc., are all *impossible*, and the character has committed

---

[54] And maybe the next thing you know they're having sex in the bathroom stall.
[55] Directed by John Carpenter; based on the novel by Stephen King.

himself to just weirder, deeper levels of loneliness, absurdity, and madness.

Then again, maybe this sort of neurotypical pity is presumptious and misplaced, even arrogant because what if the idea is that the character's love runs *so deep*, is so *systemic*, that, *purely subjectively speaking*, and even if it *is* totally self-generated, he *does experience*, or *feel*, love or at least something *substantially similar* to it with respect to the inanimate object? And indeed, the fact is that this sort of behavior (and its concomitant mental state), however outrageous it may seem, is *not* just a creature of fiction; it's a real-world condition called *objectophilia*: there are true accounts of people falling in love with and even happily "marrying" things like the Eiffel Tower or a train station— although, more common real-world examples are of people in romantic or, at least, very powerful and ostensibly satisfying (and thus probably also tumultuous) relationships with things like their stuffies, their guitars (e.g., B.B. King's "Lucille"), their bikes, etcetera.

It also turns out that objectophilia is not uncommon in people down the functional end of the autistic spectrum—which, of course, is particularly relevant here, with Henry—but we should also be mindful of the fact that folks down the functional end of the spectrum tend to really love or have extremely intense interests in not *just* inanimate physical objects, but pretty much *anything*: an animal or insect (penguins, moths . . . ), a person (an historical figure, scientist, writer, philosopher, musician, composer, or, less commonly, a friend or lover), an academic discipline (math, science, history, philosophy, music, language, or more likely a particular branch or type thereof), an activity (like playing an instrument, bird-watching, or, less commonly, a sport) . . . anything at all. The *key* is not the thing, itself, but the *intensity of the interest* in it.[56]

Still, it's clear from what we've seen just now that Henry *is* going to have an extremely intense interest in, and possibly some sort of relationship (albeit imaginary) with an inanimate physical object, i.e., the Mothson 1216 lawnmower; but it's *also* clear from what we've seen before, in earlier episodes, that Henry *already* has an extremely intense interest in, and some sort of relationship with Emily, i.e., a person (be she real or imaginary). So this is going to create a *double* extremely-intense-interest and/or *double* extremely-intense-relationship situation for Henry, which, we might reasonably expect, will present a problem for him, and not only because he's such a weirdo, but also because *everyone* has trouble moderating between competing interests, especially extremely intense ones, which brings to mind the old biblical proverb: "No one can serve two masters, for either he will hate the one and love the other, or he will be devoted to the one, and despise the other . . ."—Matthew 6:24.

But if we just strip out, or bracket out, all of the "*extremely intense*" business from this "equation," we are left with a (mere) double-interest and/or double-relationship situation that's just *totally sociologically commonplace* because many, if not most of us live with love, sex, family, or what we might call *the domestic*, on one side of our lives, and with work, money, co-workers, or *the occupational*, on the other; and we have to moderate, me-

---

[56]The functional autistic or Aspergerian ability to focus exclusively on the object of his obsession for long periods of time results (not surprisingly) in his knowing virtually everything there is to know about that thing; and, while he probably doesn't talk much generally, on *this*, his subject of expertise, he can and, indeed, does tend to yammer-on, much to his interlocutors' chagrin.

diate, negotiate, handle, whatever, the conflicts that naturally arise between the two, such that the difference between Henry and most of the rest of us vis-à-vis these categories or, rather, the specific interests and relationships that constitute them and the conflicts that ensue from them, may be, most fundamentally, a matter of degree—understanding, however, that when we increase the intensity, or degree, or *quantity* of interest in (or desire for) something enough, or *too much*, we're going to get *qualitative* cognitive-behavioral distortions and anomalies, like objectophilia, aberrant infatuations, PhDs in philosophy, and so forth.

It makes perfect sense, then, on two counts, for Noella to use extreme, or harsh, or, I guess, draconian-sounding tropes here, like "*Blinded* by the Light" and "Like a moth to flame"—which is not *explicitly* used but taunts Henry *obliquely* through the *Moth*-son name—because (i) they are properly descriptive of the intensity and qualitative abnormality of Henry's interest in the mower, and (ii) they are (also) prominent biblical[57] or quasi-biblical *cliches*,[58] which forebode that:

1. *The light by which he sees shall also be, if he looks too long at it, the very same that blinds him; and,*

2. *The fire by which he survives the night shall also be, if he gets too close, the very same that burns and kills him—*

and we don't need anyone to tell us that both warn against Henry's "overdoing it," and not only with the mower, but also with Emily since she is his other light- and (by extension) fire-signified intense-interest.

---

[57]The Apostle Paul is said to have been "blinded by the light" of God.
[58]They are, indeed, The Cliches of Light & Fire.

But we don't yet know the *exact* extent to which Henry will be affected by these two forces, Emily and the Mothson; I mean, we can be confident, given everything the narrative has been telling us lately, that he will be *to some notable extent* determined by them, but the narrative has also been telling us that this story is a sort of *Bildungsroman*, which suggests that Henry's blindness will be only temporary, that these flames will burn but not kill him, that he will *learn* from these experiences, from the *pain* of these experiences, and grow stronger from them. So what all this boils down to, it seems to me, is *free will* because either Henry has a sufficient amount of it and can use it to *overcome*, to some significant extent, the tyranny of his interests, desires, and disorders; or, he has an insufficient amount of it and will be essentially a puppet to those interests, desires, and disorders.[59]

And Noella can take it either way from here too, can't he? He can deprive Henry of the requisite amount of free will and then have him ping-pong back-and-forth helplessly between the Mothson and Emily, between work and home (or rather, probably, *sex*) and then just explode or implode or otherwise deteriorate in some dark and probably humorous fashion—which could be pretty goddamn entertaining; or, he can take the Nietzschean route, the that-which-does-not-kill-him-makes-him-

---

[59] I'm assuming that *absolute*, or *total*, free will is reserved for *impossible* beings, like God.

stronger route,[60] give him the requisite amount of free will,[61] and have him learn how to take control of, or at least manage his relationships with Emily and the Mothson—which doesn't sound nearly as entertaining or exciting, but it is more optimistic and responsible and, in the spirit of the *Bildungsroman*, grown-up.[62]

It's apparent now, too, how the moth metaphor supports all of this and more because, first of all, it sets us up for the possi-

[60] Nietzsche, *Twilight of the Idols* (1888): "*From the military school of life.*—That which does not kill me, makes me stronger." I think all Nietzsche is saying here is that these people, the military, are strong people whose motto is: "Whenever something bad happens to us, we (try, over time, to) take it as an opportunity for upbuilding and edification," and that the rest of us would do well to follow their lead on this. It's just a *normative* statement, or exhortation, like, "In the face of adversity, be strong!" or "What is the grain of sand to the oyster but an opportunity to make a pearl? So be an oyster!"—that kind of thing. It's *not* (as one might unwittingly assume) an attempt to capture some kind of *necessary truth* because we all know that that which does not kill us does not *necessarily* make us stronger (than we were before the unfortunate event). I mean, obviously, I could *never* get *physically* stronger (than I was before) as a result of an accident in which I lost both my arms and my legs; in fact, I'm sure I'd be forever physically *weaker*; and, it's obviously totally *possible* that I'd never get *psycho-emotionally* stronger (than I was before) either, because, as a result of such an accident, I could fall into despair, lose my will to live, and die in a state that was not only *not* psycho-emotionallly stronger (than I was before), but very much psycho-emotionally *weaker*.

[61] Nietzsche criticizes the notions of free will and determinism in any *absolute* sense and, instead, advocates a world where (for lack of a better way to put it here) the two are blended in a constant dynamic. You could say, then, that free will and deterministic forces are *degreed* and that their relationship with one another is one of constantly shifting degrees.

[62] Now whether there is *in principle* any free will to give Henry is a philosophical question that has never been answered to anyone's complete satisfaction, though in the law, we tend to, or perhaps *have to* (as a practical matter) go with an Ayer-ian view, which is, basically, that free will, or freedom, is the freedom *from* (undue) constraint (e.g., false imprisonment) or influence (e.g., intoxication).

bility that Henry is in the midst of a transformation, that he is metamorphosing from "caterpillar" to "moth" and that, while it might not be pretty, he will eventually learn to fly—which, of course, is consistent with our *Bildungsroman/free will* angle here; second, it (the moth metaphor) sets us up for the possibility that Henry, just like so many moths, will die mindlessly in the flame or flames to which he is drawn— which is consistent with our *deterministic/no free will* angle; third, it sets us up for the possibility that, just like a moth, Henry will be "nocturnal," or that he will operate largely under cover of night or darkness— which should actually come as no surprise because we've already seen how taken Henry was with the darkness of Carlsbad Cavern; and finally, it sets us up for the possibility that, just like a moth against the trunk of a tree or the word "moth" within the word "Mothson," Henry will hide or camouflage himself against the background of his environment—which also should come as no surprise because *hiddenness*, as we have seen already, is a family trait.

I should point out as well that, just like the metaphor of the bat and the metaphor of the snake from before, and like words with more than one definition (which, it turns out, is almost all of them), and like words that always need *more* definition (such as "this," "that," "these," "those," etc.), the metaphor of the moth is *deictic*: *prior* to use and interpretation, when it is, as it were, *at rest*, it doesn't have just one, univocal, or unambiguous, meaning; it is multivalent: it has a bunch of different, even contradictory meanings, and it's only when it is disambiguated by context, perspective, or point of view that it comes to represent, or mean (albeit only temporarily of course[63]), one thing.

---

[63] Because obviously the metaphor is always subject to being recontextualized and recast to represent one of its other meanings.

The metaphor of the moth, then, is what you might call a *hermeneutic free-agent*, at least with respect to a *selection* of different meanings (because, again, the metaphor of the moth doesn't also mean *just anything*, like shoe-string potatoes or California), and I guess the, or at least *a* broader lesson here is that most all words and metaphors are hermeneutic free-agents with respect to a selection of different meanings and that linguistic meaning is largely determined by context, perspective, or point of view—the truth of which suddenly seems painfully obvious to me. Anyway, it's safe (or saf*er*) to say, based on precedent, that, in the coming scenes, Henry will camouflage and hide himself and that, more and more, he will operate under cover of darkness; but it's harder to say how the free will issue will play out—on that one, we'll just have to wait and see.

It bears considering again, though, for a second, just what sort of *family* it is we're talking about here; I mean, we are wont to say that there are *family traits*, or *heritable characteristics*, like *hiddenness* . . . and *incestuousness*, which, naturally, imply genealogy, *ancestry*; but here, with the Henry family, we can't help but notice or, at least, highly suspect that ancestry stops—or starts, depending on how you look at it—with Mother, Uncle Avery, and, I guess, Royd: they are as far as back as we go: there are no grandparents or great-grandparents, nor any mention of them; and, despite the fact that we know there are other people in this/their world, it's like Noella wants us to think, well, not only that the Henry family is as a spatially- and temporally-autonomous universe unto itself (as we discovered on the trip to Carlsbad), but also that all of human history somehow *begins* with them, with Mother & Uncle Avery, Royd, Henry & Emily, Maybe, and, lest we forget, *us*, the audience (because it was *our birth* that literally kicked things off here, if you recall); and, if that's right: if we—all seven of us—represent human history's "first family," then we must also be a *reinterpetation and amalgamation*—or, yes, a *double*-modified reiteration—of the Adam & Eve creation myth and the Birth of Jesus story, in which *our* role is to *bear witness* and spread *the word*, the *truth*, according to this new perverted diorama, which is:

— that Adam & Eve and God & Mary—*both* sets played by Uncle Avery & Mother—are twin brother and sister whose most essential characteristic is that they are or have been consensually (by all appearances) incestuous, and whose most noteworthy accomplishment is that they conceive Jesus, or rather, in this case, *Twin Jesii*—played by *both* Henry and Emily—who also, it could be said, play Adam & Eve, *again*, and who also are (or will be) consensually incestuous;

— that Adam & Eve and God & Mary—as played by Uncle Avery & Mother—have to get a "divorce," probably because they've focused in on the parts of the Bible that do not condone incest (Leviticus, Deuteronomy)[64] and are concerned with how they will be perceived in the eyes of God, or, perhaps, because of some insight or intuition into the possibility of progenetic insult, and so Satan—played by Royd—is recruited to be Eve/Mary/Mother's husband as a *cover*, preys on Emily/Jesus until she runs away or he kills her, then conceives Maybe with Eve/Mary/Mother, and preys incestuously on her (Maybe), but where *his* incestuousness is distinguished and seriously aggravated by its also being pedophilia and rape, which are patently *non*-consensual—two further implications of which are: that there is a right way: *consensual*, and a wrong way: *non-consensual*, to commit incest, and that the, or at least

---

[64] Others parts of the Bible do condone incest, both explicitly (just think of the case of Lot and his daughters), and implicitly (which I'll get to in a second).

*a* big difference beteween God (et al.) and the Devil (et al.) here is the approach each takes to its commission; and,

— that, rightly or wrongly approached, *incest* is *the key, the tie that binds* everything together here, and, at least "In the beginning," it is what ensures humanity's survival—that seems to be Noella's *thesis* here; and, like it or not, I think it can actually be pretty soundly defended, both biblically and scientifically.

Because, biblically speaking, if Adam & Eve are the first two people on earth, well then the challenge is to explain how they propagate humanity from there *without* incest. Can't be done. If they only have a daughter, at some point (hopefully once she can consent) she's got to do it with dad; if they only have a son, at some point (hopefully once he can consent), he's got to do it with mom; if they have sons and daughters, then (hopefully once they can consent) they have to do it with one another or with mom and dad. So there's no way in hell around it: the Bible—or at least this major part of it—*entails* incest: *it's incest all the way down.*

And scientifically, or bio-evolutionarily, if non-incestuous sexual reproduction evolved from *asexual reproduction* (which it did), then non-incestuous sexual reproduction has its roots in, and *would not be but for incest* because what could be more incestuous than breeding with *yourself*? Furthermore, the *biological directive* against close incest, whose aim is to both confer fitness advantages and prevent harm to the gene pool, had to have evolved over time, through much trial and error, meaning there *was* a time when close incest, despite its developmental (or "technological") crudeness, was *not* biologically verboten, and if it was not biologically verboten, well then you can bet your ass it was not only common practice, but maybe even the best thing going in the highly motivated business of survival.

Thus, scientifically speaking as well, we are forced to accept that we would not even *be* but for incest, that we are *all* descendeants of incest.

And if that's not a big enough pill to swallow, herein also lies a proof (or at least a very strong argument) that big 'G' God doesn't exist because if close incest is genetically disadvantageous and harmful, if it results in poorer environmental fitness and in stuff like recessive gene disorders, and if God created the heavens and the earth, as the Bible claims, then either He *didn't know* how to set things up differently, non-incestuously, non-disadvantageously, non-harmfully for us (and everything else), and he is *ignorant* of something, i.e., not omniscient, and thus not God; He set things up like this to disadvantage and harm us (and other things) *on purpose*, and he is *evil*, i.e., not omnibenevolent, and thus not God; or, He *wasn't physically able* to set things up in such a way that didn't disadvantage and harm us (and everything else), and he is *weak*, i.e., not omnipotent, and thus not God. It still may be, of course, that some lesser, shittier god exists; and, of course, it may be that no kind of god exists *at all*; but if your reaction is to shake your head and protest that none of this matters because the existence of God is entirely a matter of *Faith*, then I say you can have your "Faith," but, metaphysically speaking, it will *not* be in God.

I know, that's a lot to stomach in one sitting, but, unfortunately, there's one last thing we've neglected to address here: the family *pets*, or at least Luke because all Pickles seems to me to be (as of yet anyway) is comic relief (hence the ridiculous name); but *Luke* ... Luke is, first of all, co-nominal with Luke Duke from *Dukes of Hazzard*, which, as it turns out, is not *just* a fun, post-modern, reference-complicating intertext, but also a *deeper* intertext that fits right in with Royd's odious transgressions because Tom Wopat, the the guy who played Luke on *Dukes*, was arrested for indecent assault and battery of a young woman in 2017; and, second of all, Luke is also co-nominal with St. Luke, one of whose versions of Jesus' birth in the Bible is, interestingly enough, consistent with all of this film's incest business because, according to it (specifically, Luke 3:23), Joseph was the son of Heli, *Mary's father*, and if he (Joseph), not God, impregnated Mary—which is the more likely story—well then it was an *incestuous conception*, not an immaculate one.

And with respect to Luke *qua* dog: we already know that his irksome barking is a serious impediment to Henry's being on *the other side* of the creek, to Emily's long-term return, and to Henry & Emily's ultimate physical reunion, so he (Luke) is like Cerberus, but he's Avery/God-the-Father's Cerberus, guard-dog to (an ostensible) Hell; and surely we've also noticed by now the unsavory crotch-muzzling behavior, which, because Avery suspiciously denies knowledge of its origins, rouses in us the concern that lonely old Uncle Avery has trained Luke to suck or, perhaps, lick, his (Avery's) cock, and now Luke reckons it's the thing to do with Henry as well, and can now see how both contribute to an emerging overall or comprehensive and complicated representational picture of Luke as a really irksome Cerberus-like-Bible-writing-hillbilly-actor-sex-criminal-cocksucker . . . or -licker.

W'RE SITTING in the passenger seat, looking over at Henry, who's driving; Henry is in the driver's seat now, of his El Camino. He looks serious, intent, intense, very much the way he did when he crossed the bridge to the other side of the creek for the first time. And there's no need to go on about it because it's plain as day, but it would be hard to overestimate the importance of this moment for Henry and the film: this is independence, freedom, or at least some very significant degree thereof.

We turn and look out the back window: a lawnmower, the Mothson, is riding high and proud in the flatbed . . . though there's something a little bit forlorn about it too . . . like it ought to be riding in the passenger seat instead of us. We look back at Henry then out at the road ahead of us. The word:

# LUCKY'S

appears in the sky then fades out as we roll through a flat, wide-open section of landscape, a vast bed of green populated only here and there by burly oaks and short green tufts of some kind of bush. There's a sign coming up on the right-hand side of the road . . . In black hand-painted letters against a white background, it says, "Lucky's 1 Mile Music Cocktails Beer Fun." We pass it and cut.

Now we're in the process of turning right onto a dirt road. Another hand-painted sign, which just says "Lucky's" with an arrow pointing down the dirt road, drifts across the windshield from right to left then disappears behind us. Down the road about a quarter mile, mashed between the two hard flat sheets of earth and sky, there's a white house with a black roof. There are no trees or bushes or anything around it, and, over one half of it, there's a second story—probably a bedroom. The sunlight, coming in somewhat thin and sideways, is mid-morning light.

There's a pick-up truck parked around the right side of the house; Henry sweeps the El Camino across the front of the house to the left, into a gravel parking area, makes basically a 'U' so we're pointed back the other way, then we both turn around and look through the back window as he backs up to where the gravel meets the grass. In the grass, placed seemingly randomly, there are a bunch of wooden picnic tables and benches.

We cut to Henry rolling the Mothson down out of the El Camino on a couple of two-by-fours; a man's voice says, off-screen—he's come from the house behind us—"Buenos Dias," and we cut again in order to include in the frame, with Henry and the Mothson and the grass and tables behind, a man in a white wife-beater, tan shorts, and flip-flops: it's Lyle Lovett, and if we remember from the credits at the beginning, Lyle plays himself. Thin, wiry, wildly bent and gnarled and exaggerated head and facial features, he is a caricature of himself, standing there, subtly swaying, like a dinghy in light chop, the smoking cigarette and the bottle of beer he's holding out in front of him in either hand serving, it would appear, as ballast.

Henry stands behind the Mothson, which is now on all four wheels in the grass behind the car. Lyle puts the cigarette in his mouth and, squinting against the smoke, reaches into his right front pocket and pulls out a wad of crumpled-up bills.

"Here you go," he says around the cigarette. "Feliz Domingo."

Henry comes over and takes the bills from Lyle, the top half of whose body

has, in the transaction, crossed the tipping point with the bottom, and he has to take a step forward to counter; then he steps back, gets the cigarette out of his mouth and into his right hand again, and all is well.

Henry unfolds each bill and counts them. Lyle, his right hand with the cigarette up now closer to his face, almost in front of his face, regards Henry through a gray stream of smoke.

"Eighteen," Henry says.

Lyle looks at Henry for a second, blinks a couple times, then puts the cigarette back into his mouth, reaches into his front pocket again, pulls out two more dollar bills, and hands them over to Henry.

Lyle pops the cigarette out of his mouth, between his thumb and forefinger this time, in the backwards-hand style, with the palm facing out, inhales with a sudden hiss, then says through a cloud of exhaled smoke, "See you in two weeks, Henry. And hey," he adds, pointing the butt of the cigarette at Henry, "don't forget to whack some under them tables. We don't want them little blades reachin' up and ticklin' folks' ankles, know what I mean?"

"Yes sir."

"All right then," Lyle says, turns around, and heads back toward the house.

We cut to Henry putting his left shoe up onto the Mothson's engine and pulling the cord. It starts right up. He pulls the goggles down over his face and heads off across the grass. We follow. Avoiding picnic tables here and there, we go all the way down to where the grass reaches the taller weeds and turn around. On our way back, Henry and we look to our left, toward the house, toward Lucky's: Lyle is standing in a window watching us. We keep mowing. We make a couple of turns and look back. He's gone. Fade to black.

"Henry . . . *Henry*," Mother says, and our eye pops open: we are lying on the couch in the living room, merged wth Henry, looking up at the wall and ceiling. The TV is on.

"Yeah, yes," we say, turning only as far as the TV before our attention, or at least our visual attention, is arrested by *The Dukes*, the 1983 Saturday morning cartoon version of *The Dukes of Hazzard.*

"I'm sorry to wake you, honey," she says behind us, "but Royd had to go in to work this mornin', so he's gone, and Avery just come by wantin' to take me and Maybe on a little surprise shoppin' spree over in Longview, so I just thought I should tell you so you didn't wake up and there wasn't nobody here. I also left a note on the kitchen table for Royd tellin' him where we're at too, just in case you're out whenever he gets home. Okay?"

"Okay," we say, watching *The Dukes*.

"Okay, well . . . we'll see you in a couple hours then."

"Okay," we say.

Boss Hogg has raised a bridge so the Dukes will crash and die, but the Dukes just jump the gap, yee-hawing the whole time: they are magically invincible and permanently overjoyed . . . but our eyelid sags all the same . . . and Noella fades down the sound of the TV accordingly . . . until finally the screen is totally dark and silent, except for the first breaths of sleep . . . and, finally, the long, meditative breaths of deep sleep.

If we are, indeed, still merged with Henry, then this marks the first time we have been merged with a character who is asleep. Interesting to think, too, that *we* are *awake* inside of a character as he sleeps; and if we were so deconstructively inclined, we could take this arrangement, this *situation* as symbolic or suggestive of the possibilty that there is no such thing as *pure* sleep because sleep incorporates material elements of *wakefulness* as well, which is to say mental activity, like thoughts, dreams, and perceptions (albethey virtual), and physical activity, like breathing.

After a while, like the onset of a dream, Noella cross-fades the breath of sleep with what sounds like an animal nursing: there's a lot of frantic licking and clicking and sucking and smacking going on: could be a cow or a goat, suckling from its mother's teat . . . or from the rubber nipple of some sort of feeding bottle. Whatever it is, it's fucking annoying . . . torture, actually, the longer it goes on . . . but then that pain is suddenly superseded by the more complicated pain of the sound of a man moaning with sexual pleasure *along with* the incessant licking and clicking and sucking and smacking—which tells me that we are, indeed, *not* in Kansas anymore. The moaning intensifies, and the words:

# Syrup Dispenser & Pistol

appear then fade out; then the scene fades in: Henry and we are inside the chain-link fence that surrounds his backyard, but we (the camera) are set some five yards directly behind him, and he is standing right up against the fence, with his left hand down at his crotch, as if feeding his penis through one of the fence's diamond-shaped interstices; his right hand is down by his side, a classic diner syrup dispenser dangling from its index finger; immediately on the other side, the outside, of the fence, appearing on one side of Henry and then the other in rapid succession, we see the tip of a dog's tail, wagging; and below that, through the fence and Henry's somewhat widespread legs, we see a dog's chest and legs.

Now, it is, of course, dreadfully obvious what's going on, and we are already way out over another line here, but apparently Noella is not content to leave things as they are because, keeping our eyes firmly on Henry and the dog, he moves us now in a leftward arc gradually around them, affording us better and better (or worse and worse) views of "the situation" and confirming, first, that the dog is, indeed, as we suspected, Luke, and then, as we come even with the fence, that Luke is, indeed, shlocking and shwacking away on Henry's erect penis—which, no doubt, Henry has slathered with syrup for the occasion, and which—we can only hope—is a prosthetic prop.

We're going to have to stop right here a second because . . . I mean, this scene has got to be entirely unprecedented in mainstream film, and you know there are going to be a whole lot of people who, once they get wind of it, are going to argue that it is, legally speaking, *obscene*, which is to say, patently offensive and lacking any redeeming social or artistic value, that it is therefore not *protected speech* under the First Amendment, and that it should be cut from the film. Though I'm not sure where I stand on this, exactly . . . I mean, David Lynch does a lot of shock-value stuff in his films, which I support, and generally I come down on the side of supporting artists and their judgments with respect to the inclusion of such scenes in their works because, well, I trust, I suppose, that they, artists, are the *prima facie* experts of social and artistic value in their own works. It would appear, however, that my body is at odds with my mind on this one because, for at least a moment, unconsciously and automatically, I close my eyes and plug my ears.

Keeping my ears plugged (because I seem to be *super-viscerally-sensitive* to the licking and clicking sounds), I open my eyes: Noella has arced us around to a position behind Luke now, such that the canine-oral/human-genital insult at hand is visible only obliquely, which is little consolation, but our visual attention is also drawn to the big window at the back of the house, where Pickles is jumping up and down in and out of the window frame, and there is someone, Royd, standing in the window as well. They disappear, the backdoor opens, and I unplug my ears.

Pickles bolts out the door, barking; Henry groans in what sounds like both ecstasy and disappointment, drops the syrup dispenser, falls to his knees in the grass, and half-buckles-over, holding and covering his penis with both hands. Luke barks then jumps up onto the fence to Henry's left to greet Pickles. Pickles is now at the fence both barking and whining; Luke barks again. Then Royd comes out of the house. He's coming quickly and angrily—he's angry about what Henry and Luke are doing and probably also about the note, about what Avery's doing—and he's got a pistol in his left hand. We swing fast around to the right, retracing the same arc, until we're even with the fence again, and stop. Royd walks up to the fence. Pickles is still barking—he hasn't stopped barking. Luke barks at Royd. Royd raises the pistol and shoots Luke between the eyes with a massive *bang*. Luke staggers backwards a few steps, sits down, then falls over onto his left side. Pickles barks even more. Royd turns and, with his left boot, kicks Pickles hard in the chest. Pickles yelps, flies through the air, lands several yards behind Henry with a thump, then whimpers and slinks all curled up back to the house and slips inside. Royd turns to Henry.

"All right, get up," he says, gesturing with the pistol. "*Get up.*"

"Yes, yes sir," Henry says, slowly unfolding himself. He turns away from Royd (and us) and zips and fastens his pants.

"All right, now gimme the syrup," Royd says, pointing at the syrup dispenser with the pistol.

Henry bends down and picks up the syrup dispenser.

"Now wipe it off with your shirt and hand it over."

Henry wipes off the syrup dispenser and then, without turning his body around, hands it back toward Royd with his left hand; Royd steps forward and takes it from him with his right.

"All right, now go and get the shovel and drag that piece of shit down away from here somewhere and bury it. You hear me?"

"Yes, yes sir."

"Well go on then, goddamnit."

Henry walks, still semi-doubled-over, back across the yard toward the garage; Royd heads back toward the house with the syrup dispenser and pistol; we stay put at the fence.

"*Hey*," Royd says over to Henry just before he goes into the house and Henry rounds the corner. Henry stops and turns his head slightly toward Royd. "When I say 'away from here,' I mean all the way across the damn creek, okay? I mean bury that piece of shit deep in the woods across the creek. Understand?"

"Yes sir," Henry says.

"Okay *and*," Royd says raising the pistol up with his left hand and pointing it loosely at Henry, "you don't say *nothin'* about this to *Avery* or *Mother* or *Maybe* or *nobody*, you hear me? *You hear me?*"

"Yes, yes sir, I hear you."

"This . . ."—Royd makes a small circle in the air with the pistol—"this *whole thing*, if you know what I mean, will just be our little secet, okay? *Okay?*"

"Yes, yes sir, okay."

"Okay." Royd lowers the pistol back by his side. Then he raises it back up again. "And if anybody asks about Luke, you just say you ain't seen him. That's it. You ain't seen him. Okay?"

"Yes sir, okay."

"Okay," he says, lowers the pistol, goes into the house, and shuts the door.

Henry disappears around the garage, and we're left staring at the empty backyard and the back of the house. The cicadas click on . . . or could be they've been going this whole time, but things have just calmed down enough now for us to notice them again.

Fade to black and silence.

I KNOW, it's tough, tough stuff to swallow (as it were), and, as I said before, once it gets out there (which shouldn't take long), it's not going to go down (as it were) well with the moral majority, and there will be blood. But look, if we can just step back for a minute and take it—the whole naughty, nasty episode with its bestiality, dog-murder, and everything else—as not only something to be up in arms about, but also as just *a collection of narrative facts*, then I'm sure we can make something more intelligible of it, that we can extrapolate from it, in that cool-headed analytical style with which we are now so familiar, a number of specific, narratively salient explanations and conclusions, such as the following:

(i) That Avery has taught Luke to suck, lick, whatever his (Avery's) cock; that Luke has "hinted" or "suggested" to Henry (through a number of muzzle-punches to his crotch) that he (Luke) is game to suck Henry's cock; and, that Henry has obviously taken the hint or thought well of that suggestion, having recently arranged things so that he (Henry) would benefit from having his cock sucked by Luke as well.

(ii) That, in addition to receiving, as it were, blow-jobs from his dog, Avery has strong, seemingly healthy domestic-paternal-familial desires and is going around looking for ways to satisfy them: he's gotten some satisfaction through his recent interactions with Henry, and now, with Royd conveniently gone on a Saturday morning (an absence which he is somehow (doesn't matter how) aware of), he's trying to get satisfaction through a close interaction with Mother and Maybe.

(iii) That Mother and Maybe are trying to satisfy their desire to get closer to (Uncle) Avery . . . though probably mainly they're just eager to get some new clothes.

(iv) That it has been everyone else's absence from the homestead, or compound, this Saturday morning that has afforded Henry the opportunity to have his cock sucked by Luke and his sexual desires, however depraved, satisfied.

(v) That Royd is so incensed by the note and what he perceives as Avery's surreptitious undermining of his (Royd's) authority, and is so repulsed and humilated by what Henry is doing in his backyard[65] that he feels totally justfied in shooting Luke in the head: it puts a definitive end to the bestial offense and satisfies his desire to get back at, or hurt, Avery.

Now, the screen's still dark, but we hear a little girl, Maybe, talking against a background of pulsing cicadas, but because of the distance and the fact that Noella's got some kind of tube- or phaser-effect on the whole audio track, we are only able to pick up fragments of what she's saying:

"And then . . . the ferris wheel . . . he said . . . I haven't . . . but . . . to the fair, Henry? . . . soon . . ."

Our eye cracks open and a thin splinter of white steam-like light vertically divides the screen from top to bottom then widens (but only feebly and halfway, as if we're barely alive) to reveal, through and over blurry shades of grass, a sideways (we seem to be lying sidweays in the grass) and very humid image of Henry and Maybe, sitting together in the grass as well, in the near distance.[66] Our eye, or eyelid, sleepily opens and closes on the scene. Maybe looks over at us. Then she points at us.

"What's wrong with Pickles, Henry? Why isn't he movin'?"

---

[65] Just because Royd is an incestuous-pedophilic-rapist-dog-murderer does not *entail* that he's going to condone bestiality. However strange it may seem, he can still have his limits.

[66] Suddenly it strikes me just how penile the camera and we are here, a real one-eyed sort of monster, probing around, inserting itself into everything, making scenes through "rape," by raping open situations and environments.

Henry looks at us too. Evidently, we are merged with Pickles now.

"Why isn't Pickles movin', Henry?"

Henry gets up and walks over to us until we see mostly just his shoe and lower pant leg. He kneels down. Now we can see an out-of-focus Maybe through the square-ish space framed by his butt, the right edge of the screen, the grass, and the now vertical sole of his shoe (which is propping up his butt). Henry's hand comes down in front of our eye then moves behind our head. He lifts up our head and drops it into the grass: we are a dead or a very nearly dead dog—and it was Royd's boot, we have to think, that killed or very nearly killed him.

Henry stands up. Through a still bleary and only half-open eye, all we see now are his lower pant leg and Maybe in the distance. We hear a high-pitched whistling sound, like a tea kettle. It's Maybe, crying. Fade to black and silence. The words:

# BURIED ALIVE

appear (in red) then fade out. When we fade in again, we're still lying sideways and bleary-eyed in the grass, but Maybe's gone. We hear the backdoor shut then footsteps in the grass, approaching. Someone, probably Henry, stops, kneels down beside us, and drops something, some kind of dark, minimally translucent material, just in front of our eye, so all we see is a kind of deep amber shadow, which he starts moving around in front of us, then he grabs us and starts moving us around too; flashes of sunlight reveal that what he's trying to do is put us into a sack, like a burlap potato sack. As he struggles to do this, we are aware only of the sounds of his effort and a tumult of images, mostly dark, some, occasionally, blindingly bright, until finally we drop unceremoniously into the bottom of the sack, out of the top of which now, we can see Henry and the sky, until he closes it up. Now, but for a diffuse sheen of brown light that manages to soak through the hairy pores of the sack, we are blind.

"Here's a shovel, Henry," Mother calls out. "Bury him down by the big oak or somethin.'"

We hear Henry walk over to get the shovel from Mother (Noella, amplifying the light crunch of Henry's footsteps in the grass). He comes back, picks us up, and carries us the short distance over to what has to be the chain-link gate at the far corner of the yard, which he opens, closes behind him, then heads down, presumably, to the big oak (his footsteps still emphasized, along with the swish of his pant leg against us). Before too long, we cross into shade, Henry drops us onto the ground, and starts digging.

A small crack of dull gray light has appeared in the upper right quadrant of our visual field (i.e., the screen)—a small opening at the top of the sack, no doubt—which we hang onto as the shovel cuts repeatedly into the earth nearby. Occasionally, Noella has us blink, each instance of which (there are some three or four) we are ultimately able to infer, represents a small but not insignificant jump forward in time, through the too-long and redundant and tedious process of listening to someone dig a good, Pickles-sized grave, because it's not long before Henry picks us up, drops us into the hole, and starts shoveling dirt back on top of us. With each shovelfull, whatever light is left is darkened to pitch by large bundles of degrees, so that after only a few tosses of dirt, there is no light left at all; the sounds of Henry stabbing dirt and throwing it on us die out by bundles of degrees as well, and, very soon, we find ourselves in total dark-ness and silence once again.

Now this is the first time we've been in such a state *as a dog*, and the first time that we've been, in *effect* anyway, *buried alive*. Although, I don't know that our being one with Pickles here means anything *in itself*; that is, I don't think Noella is trying to say that we, the audience or the camera, are, in some important respect, *dogs*, or that we are, *ourselves*, in some way (and for some reason), very nearly dead and being buried alive; what Noella *is* doing, though, undoubtedly—beyond just creat-ing fun and entertaining cinema—is drawing our attention to, and thus, by extension, suggesting that we ponder the signifi-cance of Pickles-the-dog's live burial and death *in this narrative*, in this film.

And when we do that, I'm pretty soon thinking about how, in fiction, both literal and figurative worlds are often taken up and combined, or *merged* (as we seem to be in the habit of say-ing now), such that being *buried alive* here implies *not only* that something is literally going to *die*, it *also* implies that something figurative is going to die *and* that something figurative is going to *live*, to *persist*, to *survive*, *in* and *through* death and almost as-suredly *reappear* in some form or another down the line—and, if you have any doubt about this last part, just say it out loud: say "buried *alive*," emphasizing the "*alive*," and you'll see what I'm driving at.

Now the French, notorious theorists of paradox that they are, say that when we encounter paradox, we come down with a sort of sickness or flu: "une maladie paradoxale" they call it, the symptoms of which are nausea and light-headedness, or, again, in the French, "la nausée et l'effervescence synaptique." When asked, during one of his lectures on his big book, *Études de Paradoxe*, to elaborate on what *exactly* is meant by the beguiling words "l'effervescence synaptique," Emile Meniers said, to the delight of his audience, "C'est comme une Sprite fraîchement versé dans le cerveau": "It's like a freshly poured Sprite in the brain."

So I wouldn't be totally surprised if some of you aren't feeling all that good right now because there *is* the paradox here that *Pickles-the-dog both dies from and survives being buried alive; but,* since this is *not* a hard-case type paradox, *and* since we've pretty much already explained it (just above), any *maladie paradoxale* you may have contracted should be cured *toute suite*; I mean, all you have to see to dissolve the contradiction at its (the paradox's) heart is that the subject term "Pickles-the-dog" *equivocates*, or is ambiguous, in its meaning: if it means Pickles' *literal-material* being, then it dies; if it means some *figurative-immaterial* aspect of Pickles' being, or something the dog *represents*, then it either dies or it survives, depending.[67]

It goes wthout saying, then, that Pickles' *literal-material* being is going to die here. No, I'm sorry. That's over-stating it because it doesn't just *go without saying* that Pickles' *literal-material* being is going to die here; this is fiction; anything is possible; thus, Pickles' physical body *could* survive being buried alive, but if it did, what we *would* be certain of is that our story had suddenly gone the way of *Pet Sematary* (Stephen King: 1983 book, 1989 film),[68] and the likelihood of *that*, I'll wager, is low—not impossible, but low—because it falls outside the range

---

[67] An even easier example: the contradiction at the heart of the paradoxical statement "The cake is so good and so bad" dissolves when you see that the meaning of the term "cake" equivocates: when it means *that tasty stuff*, it's good; when it means *that fattening stuff*, it's bad.

[68] And I guess, less directly, all the other living-dead-type books and films out there.

of *way* more probable developments given, or implied by, the events of the story thus far.

This is *not* to say, mind you, that it wouldn't be really cool and hilarious and subversive of our narrative paradigms, expectations, biases, etc., if Pickles were to come back a zombie; I'm just saying that—you know, unless I've missed something really big and there's a massive lacuna in my understanding of this film up to this point—that the chances we'll see Pickles-the-zombie-dog in the coming scenes are slim or slimmer than other possibilities because nothing so far has really set us up for such an eventuality.

On the other hand, zombie dogs are surely more likely than the remainder of this film suddenly turning into a documentary history of the shoestring potato. So ultimately we can probably say something like that there's about a ninety-percent chance the film will continue on concerning itself with Henry and Emily without introducing Pickles-the-zombie-dog; a nine percent chance that Pickles will turn into a zombie dog, and a one percent chance (just to keep it simple because it's probably way less) that the film will soon be about shoestring potatoes.[69]

Things are more complicated with Pickles' *figurative-immaterial* being. If Pickles represents a sort of mindless, intentionless idiot . . . or, more charitably, if he represents a kind of infantile consciousness, then his death will signify the end,

---

[69]Laird Hunt's 2001 book *The Impossibly* does a one-eighty mid-way through, changing suddenly from a full-on mafia crime story into a full-on ghost story. Theoretically speaking, it's pretty cool, *banging* together these two disparate master narratives; *but*, the force-job is, actually and in fact, set up by the also banged-together title, by the noun-adverb "The Impossibly"; what's more, in my humble opinion, the book, and, specifically, the force-job, doesn't *really* work; it's not a good read; it's a hamfistedly illustrative theoretical gambit: it's *The Hamfistedly*.

the *real* end in Henry, of that sort of consciousness; with Pickles' death, the preamble to change is over, the vague transition period is complete, and we have our watershed moment: from here on out, Henry is no longer a child, but a young adult, in earnest; and this is driven home by the fact that Henry is the one who has to do the very adult job of *literally killing* Pickles: Pickles may have been going to die anyway, and very soon, but it was Henry's shovelfulls of dirt that *actually* killed him, that were the proximate cause of his death.[70]

So Henry *himself* puts the finishing touches on his childhood, and, consistent with that, we see him cotemporaneously discover his true vocational calling as a lawnmower, which will bring with it a paycheck, a living, a life, and a newfound independence from Royd, his mother, and her watchful and voyeuristic eye. We can see this newfound independence in the last episode in Henry's more prideful comportment and in his ability to move on, or rather *mow* on, *regardless* of Mother's status in the window, and it is further signified by Mother's ultimate disappearance from the window all together, the message-in-metaphor of which is that Mother is no longer the ubiquitous presence in Henry's thoughts that she once was and that he no longer cares what she thinks about him, at least not in the way he did before. She has, then, in other words, at least in an important psychological-developmental sense, "died" to him.

This turn, or move, or paradigm shift, from thinking about what *the watcher in the house*, his mother, thinks about him, to thinking about what *the watcher in the woods*, his (same age)

---

[70] Which is a really, I think, poignant and effective intertext with, and modified reiteration of the tragic scene in *Old Yeller* when the boy has to take Old Yeller (his dog) out back and shoot him, to put him down, because Old Yeller is terminally ill or is going to die soon anyway or some such thing.

love interest, thinks about him shouldn't *totally* surprise us, at least on a social-developmental level, because it is, after all, normal for young adults to shift their allegiance from their parents to their friends; but on a strictly psychological level, the implication is that Henry no longer wants to love and perhaps have sex with his mother, but that he wants to love and have sex with his sister, and it's this Freudian incest stuff (among other things) that many of us are struggling with here, that we're both drawn to and repulsed by, right?

What this, the fact of this struggle between fascination and repulsion vis-à-vis incest, suggests to me now is that there is a profound conflict between the primary instinct to have sex and the secondary or evolved (or epigenetic) instinct to *not* have sex with a close family member, to commit incest. It's a conflict, which, given the usually wide variety of sexual partners and procreative options, the instinct not to commit incest usually wins hands down; but the problem here, with Henry, is that there are, apparently, no other potential partners around or available but Emily. Henry and Emily are, in effect, sealed off from the rest of the world, such that the only hope for the survival of their genetic line *is* incest. This further suggests—though not surprisingly—that the deeper survival and sex instincts are in cahoots because, together, in dire straits (like the one dramatized here), they'll do whatever they can, even outstrip the prohibition against incest, in order to procreate.[71]

I am reminded of the biblical story of Lot and his two daughters (who, for some reason, go unnamed). Lot's daughters, because the three of them are so severely and seemingly endessly isolated in the mountains, deem it necessary to have sex with

---

[71]See Dawkins' *The Selfish Gene.*

their father in order to preserve their genetic line. So, they force dad to go on a two-day wine bender, fuck him multiple times while he's asleep (the acts of which, he is reported to have said, he was entirely unaware—yeah *right!*), succeed in getting pregnant—both of them—and finally give birth to Moab and Ammon.

In any case, if Pickles also represents *Maybe's innocence*: her childhood innocence, her sexual innocence, her psycho-emotional innocence—and I think he does because dogs just *are* morally innocent, and Pickles was brought into the family *because of*, and *for* Maybe—then, very likely, it (Maybe's innocence) is going to die, and it's going to die because of, or at the hands of, Royd. We have seen, up to this point, some serious *threats* to Maybe's innocence: Royd's icky doting on her, his slipping naked into bed with her at that hotel under cover of night, and, metaphorically speaking, his failed attempt to lead her down into the "cave" (Carlsbad); but here, now, with Pickles' death, we can be fairly certain, her innocence is about to die *for real*.

Pickles could also represent (metonymously) this whole nuclear family, this whole numerical-familial unit: Mother-Royd-Henry-Maybe-Pickles. *The family dog* is, after all, one of those ubiquitous symbols of *family unity*, perhaps especially in the US, and so Pickles' death here can be seen as a clear sign that our family (qua *family*) is dead, or is about to be dead, and that, very soon, its members will disband or, in some important respect, go their separate ways.

Now, with respect to *figurative-immaterial* aspects of Pickles that will *survive*, if we can accept, in addition to everything else here, that Pickles, qua *dog*, can stand for *animality* more generally and in its most pejorative, most dissolute and/or savage sense—and I think we can because it is common knowledge that dogs sniff and huff each other's assholes; that they, often enough, piss and shit in the public spaces of their own homes; that they eat their own and other dogs' shit; that they bite, rape, and otherwise physically brutalize each other; that they vocally assault (through ballistic volleys of violent barking) people, other dogs and animals, and vehicles; that they run down and otherwise try to intimidate same, generating in them (or their drivers and passengers) the apprehension of immediate bodily harm; that they frequently bite people, and that they occasionally tear young children and babies apart limb from limb—then we can also accept that Pickles represents *moral vacancy* and that it will be a dissolute and/or savage sort of thing that is going to *persist* through Pickles' *literal-material* death and show up later on.[72]

Pickles, then, and *dogs* more generally are, like our bats, snakes, and moths from before, a deictic or context-determined metaphor. And perhaps you've noticed, as I just have, that the fluid nature of this sort of metaphor totally supports our being able to make *paradoxical* statements, like "Pickles/Dogs represent both moral innocence and moral vacancy" and "Pickles/Dogs represent both good and evil," because it (this sort of metaphor) allows the meaning of the subject term, "Pickles/Dogs" to *equivocate*: when we take it to mean (*Maybe's*) *cute (if stupid) little domestic pet*, then he represents *moral innocence and good*; when we take it to mean *dissolute and savage ani-*

---

[72]It occurs to me to state a fact here: *men are more brutal and violent than women*—and then to extrapolate that men's talents as violent brutes are obsolete: *what may have been an asset on the savannah is a liability in the city.* This is of great concern today. Leaders today should not be morally obtuse, savage animals.

*mal*, then he represents *moral vacancy and evil*—but where, of course, in the same breath, we also dissolve, or explain away, the contradiction at the heart of the paradox because, as we now know, when the meaning of the subject term equivocates, there is no contradiction, and the paradox is discharged.

It's not *new* news, but it's always interesting (to me) to note that, in dogs, or in animals that are largely or pretty much pre- or non-moral (I qualify this because they do have *some* (albeit limited) sense of right and wrong—which they get mostly from their social settings), *moral innocence* and *savagery* are not inconsistent, are not contradictory: such an animal is a *morally innocent savage*: when it eats shit or mauls a baby, it doesn't know what it's doing; I mean, *we* might punish it, but *it*, deep down, is not *really* responsible or guilty; it doesn't *understand*.

We humans, on the other hand, think of ourselves as *infinitely* different from such "wild" animals, and we do take responsibility and experience guilt, and we do, very often, understand; but what if the savage forces within us are not as constrained as we'd like to think, if they are operating in and amongst us without a license: automatically, largely unbeknownst to us, and very often out of our control—then are we *so* different from these *animals* after all? Maybe the buried animal has survived, in us, and we are not as in control, responsible, guilty, and intelligent as we thought. If this is right, then—and let me be perfectly clear—I am *not* saying that we *are* (metaphysically speaking) and *should be* (psychologically and socially speaking) exonerated or free to act on whatever savage urges overcome us: no, this is *not* a license to kill; it's a plea, an appeal, a *call* to live up to, to become what we thought we were.

There's some intratextual stuff going on here too because Pickles' being buried alive is an internal modified reiteration of, not only Luke's recent live burial (obviously), but also of both Henry's passing out in, then re-emerging from Carlsbad Cavern, and, to a lesser extent, his surviving the fall from Mrs. Caldwell's attic; so we see a kind of Nietzschean *what doesn't kill him makes him stronger* pattern of evolution, a *positive* dialectical pattern of evolution, going on with Henry right now: he's growing up, and as he does, old paradigms give way to new, and, for the moment anyway—because this sense of progress needn't last forever—it seems like Henry is definitely *going somewhere*.

Now *where*, exactly, he is going, we cannot be absolutely certain, of course, but there is, I think, some pretty palpable foreshadowing in this episode for us to hang on to for the time being; and if foreshadowing is just the oblique revelation of ostensible future sites of intratextuality: the sense that a given current narrative moment or event is, like a *forward-thrown* thread, going to be reiterated in some fashion or other down the narrative line—then, if I had to guess, I'd say Noella wants us to intuit that Pickles' being buried alive looks forward to some future experience Henry will have or even to a life he will live *underground*, be it literal, metaphorical, or both;[73] and if this is right, if Pickles' being buried alive looks forward in this way *and*, as we've been saying, reaches *back* into the past to take up again, especially, Henry's experience down in Carlsbad Cavern, then Pickles' being buried alive is a *bridge*, an intratextual bridge, between Henry's past and his future, between Carlsbad and whatever Carlsbad-like situation is to come. The scene casts a line into the past and into the future at the same time.

[73] I can't help but think here of Dostoevsky's Underground Man from *Notes from Underground*.

Finally, I think Maybe's garbled, bad-trippy sounding talk about "the fair" and "he said" and "the ferris wheel . . . soon" is foreshadowing too, but in a more straightforward sense: it tells us that someone, almost certainly Royd, has promised to take her to the fair, but where the fear, the foreboding is that it's a lure, a trick, the result of which will see a child's dream turn into an adult nightmare.

A FTER THE LAST SHOVELFULL of dirt was thrown over us (the last one we were able to perceive anyway), the screen went dark and silent for some time, and that is how things stand now . . . .until the silence is broken by a loud metal clank, followed immediately by the heavy grinding of the steel wheels of a railway car, slowly starting to roll off over the tracks. These are the sounds of our mining car, from back at Carlsbad, but this time, we don't speed up but continue to travel at a slow, even speed. We are, presumably (because there's still no light), moving over level ground.

In the distance, pick-axes strike rock in broken rhythms, like men working in a mine, and, as we roll on, they grow louder: we are approaching them . . . but when we reach them, we do not stop; we pass them by, and their sounds fall quickly behind us, diminishing steadily by degrees. But before they fade out all together, Noella dials up, in their place, the sounds of breathing and the up-and-down crank of some kind of lever, as if we or whoever we're with are having to work hard now . . . to power the car . . . a handcar . . . up and out of the mine.

This goes on for about thirty seconds, then Noella fades out the sound of the crank, and all we are left with is breathing . . . but it's no longer labored; it's measured and even. It's hard to say why, exactly, but the assumption is that it's Royd and that it is he who has risen metempsychotically (or transmigrationally) from Pickles and come up through the mine to wherever it is we are now.

A door creaks open slowly, crypt-like, and a grainy deep-amber light spreads behind its sweeping black shadow, left across the screen, brightens a bit, then resolves into Henry and Maybe's room, which recalls for us, though in a new way, of course, the scene back at East-Tex Insulation where Royd slowly pushes open the door to the office to the sound of the Bee Gee's "Stayin' Alive"; thus, it also should alert us, more generally, to the possibility that the concept, trope, theme, metaphor, whatever you want to call it, of "the door" (however well-heeled it may be) is beginning to see some real action here. Indeed, Noella's use of "Stayin' Alive" in connection with dark passages and their doors might suddenly take on new meaning: dark passages and their doors provide the means by which repressed urges, instincts, traumas, etc., *stay alive*, survive, are born again, and resurface.

Maybe is asleep in her bed; Henry is asleep in his, tucked-in funereally again. We slide right along the near wall, stop in the corner, rotate back towards the door, descend, and settle down at Henry's left shoulder. Royd (it is Royd; the light is sufficient enough to be sure) is walking quietly around the foot of Henry's bed and over to Maybe's. He stops at Maybe's bedside and stands over her. He reaches down and pulls back the covers. She's sleeping on her side, curled up, facing the opposite wall. She doesn't move. Royd leans over and, with both arms, scoops her up out of bed. She squirms and resists a bit; she doesn't know what's happening.

"Shh, baby girl," Royd whispers. "Time to go to the fair."

She settles down into his arms. Royd turns and carries her out of the room, into the dark hallway. The words:

# BODY SNATCHER

appear (in light gray against the darkness) then fade out. Henry's face, in profile, moves into and takes up the right half of the screen: he has raised his head. He sits up on his elbows, and we fall behind his left shoulder but then swing out and around and over to a position at the foot of Maybe's bed to watch him. The front door to the house creaks open . . . creaks closed . . . snaps shut. Henry throws off the covers, jumps out of bed (wearing only his white underpants (again)), runs into the dimly-lit hallway, and starts banging furiously on Mother's bedroom door.

"What! What is it?" Mother yells from behind the door.

"Royd took Maybe! Royd took Maybe!"

"What? Oh . . . No, Henry, that's . . . It's all right . . . Henry, open the door a second, okay?"

Henry opens the door, but no light spreads behind it: it's a different sort of door than his . . . and a different sort of room: nothing is revealed by it, and nothing resolves in it; and while we should not say that they, or, specifically, the *room*, *Mother's* room, is unique—because it is, just like Royd's window-less office at East-Tex, a sort of *dead end* place—we *should* say that, as an intransigent black cavity, or black hole, it goes much further than East-Tex . . . or any other room we've encountered so far, and is thus clearly distinguished.

"It's all right, honey," Mother says disembodied through the dark. "Royd's just taking Maybe to the fair today, and it's all the way over in Ruston, so they had to leave real early . . . but they'll be back tonight."

We strain hard to see her, but still there's nothing.

"I'm sorry, Henry. I thought we talked about this. They were gonna go, and we were gonna stay here . . . because I don't like fairs, and you're too old for that stuff, remember?"

Henry just stands there.

"Well . . . anyway, Henry. Everthing's okay, okay sweetheart? Now go on and close the door, please, and go back to bed."

Henry pulls the door closed and stands in front of it.

He turns around and looks down the hallway at the front door.

The Buick starts up outside.

He walks to the front door and stands in front of it.

The Buick clanks into gear and starts to roll off over the gravel.

Henry opens the door: the El Camino is parked at the far end of the parking area, and there is a car parked in front of the house, but it's not the Buick; it's a Chrysler Cordoba[74]; the Buick is, indeed, headed down the access road.

Henry watches it a second, then he steps outside, walks right, past the parked car, and starts to jog . . . then he starts to run. We run after him but, because of the burden of the camera, we quickly fall behind.

Henry's running as fast as he can now down the access road after the Buick . . . and he's catching up to it . . . but then Royd—probably alarmed to discover, in his rearview mirror, Henry, running after them in his underwear—slams on the brakes.

Henry stops, lit red by the brake lamps.

We stop.

Then Royd guns it. The tires spin caustically in the dirt before they gain traction and the Buick speeds off.

Henry disappears completely in a cloud of dust.

The Buick turns right up at the main road and is gone.

Now there should be little doubt that Royd is kidnapping Maybe here and that this trip to the fair provides him the per-

---

[74] The car Ricardo Montalban famously hustled back in the '80s, supported by the song, "Volaré," which means *I will fly.*

fect opportunity to make off with her without interference from Mother or Henry; and because we saw it coming, and because Mother suspected nothing (of course) and Henry smelled the rat a little too late, we have been filled with a strong sense of dramatic irony, of helpless doomed-ness and despair with respect to Maybe, the worst part of which is knowing that not only is her *body* in jeopardy, but also her *mind*, her psyche, her soul, her self: taking and using someone's body to one's own ends like this entails seriously and probably irreparably damaging that person to the *core* of her psycho-emotional being; indeed, recall in *Invasion of the Body Snatchers*[75] - our most obvious and direct intertextual reference here—how, when the alien pod organism duplicates a person's body, it completely destroys that person's psycho-emotional self, leaving only a *zombie*.

[75] Film—1956 original and 1978 remake (with Donald Sutherland).

W E WALK toward the cloud as it hangs over the road in the moonlight, pale and opaque, like a smudged erasure. The word:

# EMILY

appears (in black against the cloud) then fades out. Henry materializes out of the cloud, walking, back toward us and the house; he, his whole body, his skin, is pale too, as if he, too, were made of dust.

As we approach one another, we see his face: jaundiced, spectral, bereft . . . except for his eyes, which, while apparently directed at the ground in front of him, are frozen and, as it were, turned inward, staring fixedly at something entirely internal. We swing around behind him, behind his left shoulder, and follow.

There is a sharp "ting," like the sound of a steel triangle being rung, and, at exactly the same moment, as if the two are connected, a bright white light switches on down by the creek.

Henry stops and looks up at the light *very much as if it is the ting that makes him do so*, which is, to us, like being rudely snapped out of an engrossing dream because we all know there's no thing that would go "ting" *outside* in the world, outside in Henry's world like this right now; so we're groping around for some defensible explanation, and the first one that occurs to me is that if the ting doesn't come from Henry's *external world*, then it must come from his *internal world*, that he must hear or experience the ting from *inside himself*, from *inside his head*, and that its function is to alert him to the light, to make him look up and see the light, which must be *outside* of him, in the *external world* because why, indeed, would he have to raise his head and eyes to see a light that is wholly *inside* of him?

And then it only makes sense to think that it is *Emily*[76] who is responsible for switching on the light; that she, too, is *outside*, in Henry's *external world*; and since she and Henry are *telepathic* (or some such thing), that *she* is the one who has planted, or caused, the ting in Henry's mind—to get him to look up and see her light[77] and come across the creek to find her, just as she had instructed him to do—*telepathically*—down in Carlsbad Cavern. And if this is right, then it also means or at least strongly suggests that Henry really *did* see a light across the creek back when he and Mother and Royd were sitting around in the backyard a few years ago, and that the garbage that was strewn about in the parking area upon their return from Carlsbad was strewn about *not* by a racoon but by *Emily*, who had been rooting around in the cans for food.

This is a pretty reasonable explanation or, rather, *theory* of the ting—let's call it the *Emily is in Henry's External World Theory*—and it is, of course, what *Henry* believes; but it's pretty obvious, painfully obvious actually, that the ting *also* serves as an *extra*-diegetic, *outside-the-main-narrative*, communication *from Noella to us, the audience*, the function of which is to alert *us* that Henry has just had a really bright *idea*. For *who*, I ask you, could possibly have been ultimately responsible for insin-

---

[76] And not Pickles-the-zombie-dog or a shoestring potato . . .

[77] If this reading is right, then Noella has just granted us, if only for an instant, access inside Henry's mind, which would be a first and perhaps the closest thing we're going to get to internal monologue here. Though granted, it is a little disconcerting to finally be let inside Henry's mind only to get a ting. I am reminded here, as well, that during those times we have been merged sensory-perceptually with Henry, we have nevertheless been locked out of his *reflective* consciousness.

uating such an obtrusive and artifcial effect as this ting into the film other than the writer/director? And *who*, I ask you, is apt to have bestowed upon him a ting of this nature at exactly the same moment that a light pops on for him but a fictional character in a movie or cartoon for whom, the audience is to understand, a deep train of thought has just culminated in a bright idea? "Ting!"

The implication *here*, though, totally *contra* the *Emily is in Henry's External World Theory*, is that, because it occurs extra-diegetically, or outside the main narrative, *only we, the audience,* hear the ting, that Henry does *not* hear the ting at all, that the light captures his attention on its own—which is, actually, perfectly believable as well—and, most importantly, that the light, Emily, and her message to him to come across the creek and find her are the *constituents* of Henry's bright *idea* and thus all *only in Henry's internal world, in his imagination: hallucinations of things in the external world*—because an *idea* or *ideas* do not take place outside, in the external world; they take place *entirely inside one's head*, do they not?

On *this* view, then, what is communicated *to us* via this device, this ting, is that the light, Emily, Henry's initial sighting of the light, and his experience of, or with Emily down on the floor of Carlsbad Cavern, are *not* telepathic communications from some source in Henry's external world (i.e., Emily), but *ideas*, fantasies, dreams, illusions, fictions, super-convincing *hallucinations of things in his external world*, which are *actually* produced and take place entirely within the confines of his *internal world*, or *imagination*. It follows, of course, as well, that the garbage was strewn around *not* by Emily, but, in fact, by (mere) racoons. This too—let's call it the *Emily is Only in Henry's Internal World Theory*—is a perfectly reasonable, equally defensible theory of the ting, and it is, I think, just as consistent with the facts of the narrative as the *Emily is in Henry's External World Theory.*

So, now, regardless of your positions on telepathy and super-veridical-seeming-hallucinations, both of these diametrically opposed theories are equally consistent with the facts as they are presented in the fictional narrative that is this film; and, in the absence of any further, better, more dispositive theory or explanation—and none is forthcoming (at least to me)—we have to ask: *Which one of these theories is right?* Because we all know, on pain of contradiction, that Emily can't exist both *all or only* inside Henry's head and *also* in the external world at the same time. So one of these two theories *must* be wrong . . . *right?*

No. Not necessarily because the situation is a lot like Shröedinger's Cat's. With Schröedinger's Cat, we know, *metaphysically* speaking, that the cat will be either alive or dead inside the box when we open it, that it cannot be both; *but,* since there's no dispositive way for us to *know* for sure which one it will be *before* we open the box, we have no choice, *epistemologically* speaking, but to process the two possibilities side-by-side, at the same time, as if they're both true; and it is in this solely epistemological sense, I think, that, before we open the box, the cat is both alive and dead at the same time. And here, in *Lawnmower,* we know that, *metaphysically* speaking, Emily cannot exist both in the external world and only inside Henry's head at the same time, but since there's no dispositive way to know which is metaphysically true given the evidence, we have no choice, *epistemologically* speaking, but to accept and process the two possibilities simultaneously as if they're both true, as if

Emily exists *both* externally *and* only internally to Henry *at the same time.*[78]

The light starts moving ... to one side ... then the other, slowly and deliberately, back and forth now in small arcs, as if slowly waving.

Henry starts walking again. We follow.

The light starts switching on and off.

Henry stops.

The light holds still.

Henry walks.

The light switches on and off.

As Henry approaches the house, the light starts waving again.

He walks past the house, and the light goes back to switching on and off.

Henry heads down to the bridge, the light switching on and off all the time.

As Henry crosses the bridge, the light, still switching on and off, starts receding into the trees.

Henry walks up the other side of the creek, but the flashing light continues to withdraw into the woods, so he turns into the woods and follows.

It's much darker under the trees; the tree trunks, as we pass through them, are darker than the darkness itself.

The light stops receding; it holds steady, lighting up more and more space for us as we approach, and we can see now that

---

[78] These sorts of considerations might prompt us to wonder, more generally, whether some traditional metaphysical questions are, quite simply, *impossible* to answer, and whether (as Quine might have it) epistemology is, as it were, more metaphysical than metaphysics, more basic than metaphysics, more ontological than metaphysics, or ontologically prior to metaphysics.

we are no longer following behind Henry; we have merged with him somewhere back in the dark sub-rosa.

Now the light is close and very bright. The darkness is fractured across the lens with bright silver shards.

We push through a thicket of dense underbrush, and the light angles directly into our eye, blinding us completely. We stumble and the light switches off just as we hit the ground.[79]

We hear light footsteps on the forest floor, approaching . . . then a grainy white object . . . a grainy white vaguely triangular object starts pushing through the darkness, steadily materializing, floating in our direction.

Our eye adjusts, and we can see, by the full-moon-light now, that the approaching object is a dress . . . it's a teenage girl, fifteen-sixteen, in a very small, in a way-too-small sleeveless A-line flared white sundress. The bottom of the dress barely reaches the bottom of her underwear. She stops in front of us. Except for the dress and underwear, her skin is bare, including her feet.

She sits down on her knees in front of us. She looks exactly like Henry: brown hair, parted from left to right across her forehead, brown-skin, somewhat gaunt but attractive.[80] There's dirt or mud on her face, and she's tried (unsuccessfully) to cut and brush or straighten her hair. She stares at us a second. Then she

---

[79] Of course, Noella's having whoever it is with the flashlight (you know who it is) switch it off at just this moment is purely for dramatic-cinematic effect. Obviously, it would've been way more natural, not to mention *helpful*, to leave it on.

[80] Looking back to the list of actresses and actors, I'm thinking this girl must be Joss Christiana Hoffman, that *this Emily* is Joss Christiana Hoffman, and *this Henry* is her real-life identical twin brother, Joff Christian Hoffman. And I guess Joss is to Jess and Joff is to Jeff . . . I don't know.

sits up on her knees, reaches down with both hands, and pulls the dress off up over head.

The screen goes dark, but we can still hear them breathing.

"Don't tell nobody about this, Henry," Emily whispers (as if in our ear). "If you want me . . . and you wanna keep me, then this will just be our little secret."

We cut, in the darkness, to the sound of heavy breathing, which surprises no one . . . but then the image appears of us—still merged with Henry—running up to the chain-link gate at the back of Henry's house, which *is* a bit of a surprise—and it's obviously Noella having a bit of fun with us here; but, in any case, the assumption is, I think, that we have done the deed with Emily, either in our imagination or for real (or both), and now we're trying to get back into the house and get situated before Mother gets up . . . but morning has broken.

We come through the gate, walk quickly across the backyard to the back door, and open it.

Mother is down the hallway, caught, apparently, crossing between the two bedrooms.

"Oh thank *god*," she says, bringing her hand to her chest. "I been worried *sick*."

She comes down the hall; we come into the house and shut the door behind us. She gives us a big hug then pulls back and holds us by the shoulders.

"Where have you *been*, Henry?"

"Out, outside. I just been outside."

"In your underpants? At six in the morning? Why, honey?"

She lets go of our shoulders.

"'Cause . . . after Royd lef', and Maybe lef', I couldn't sleep no more, so I just went outside . . . just down by the creek."[81]

"Well what'd you do with all of Maybe's clothes then? And, and Royd's suitcase?"

We don't say anything.

"Were, were you trying to pack some clothes and go with 'em or somethin'? And you just packed Maybe's clothes instead of your own, by accident?"

"No, I just . . ."

She takes us by the shoulders again.

"*Henry. Tell me that's what you did. Tell me that's what you did and you bring back that suitcase and Maybe's clothes right now, you hear me.*"

She lets go of our shoulders.

"*Go on, then,*" she says. "*Git.*"

But we don't go anywhere.

Mother falls to her knees and starts crying and praying inconsolably at our feet.

Fade to black and silence.

---

[81] It's obvious that Henry is having a hard time lying to his mother here, but it's common for people on the Spectrum to have diffculty lying; but it's *also* probably his first time to lie to her in any really *material* kind of way because if he tells her the truth, then Emily—the truth, the reality, the whole subject of Emily—is no longer his and his alone; and, indeed, it's not hard to imagine that, once Mother believed him, she (and Avery) would march across the creek, and hunt Emily down, and otherwise ravage the subject until absolutely none of it, of her, of Emily, was left for Henry—and he can't have that, not at this point in his life; so, this marks (yet) another big, watershed-type developmental moment for Henry: in active defiance of Mother's heretofore unassailable power to extract material truths from him and invade the realities of *his* heretofore entirely porous "domain," *this* time, he says, *No, fuck you, this is mine.*

Now Mother is ruined. And it's hard to imagine any scenario, other than Henry's killing the shit out of Royd and getting Maybe back, that could save or redeem her (Mother); but one gets the distinct sense, given the precious little time left in the film (less than twenty-five minutes remain) and the way things are trajecting, that *that* is not going to happen—it's not *impossible*, obviously, but the chances, I think, are slim . . . and this *despite* any prior narrative indications or interpretations or expectations or wishful-thinkings to the contrary because, I mean, haven't we all been thinking, hoping, etc., pretty much this whole time, that Henry will at some point, probably near the end, as the big climax, kill the shit out of Royd?

Whether they are explicitly generated for us (the audience or reader) by the text, or they are creatively constructed by us out of the text, *expectations* that we develop over the course of a narrative that ultimately go unrequited function as a type of *red herring*: we expect, that is, we believe, fear, hope/want very much, etc., that some particular event (like Henry killing Royd) is going to happen, which fills us with *suspense*, but when the story ignores those expectations, this drains us of all that *suspense* and leaves us feeling *let down*, or disapppointed, with an empty sense of *bathetic irony*, which is something you might think should be avoided in story-making, but it can actually have quite a powerful effect, one that smacks hard of life as it often *really is* because it's true: expectations *are* often thwarted; fears, often unfounded; hopes, often dashed; and wishes, often unfulfilled.

Fiction . . . and non-fiction too, come to think of it, are often guilty of *artifically* tying up all their loose expectational threads into nice little bows at the end. So *this* move, to *thwart* expectations at or through the end, is a *realist* one: it subverts the tendency to magically tidy everything up upon completion: it *denies final closure*. Though, of course, it would also be *unrealistic* to deny final closure to *every* thread because *some* threads, in life as we know it, *do* tie up nicely in the end.[82] But Emily's return (be she real or imaginary or both) here, at (or near) the end, which we have no doubt been expecting since the beginning, is a good example of Noella closing, or at least *initating* the closure, or tying-up, of that thread. And it probably goes without saying, but, in the interest of being thorough, it occurs to me to add here that if *none* of our expectations were *ever* satisfied *over the whole temporal course* of a narrative, from beginning to middle to end, then that narrative would be non-evolving, non-continuous, well-nigh unintelligible, and probably not even really a *narrative* at all, but just a *collage* of flimsily- or un-related images.

In any case, if Royd and Maybe are, indeed, gone forever, then I predict that we are about to see in Mother a steady, guilt-fueled decline. Being the kind of person or character she is, a *blind pleaser*, and being still (and perhaps perpetually or at least indefinitely) *gaslighted*, she'll be hounded by the idea that her inadequacies (as wife, mother, person, whatever) were the cause of, or the reason for, Royd's and Maybe's departure, *and/or* she'll realize that she knew in her heart of hearts that Royd was evil but then torture herself for never having had the courage to face up to that fact or do anything about it.

Interestingly, though, if this is right, then, *to Mother*, the whole tragic thing will end up being *all about her*, which, one

---

[82] Charlotte Bronte's *Jane Eyre* versus Emily Bronte's *Wuthering Heights* is a great case study on closure v. non-closure through the end (respectively).

might rightly argue, constitutes a weird sort of *narcissism*: a *negative* or *ironic* or *perverted* or *inverted narcissism*, where she won't be able see anything *except a horrible image of herself* whenever she reflects on the whole, obviously more complex (than she's making it) situation: she'll be *chronicly, obsessively, and all-pervasively self-blaming*. Which prompts me to wonder whether *gaslighting*, perpetrated by *typical narcissistic* psycho- and sociopaths (like Royd), causes or at least seriously amplifies and exacerbates in its victims (like Mother), this *weird*, sad type of *negative* or *inverted narcissism*.

Anyway, this is what happens when the *blind pleaser* character- or personality- type (or adaptation or *mal*adaptation) bumbles through the dim gaslight and into harm's way. The words:

# TWO MONTHS LATER

appear on the screen then fade out. Then the scene fades in: we're standing in the living room, looking at Henry, who's sitting at the dining room table, in Royd's chair now (notably), staring intently into the box or cage he's formed with his hands and fingers in front of him.

Henry, then, evidently, is not ruined at all but really rather on the make: he's got him a Mothson, an Edgmaster, an El Camino, a blue gas station suit, a job, an income; he got his dick sucked (albeit by a dog), which was, in itself, of course, remarkable, but it also brought about (albeit indirectly and unintentionally) the dog's, Luke's, death, which, because it was the same as, or identical to, the vanquishment of the irksome guard-dog of the other side ("Cerberus"), also enabled him to have sex *with a girl* (albeit his twin sister, be she real or imaginary or both) for the first time; and now, finally, he's sitting at the head of the table, the man of the house.

Mother enters the frame from the left, from the hallway. She's wearing high-heels; a short denim skirt; a tight, red, spaghetti-strap-type tank-top blouse; a big black purse, and a lot of make-up. She looks too old and out of shape to be dressed like this, and the make-up makes her look like a clown.

"Okay, Henry," she says, jangling her keys out of her purse— Henry looks up from his cage—"I gotta go to work now ... down at Lucky's, God forgive me. And I won't be back 'til late. I'm sorry. But I'll see you in the mornin', okay?"

Henry doesn't say anything; he just looks bewildered.

"Ain't got no choice, Henry. We both gotta work now." She identifies her car key. "I'll see you in the mornin'," she says, then walks down the hallway and out the front door.

Henry looks back at his hands.

We hear the Cordoba start up then pull away over the gravel. Royd must have gotten the Cordoba for Mother so that, in the absence of the Buick, she'd have a car: a strangely thoughtful gesture tucked inside an act of otherwise pure evil.

W E CUT TO HENRY, lying in bed, on his back, tightly, funereally tucked-in (somehow), asleep. The word:

# ABRAHAM

appears (above Henry's head) then fades out. We are standing at the feet of the two beds, between them, watching him. He is illuminated (albeit barely) by a vague shard of weak yellow light, coming through his fractionally open door. Perhaps he has left the light on in the kitchen for Mother, for when she comes home.

We hear the front door click open, and Henry's eyes open toward the ceiling. There's laughing, a man and a woman's, Mother's.

"Shh," Mother says and laughs. "Shh."

"Okay, okay." The man laughs.

The front door clicks closed.

Mother and the man go down the hallway into the kitchen.

Henry gets out of bed and goes over to the bedroom door and looks down the hall after them. We step in behind and over him and look down the hall as well.

We hear Mother and the man open the refrigerator and pop two cans of beer. They laugh and talk. Then they get quiet and Mother starts moaning.

"Stop," she says and laughs.

The man says something.

They come down the hall; Henry and we step back.

They go into Mother's room and shut the door.

We stay where we are, just inside Henry's bedroom door. Everything's quiet.

Then Mother starts moaning again ... louder and louder. Presumably, Henry knows what this means now.

After a while, everything goes quiet again.

We cut to Henry, sitting at the kitchen table, at the head of the table, eating Cheerios, properly, with milk and a spoon, and he's fully dressed (jeans, plain white t-shirt, tennis shoes). We are above and behind his left shoulder. It's early in the morning. The sun is barely up.

Henry and we hear Mother's bedroom door come open. Henry stops eating and looks up. The door shuts.

Someone's coming down the hall.

A tall, slender, gaunt man with dark disheveled hair materializes out of the lightless hallway and stops. He's wearing a black trenchcoat, which is hanging open to reveal a wrinkled, soiled t-shirt that says FUCK YOU, I'M FROM TEXAS,[83] torn black jeans, and black combat boots. He stares at Henry a moment. He looks remarkably like Abraham Lincoln, but sick. His eyes and cheeks are sunken in shadow, and there are scabs here and there on his face.[84]

He—or, I suppose it's Abraham—smiles and nods at Henry, but it's not in the way one way one would smile and nod in

---

[83] Believe it or not, this is an actual shirt. It first appeared in the eighties, and it was really popular back then, in Texas. I had a friend who liked to wear his, but I told him I wouldn't go out in public with him unless he took it off. It's still available for purchase now. It has always astonished me the level of ham-headed hubris it took to make, much less *wear* something like this. I mean, if anything ever said, "I am a big fat violent idiot with a really tiny penis," well this is it.

[84] Given that we're in the mid-nineteen-eighties, it is hard not to think that this is AIDS, that Noella is referencing AIDS here.

greeting a stranger, but in a familiar way, a way that suggests that the whole point of his coming down the hall is to confirm with Henry the completion of some task . . . and that Henry is his commanding or superior officer. Then he turns around and disappears into the darkness of the hallway.

The front door opens and shuts.

Henry gets up and goes out the backdoor. We follow.

We creep left, along the side of the house, stop at the corner, and look around it.

Abraham is walking away up the access road, cicadas screaming, the sun at his back, bright and harsh and hot . . .

Now, *one* way to read this scene and Abraham, in particular, is *psychoanalytically-archetypally*, where Henry represents the *typical*, or *arche-typical*, heterosexual male, and Abraham represents a creature of his subconscious, of his subconscious desires, whom he (Henry, the archetypical hetero-male) has summoned (unwittingly, of course) to complete a task, which is: to have sex with and thus murder (or at least—because deadly diseases do not kill instantly—*initiate* the murder of) his mother so that he (Henry, the archetypical hetero-male) can (or can more easily) have sex with his sister.

However, unlike with *The Oedipus* and *Electra Complexes* (wherein, as you know, heterosexual boys want to "kill" their fathers so they can have "sex" with their mothers, and heterosexual girls want to "kill" their mothers so they can have "sex" with their fathers, respectively), there is neither Greek (or otherwise) myth or story, nor psychoanalytic theory or account on which to base this reading or any sort of *Sibling-Incest Complex*, which makes it look, at least on the surface, like maybe Noella is just perverting these traditional psychoanalytic paradigms for kicks or to be provocative.

It turns out, however, on looking a little deeper, that this *psychoanalytic-archetypal* reading and its centerpeice, this ostensible *Sibling-Incest Complex*, may not be *that* far off base; I mean, they will, to be sure, be subject to some serious criticism, but they may also be worthy of some serious consideration because . . . well, for the following reasons:

(1) First of all, we have to remember that, in *real life*, these sorts of Complexes almost always deal only in *repressed*, i.e., *unrealized*, *desires* to murder and commit incest and *not*, as their supporting myths and stories always do, in the *actual* commission of murder and incest. The myths and stories exaggerate or literalize to make their points, but, in real life, heterosexual boys repress desires to kill their fathers and have sex with their mothers, and heterosexual girls repress desires to kill their mothers and have sex with their fathers, such that those desires almost never break loose and result in real-life murder and incest, and they almost always show up, or manifest, as (mere) *animosity* toward one parent and (mere) *affection* toward the other. If this is right, then the bar is obviously set really low for someone to qualify as having one of these sorts of Complexes, *including* our newly proposed *Sibling-Incest Complex*, and it stands to reason because these sorts of Complexes are supposed to capture something really sweeping about large swaths of human nature.

(2) I think it would be pretty hard to disagree—and I'll wager that the majority of psych professionals would corroborate this—that most heterosexual males with sisters will, at some point in their development (probably usually in their pre- and early-teens, but later for Henry, of course, because of his condition) have at least *some* natural, aboriginal sexual interest in those sisters (and their (different, provocative) body parts—if only by virtue of proximity and access), which is going to mani-

fest most often as attention and affection toward them, however subconsciously and surreptitiously or ironically or even imaginatively and/or masturbatorily those attentions and affections are expressed.

If this is right, then it's also not hard to imagine that mother will stand as an unwelcome impediment because the boy can't *really* focus his attention and affection on his sister while she (his mother) is front and center in his world, getting in the way, requiring his time and love and affection and attention as well, and, as it were, *standing in the window*, keeping an eye on him, *judging* him, making him feel *guilt* and *shame* for things he's trying to do and establish for himself as an ostensible independent agent; in other words, he cannot *really* be *free* to focus his attention and affection on his sister and be an independent agent unless mother is sufficiently out of the way. So it's also about *freedom*: freedom *from* obligations, authority, judgment, guilt, shame, etc., and freedom *to* make his own decisions, to be an independent agent, etc., come what may.

(3) And, if we give credence to *The Oedipus Complex*, then it makes at least some sense to suggest that what's going on here is that the boy, Henry, is exactly in the ambiguous midst of the transition *out of* the *Oedipal* stage and *into* the *Sibling-Incest* stage of typical heterosexual male development; he is, as it were, *on the bridge* between the *Oedipal* and *Sibling-Incest* stages, such that the old object of his desire, his mother, and the new, his sister, are commingled, conflated, or *not-as-yet-disambiguated*, which would explain why, in the case at hand, Henry wants to *both* have sex with *and* (thus) kill his mother, *and* have sex with his sister.

So, yes, it's a somewhat wild but certainly *not totally insane* reading, or theory, especially when you consider that the *next* stage of typical heterosexual male development would be from, or out of, this *Sibling-Incest* stage and into the mature, or fully-developed, *Outsider-Outcest* stage.

But look, if you're uncomfortable making and trying to defend big *universal* or *essential* claims about large swaths of human nature, as this *psychoanalytic-archetypal* reading, with its *Sibling-Incest Complex*, does, then alternatively, but similarly, and a lot less (but not entirely un-) controversially, we can read the scene *psychoanalytically-subjectively*, which is to say, more *specifically*, as if the scene were someone's, an *indivdual's*, dream,[85] to which we then apply a sort of Freudian interpretation. And here, of course, the dream is, undoubtedly, *not* Henry's, but *Noella's* (because Henry *is* Noella's dream), and the reading, or interpretation, of that dream is simply: that Noella wants to kill his mother, through sex, in order to (more easily) have sex with his sister—and, indeed, Noella *does* have a sister, one sister: Christina.

And with respect to the problem or complication that he wants to kill his mother *by having sex with her*, one could argue (albeit perhaps not *entirely* convincingly) that, since Noella's *ultimate* goal is sex with his *sister*, then sex with his *mother* is *not* something he desires *in and of itself*, as an *end* in itself, but merely as a *means*, something he *has* to do, in order to get what he *really* wants; *sex*, in other words, is, in this case, just like a

---

[85]The whole scene also pretty obviously intentionally *re-calls*, or *re-collects*, or *re-members* (or, yes, is an *external modified reiteration* of) the scene from David Lynch's *Lost Highway*—a super-internal-psychological director and a super-internal-psychological film—where Fred Madison (Bill Pullman) is looking all around his house for his weird, super-stoic, totally taciturn wife, Renee (Patricia Arquette), when, finally, she slowly, quietly, eerily, nightmarishly emerges/ materializes out of a pitch-dark hallway or closet as if from the dark depths of his own mind.

knife or a gun or a bat: it's merely his or, rather, his *subconscious'* instrument or murder weapon of choice at the moment, which means it's *fungible* and can be *reduced out,* such that the assertion becomes not: *he wants to kill his mother through sex so he can (more easily) have sex with his sister,* but the much more managable and satisfiable: *he wants to kill his mother (somehow or another) so he can (more easily) have sex with his sister.*

In any case, while we're in the spirit of invoking and manipulating traditional paradigms, we should also introduce the idea or possibility that Henry's subconscious is like a sort of *minor deity,* or *lesser god,* or, better yet, *pseudo-god* here, *in itself,* on the theory that it has been (invisibly) orchestrating things . . . or at least materially increasing the probabilities of certain things or events, like Mother's death (in due course) and Luke's death, both of which pave the way for Emily and him to do as they please on the other side of the creek. And if we like this sort of expansion into the *theological,* or *pseudo-theological,* then our *psychoanalytic* readings (either or both of them) become *psychoanalytic-pseudo-theological* readings, where the idea, more generally,[86] is that the human subconscious is often more powerful than we think (or even *can* think) and that it, at least sometimes, runs our lives as if we were puppets and in such a way that is oblivious to, or prior to, or just somehow *beyond* our distinction between good and bad and good and evil.

---

[86] Because fiction very often logically fallaciously *generalizes from the particular* in order to make philosophical points: a liberty fiction gets to take that philosophy, itself, does not.

Which dovetails nicely with or into a more specifically *biblical* or, rather, *pseudo-biblical* reading[87] because it is, of course, *Abraham* who (in the Bible) puts secular or moral-ethical considerations of right and wrong and good and evil aside in order to follow God's command to murder[88] his son, Isaac;[89] *but*, since it has already been shown (I think dispositively) in this film (or via our extrapolations therefrom) that the Big 'G' God does not exist, then the, or at least one big possibility here does, indeed, seem to be that Henry's subconscious is the relevant god and that, at its behest and in the name of Henry's freedom, Abraham, *this* Abraham, unlike the one from the Bible, actually *commits* murder, or, as I said, at least *initiates* the commission of murder . . . of Henry's mother.

All of which—it suddenly occurs to me—*also* invokes the story of Abraham *Lincoln* because what is the *sine qua non* of the Abraham Lincoln story if not his emancipation of the slaves in the United States? And what is going on *here*, at least on one important level, if not the emancipation of Henry from his family and the family compound? So, tacked- or stapled-on here, very post-modernly, is *also* a relatively contemporary *socio-political* reading.

That's a lot of readings and paradigms, dovetailing, interpenetrating, overlapping, interconnecting, diving in and out of

---

[87] A reading which is obviously contemplated by Noella and clearly reflected in the text of the film.

[88] . . . or at least *totally and unconditionally commit* to murder his son, Isaac, because, as you know, God doesn't *ultimately* make Abraham go through with it.

[89] Which, one could argue, was an evil (i.e., non-omni-beneficent) thing for "God" to do to Abraham (despite not ultimately making Abraham kill Isaac) and proof, at least, that whatever god is represented at that point in the Bible is not the Big 'G' God.

one another ... and so much concomitant dynamic interpretive polyvalence that we're faced with a veritable hermeneutic Frankenstein's monster; and, not to *pile on*, but there's one more reading (that I can think of at the moment); it's more straightforward, more narrative-facts-based than the others, so let's call it the *commonsense* reading, and it is: that, given Mother's overall weakness of character (or will) and her current state of maximum desperation and self-denigration, it makes good (narrative) sense, or is totally (narratively) fitting, that she would get tanked on her first night working (waitressing, I'm assuming) at Lucky's[90] and then be blind (or suicidal) enough to bring home for sex someone who is so obviously disease-ridden that her death is now simply a matter of time—I mean, if we were confident about Mother's ruin before, now, we know, it's a *fait accompli.*

[90]The painful irony of the name goes without saying.

W E CUT TO US coming through the pines, presumably on the other side of the creek. We hear the sound of a shovel cutting earth; then, in the distance, through the colonnade of branchless pine trunks, we see someone digging, and, of course, chances are, it's Henry. The words:

# DIGGING FOR EMILY

appear then fade out. As we approach, we see, in a clearing (perhaps, the same one in which they met), Henry, shirt off, standing part-way in a hole, digging; and Emily, sitting in front of him, back up against a big pine, arms wrapped around her knees, shamelessly exposing herself to Henry. We emerge from the pines, stop, and take the scene in from the side: Henry to our left; Emily to our right. Emily is talking . . .

"*Listen* to me, Henry." Henry stops digging. "I . . . I"—she drops her legs and brings her right hand to her chest—"am your *twin* sister, *Emily*. That is who I am. Maybe is just your *half*-sister. And that means that you and Maybe *and me* have the same mother, okay, but *Royd* is *Maybe's* dad, and *Avery* is *our* dad. You understand what I'm sayin'? Avery, *Uncle* Avery, is *our* dad, *your and my dad*. But 'cause he's Mother's brother *too*, he's *also* our uncle, okay?" Henry starts digging again.

"And if you're wonderin' how I know'd all this, it's 'cause I was *listenin'*, Henry. I reckon it was different for you, maybe on account your . . . being different or sick or whatever it is, but when we was around four, a lot of times, when Royd was gone to work, Avery come over and talk to Mother, and you and me'd just be settin' there on the floor with 'em, or just over in the

next room, and never once thinkin' we or I might could understand what they was sayin', they'd git to arguin' about how Avery
wanted Mother to git rid of Royd and how he wanted her and us
to move over into his house and live with him 'cause he was the
dad and ever'thing, but—and it's funny, 'cause I don't remember Mother ever standing up for much—but she wouldn't do it,
Henry. She wouldn't budge on this 'un on account of she said
it was against God's rules, what they done, and 'at they needed
to make things right, to set things aright in the eyes of God, she
said, and 'at's why she brung Royd home with her from Lucky's,
what when we was just little, just two or three or whatever it
was, 'cause Royd bein' the dad set things aright.

"Then Avery'd say it wadn't like she could *trick* God, and
she'd say it wadn't about trickin' Him but makin' things aright
*before* Him, making *amends*, she called it, and, what's more,
she didn't want her kids, *us*, knowin' that their uncle was their
daddy too or that we was the result of what she called *insets*,
but, at first, Avery'd say since *he* was the one built this place
up from dirt, then *he* was the one got to make the rules, and
fu'thermore, he said he didn't see no harm in it, bein' that they
was consentin' adults and way out here away from ever'body
'n' whatnot, then he said, cryin', that it was just 'cause he loved
her so much, which was sad . . . but she wouldn't budge, Henry,
and finally she got him to promise he'd quit talkin' about it and
comin' around like 'at pickin' fights and to never ever talk to us
about it neither.

"Anyway, 'cause me and you was *inside* Mother at the same
time, and we was *born* at the same time, that makes us *twins*,
Henry, and that's what give us that connection . . . 'cept it don't
seem to been as good as I thought 'cause even though you *got*
my message down in Carlsbad Cavern, you *still* didn't know

who I was or 'member who I am . . . *and* you ain't never done nothin' 'bout that Luke neither, like I ast you." Henry starts digging again. "*Which*, by the way, Henry, I seen that whole business the other day, in your backyard, 'cause even though I could nary to hang around here too long, *'cause of that dog*, I *could* check-in on what you was doin' a little bit ever once in a while, and what I saw the other day was that you had Luke . . . What's the word? *Busy*, I guess, and then Royd come out and shot him dead, so I know it wadn't you that finally did somethin' about that damn dog . . .

"But I cain't blame you for it, Henry. I cain't blame you for messin' with that dog like 'at 'cause you don't know . . . You ain't never been taught right from wrong . . . more like you just been taught *wrong*." She laughs. "*And* you was lonely. And I cain't blame you for not doin' nothin' about Luke all them years neither 'cause, now I know, you didn't know who I was, and why would you go and kill Luke just 'cause some girl stranger come out of a tree in a dream you had in some cave and aksed you to? You wouldn't. And you didn't. *Although*, I reckon it's true, Henry, that if you hadn't been messin' with Luke like 'at, then Royd wouldn't 'a' shot him neither, so maybe you *did* do somethin' about Luke after all." She laughs.

"Anyhow, the important thing, it's done, and now I'm here, where what I was tellin' you is that we're twins, and we growed up together too, for some years . . . five or six years I guess it was 'cause I remember it was some time after my fifth birthday Royd started what he called *playin'* with me. You remember any of that Henry?" Henry stops and looks up a second but then keeps digging. "'Cause you was in the room with us at first. Mother thought he was just bein' a good ol' dad, playin' with his kids, when he was really in there, in our room, just playin' with *me*. Then, pretty soon, once he got tired of tryin' to cover it up in front of you, and he wanted to git more serious with me, he started tellin' Mother me and him was goin' lookin' for butterflies and bringin' me over here, acrost the creek." She looks down a second, then back up. "Then, after I was gone, I reckon he figured he'd better git busy and try and make him another one with Mother so he could play with her too, poor thing . . . fixin' to be dead or ruint one way or 'nother now, believe me, 'cause if *anything* is against God's rules, Henry, it's *that*, and not what Mother and Avery was doin' or what we's doin' 'cause we all the same age and of the same mind about thangs and they ain't nobody elst around. But *Royd*, he was a *growed man*, and I was just a chile, and I did *not* want to, Henry, and that's why I'm out here in the woods, where, I know you could imagine, it ain't been easy, but at least I was free of *that*.

"And it *was* hard at first, Henry, but perty quick, I learnt to scrounge from watchin' 'em 'coons. I seen they how they git into peoples' garbage cans at night, so I started doin' the same, but I was much better at it than them 'cause I know'd how to be quiet. Them 'coons git to makin' so much a racket tryin' to get in them cans, bangin' them lids all around and knockin' 'em over, people come out and shoot at 'em half the time, but with me, you know, I got hands"—she rasies her two hands and shows them to Henry then sets them down on top of her thighs—"so I can get into them cans as quiet as a mouse, and ain't nobody ever once come out and shot me." She laughs.

"And there ain't just food in them cans, Henry; people put all kind of good stuff in them thangs: lot of time clothes, this dress; I got my first sleepin' bag outta somebody's garbage can, up in a small town near here. But I also gotten to where sometimes I hang around in the woods 'hind peoples' house and watch to see if they leave they garage open, and sometime they did, never thinkin' someone might be watchin' and waitin' in the wood to sneak up in there and take their shit. Don't happen much, but I done stole a saw and some lighters, which I was needin' to make a fire, and a big blue plastic sheet, for the rain, a big duffle bag, couple water bottles, and . . . lemme see . . . couple flashlights and batteries one time—that was good . . . and some boots one time, all from peoples' garage. "And in the bigger towns, Henry, behind them stores and shoppin' places and whatnot, they got bigger garbage cans, big square garbage cans, and they's even this one place, this one store I guess it is, in this big town up yonder, where people just drop off old shit they don't want no more, and a lot of time, they just leave it outside, and I snuck up and got my good coat and my good camp backpack and sleepin' bag there one night. I didn't even know the sleepin' bag was all smushed up in this other little tiny bag deep inside the backpack, so that was a happy surprise when I got back and there it was. And I 'member this got me to thinkin' about could I maybe go back to see if they got a tent settin' out there I could pick up too, but I never did go back on account of bein' too scared to git caught. They got good stuff, but 'cause of all the people, the chances to git caught go up at places like 'at, in bigger towns.

"I been keepin' my eye out for a tent ever since then, 'cept I also reckon maybe I don't want no tent 'cause they make me too easy to spot and too easy to sneak up on, and it'd be heavier to carry, so whenever it gets cold or rainy, I just put on all my clothes and coat and wrap up in my big plastic sheet, in this special way I got, and make do. That's probably been the worst of it though, Henry, the cold and rain. But it don't git that cold around here much, so . . .

"I guess, after while, I also do git downright sick of eatin' old food outta peoples' garbage cans, but I reckon not sick enough yet to start killin' and eatin' peoples' animals and pets. 'Cept, believe me, I have thought about it, a lot, 'cause they're ever'where: cows, horses, chickens, dogs, cats, squirrels, birds . . . 'coons. But I just ain't been able to bring myself to it. Probably mostly 'cause they really is plenty of easy pickins in peoples' garbage cans, which, like I said, I'm good at that, and I don't know nothin' 'bout no huntin' or catchin' or killin' a animal or cuttin' it all up and cookin' it. Plus, I just ain't felt much like killin' and eatin' a animal, seein' as I perty much am one of 'em myself." She laughs. "Be like killin' and eatin' *you*."[91]

She laughs. Then the image fades to black, but the sounds of Henry's digging continue, and, it occurs to me, that "Digging for Emily" can be analyzed according to our two theories: the *Emily is in Henry's External World Theory* and the *Emily is Only in Henry's Internal World Theory* (or the *External* and *Internal Theories* for short), where, on the *External Theory*, "digging for Emily" means Henry is digging a cavern or a home or a grave or all three for a *real-live* Emily and himself, and she, as the one with the superior intellect and memory, is providing Henry with (and confirming for us) critical missing information concerning what happened in that first multi-year gap and about what she's done to survive all these years.

And on the *Internal Theory*, "digging for Emily" means Henry is digging a cavern or a home or a grave or all three for an *imaginary* Emily and himself; he may also be unwittingly digging for a *real-dead* Emily (i.e., her dead body), which has been buried, by Royd, in the woods on the other side of

---

[91]Cannibalism—perhaps the only colossal no-no that has not been exploited in this film.

the creek; and, he is digging into his own subconscious memories for Emily, and, in finding "her" there, "she" becomes the internal-to-Henry psychological vehicle by which he is now retrieving (and confirming for us) information buried in that first multi-year gap, and he is extrapolating from that information—with a lot of help from what he's learned from TV, no doubt—what Emily's life *might have* been like, surviving out in the world alone.

Importantly, though, the facts continue to serve both theories equally well, such that, as things stand, they both are, *for us*, still true. *Henry*, on the other hand, surely still believes that Emily is real, a creature of his external world.

T HE SOUNDS OF DIGGING fade out, then the words:

# PART FIVE

# GOD IS DEAD

appear in white against the black. Then they too fade out, and we cut to the inside of an old pick-up truck, where Uncle Avery (the same actor but older looking and fatter now) is laughing as he looks out over the steering wheel at a two-lane road at dusk.

"Oh man," he says, "I do love that joke. Don't you think that's a good 'n', Henry?" he asks, looking to his right, past us, and over at Henry (who is older as well, probably twenty, twenty-one, but played by a different actor, one who looks a suspiciously lot like Billy Bob Thornton in *Slingblade*), but all or most of Henry's attention seems to be focused out in front of him, out the front and side windows, at the passing environs.

Both Avery and Henry are wearing their blue gas station suits.

"You do git it, don't'cha?" Avery asks.

"Yeah, I git it," Henry says, still looking out at the road. "It's 'cause the Texas guy's pecker's longer'n' the Alabama guy's one."

"Yeah, exactly. So why ain't you laughin' then? Ain't that funny?" Avery says, smiling and looking to Henry again.

Henry appears to think about it for a second; then he says, "Be better if he could drink with it too."

Avery laughs once, then he looks back out over the wheel.

"What? Like a elephant?"

"Mm Hm."

"And that'd be funnier too?"

"Yeah."

"Okay . . . well . . . it'd definitely be weirder," Avery says, mainly to himself. He's got a can of beer wedged in his crotch area which he takes and drinks from now. He finishes the can—it's Miller Lite—and drops it behind Henry's side of the bench-seat. It clatters among a bunch of other empty cans. "Go on and grab you a beer, Henry, like I told you before, and drink up. Be good for you. And grab me another 'un while your at it, would you?"

Henry reaches down, takes two cans of beer from the case at his feet, hands one to Avery, takes the other, pops it open, and takes a sip.

"Oh come on now, son. You don't just peck at it. Drink that thing. Take a slug."

Avery opens his can and demonstrates.

Henry takes a bigger drink of beer.

"There you go," Avery says. "Now, I know you cain't read and all, so it ain't like all these signs or a map is gonna do you any good, but I still want you to know where we're at and where we're goin' because . . ."

"I, I do, I do know where we're at," Henry interrupts. "I come this-a-way with Royd when we, when we blowed insulation that time. We went to a old lady's house in a, in a place called Craig. I remember. I'm good at that. I'm good at direction."

"Well, we goin' just past Craig to a little camp spot of mine at Cherokee Lake. But you ain't never tol' me that, Henry, about bein' good at direction. That's quite a . . . a asset, son." Avery smiles over at Henry. "So what's your secret then? I mean, if you cain't read a map, then how do you do it?"

"I just look outside, at all the stuff, and rememberize it, like a movin' pitcher."

"Hm. Well what about when it gits dark then, or like it is now?"

"It's harder. It's harder when it's dark 'cause I cain't see so good, but I can still do it. They's still enough light I can see and rememberize things."

"Wow. Well that's . . . good," Avery says, suddenly sounding more intoxicated than before, "'cause what with Mother bein' as sick as she is and not bein' able to work and all, and Mrs. Smickers sayin' they ain't nothin' to be done 'cept let her rest and wait and see, well then it's gonna be up to you to pick up the slack with your mowin', to put food on your table, and 'at's gonna mean drivin' out farther'n' usual for you, farther 'n' just around Henry's Chapel."[92] Avery looks over at Henry. "Which, by the way, did Mother ever tell you that's where you got your name?"

"No."

"Well, it is . . . But anyway, as you well know, they ain't nothin' at Henry's Chapel, 'cept a chapel, and you cain't mow it 'cause, well, for one thing, they already got somebody mows it, but it's also run by *official* people, and we cain't have no dealin's with *official* people, Henry, where what I mean is people who might be inclined, for one reason or 'nother or at some point or 'nother, to start askin' questions about who we is and where we live and whatnot. See what I'm sayin'?"

"Yeah."

---

[92] Henry's Chapel, TX, is at the intersection of TX 13 and TX 856. It's not a proper town; more just a site: the site of a small chapel. It's about one hundred and thirty miles east/southeast of Dallas, ninety-five miles west/southwest of Shreveport, LA, and sixty miles north/northwest of Nacogdoches, TX; that is, smack dab in the middle of nowhere

"But yer still gonna have to pick you up some new accounts now, other 'n' just mine and Lyle's. Which is somethin' I was hopin' you'd do yourse'f whenever I give you that El Camina and 'at Mothson. But hey, I understand, Henry. These sorts of . . . limitations is on account of your, your condition. But yer still gonna have to do it 'cause sometimes they's things you just got to do, like it or not, to be a man." Avery looks over at Henry. "Now, I already done . . . felicitated things for you by settin' you up to mow Joe's . . . Garage and Mrs. Smickers' place, up in Kilgore, startin' next week, but you gonna have to pick you up a couple more yourself, you understand?"

"Yeah."

"Now, it ain't gonna make you a millionaire, mowin' five yards ever' two weeks, obviously, and it don't do nothin' for you in the wintertime, when they ain't no mowin' to do at all, but it'll be enough to put food on the table for you and Mother a lot of the time, and 'at's all you got to do money-wise and food-wise, Henry, 'cause—and I ain't never told you this—but I got bunch of money saved up for us, okay . . . for whenever times git lean like 'is or in a emergency or just for retiring or whatever, which I got buried around different places on the property, or the *compound* as I call it, and which I'll show you where it's all at one of these days, when we git back. So we got some *in*surance monies, as it were, is what I'm sayin'. But they's still a whole bunch of more shit I'm gonna have to show you and which you're gonna have to learn to do, Henry, all around the compound, so if somethin' ever happened to *me*, it don't all just go to hell. You hear me?"

"Yeah," Henry says.

It's totally dark outside now, and Henry and Avery are cast sort of Rembrandtianly in the dashboard lights. Avery finishes his can of beer and drops it behind the seat. "Here, hand me another one of them, would you?"

Henry does so.

Avery pops it open and takes a slug.

"Okay 'cause look, a long time ago, in the beginning, I—well, I had me a little help—but let's just say I built this place, our place, the compound and ever'thing, up from nothin', Henry, with my own two hands. I put up them two houses. I dug that well. I put in the septic, for the toilets. I ran the 'lectric in from off the main road line—borrowed it, you might say." Avery smiles. "I set up them phones between the two houses. I took care of the garbage. Correction, I *take* care of the garbage. I'm the one takes it away to the dump, Henry, in case you didn't know. I make our car tags, which you *did* know. And what I'm gonna need you to do is, *additional* to pickin' up them mowin' jobs, Henry, is foller me around the compound, probably a bunch of times, and learn how to deal with all this shit, okay, 'cause if you don't look after the well once in a while, your wa-ter'll go south on you; if you don't check the 'lectric lines ever' once in a while and fix 'em, they git frazzled and your 'lectric'll go south on you; if you don't take the garbage to the dump over in Palestine or Henderson or one of them, pretty soon you'll be livin' in a garbage dump of your *own* makin'; if you don't tend the septic, if, if you don't go out and rent the septic truck from Joe, then suck all that shit outta the tank at the compound, then dump all the shit outta the truck into another tank over in Troup, you'll find yourse'f swimmin' in shit forthwith, let me tell you; and if you don't make a new sticker for them cars ever' year, you cain't drive 'em 'cause if you git pult over, well that's it, Henry, the gig is up, over and done, 'cause we ain't on no tax roll or nothin', you understand?"

"Yeah," Henry says, still looking out the windows.

"Hey. I'm gonna need more than just a 'yeah' on this, Henry. This is some *serious shit*, son, and while it is definitely about not just letting the compound go to hell, it's about more than that too. It's about freedom. *Freedom.* It's about the freedom *to* do what we want, and freedom *from* other people, especially all them *official* people and all they goddamn meddlin'. You ever seen that flag, the one with the rattlesnake on it? That's rattlin' and fixin' to strike? And that says . . . well, it says 'don't tread on me' on it, and 'at means, git the fuck off me or git bit, or die, 'scuse my French. You understand what I'm sayin' here, Henry?" Avery looks hard at Henry.

"Yeah . . . I git it. I understand."

"All right then." Avery looks back out over the wheel. "And look it. They's even a little more to it 'an that, which your gonna have to learn too. I mean, you can trust Joe and Lyle and Mrs. Smickers, but ever' one elst, you got to treat with suspicion. Don't git in no personal thing with nobody, Henry. Don't be chitter-chattin' with your new clients. Just do your job, git the money, and git out. And don't, don't go to the same gas station or grocery store or even the same dump two times in a row. And don't chitter-chat with none of *them* people neither, okay?"

"Okay."

"I'll show you what I mean about all this shit too, when we git back, Henry, but I guest the main of it is, if you want to be free, then take care of your own shit, and don't stick out as somebody other people, especially *official* people, might git to know or reco'nize or remember or be able to identify sometime." Avery takes a big drink then drops his can behind the seat. "Th'ow me another one of them things, would you?"

Henry gets Avery another beer.

"I do reckon it's hightime you learnt all this shit, what with you bein' twenty-one and all, but I also reckon we wouldn't be gittin' into it right this minute if wadn't for Royd doin' what he did and Mother gittin' all sick," Avery says, his voice cracking with emotion at the end. "What Royd done . . ."—he's on the verge of tears now—"he might as well 'a' just kilt your mother." He shakes his head. "Motherfucker." He says, his right jaw muscle forming a tight knob. "If I'd 'a' found him, I'd 'a' kilt him. I'd 'a' kilt him and been happy . . . 'cause it wadn't the first time . . . it wadn't the first time," he says bad-dreamily out over the wheel to the dark road ahead of him. "Just woke up one mornin' and she was gone . . ." He stares blankly for a moment. "I told her, I told Mother, but she wouldn't listen . . . she wouldn't listen to me.

"But look it, Henry," he says, collecting himself. "Mother don't want me talkin' about it—we ain't always seen eye to eye on everything—but . . ." He pauses. Then he looks at Henry, and we look at Henry. "Did you know, or do you remember, that, *before* Maybe, you had you a sister, a twin sister, Henry?"

"Cow," Henry says.

"What?" Avery says, still looking at Henry.

"Cow," Henry says, pointing out the windshield.

Avery and we look back at the road and see a brightly lit cow standing frozen in front of the truck. Avery swerves hard right, misses the cow, and slams into a utility pole. Henry's body is thrown forward violently but is held in place by his seat-belt, and we are somehow affixed to the seat as well, but at the margins of our perception, we sense Uncle Avery, in the form of a thick black streak, rise up and out of his seat then exit the vehicle through the windshield in a great splash of glass, after which we are left only with a foreboding hiss.

Henry is slumped in his seat, as if asleep, the old-type seat-belt holding him only across the lap. The windshield in front of us is webbed with crack-lines, and, to our left, there is a large, glass-fanged, blood-stained hole, where Avery went through . . . or most of him went through because in the seat where he sat, is now one of his blue-trousered legs, and one of his blue-sleeved arms is reaching up from the foot-well, held up in the crease between the seat and the door, his hand half open, in a sort of semi-circle, as if still holding the wheel. On the bench-seat directly below us is Avery's other leg, the boot of which is in Henry's lap, and down in Henry's foot-well, resting across his feet, is Avery's other arm. Fade to black and silence.

When we fade back in, the scene is the same, but the hiss has intensified . . . and we have moved over to the right . . . we have merged with Henry, who has regained consciousness.

We move Avery's leg, undo our seat-belt, and get out of the truck.

We walk through the headlights toward what looks like a large suitcase, lying in the grass.

When we get up to it, we look down. It's Uncle Avery, his head and his torso, and his eyes are open, gazing up at the sky. He sees us and smiles.

"Hey," he says.

We kneel down beside him.

"Here," he says. He looks down and to his right, his chin doubling against his chest, as if he's trying to get something out his right front pocket. He looks back up. "These . . . *these* are the keys to the kingdom, son." His right shoulder moves a little, as if he's handing us the keys.

We don't do anything.

"Go on. Take 'em. I want you to have 'em." He smiles.

We hesitate again, but finally, tentatively, with our right hand, we reach into the empty space where the keys would be if Avery were handing them to us and pretend to take them from him.

"There you go. Now go on, git," he says.

There is a massive explosion behind us, and everything turns yellow-gold.

Avery's face shines with firelight. Then, as if beheld by a beatific vision, he expires.

We stand up and look out over the amber-lit field.

We turn around and see Henry—suddenly de-merged from us—walking toward the burning truck. He walks past it then disappears into the darkness beyond. We follow. Fade to black and silence.

W E FADE IN ON HENRY, seated at a card-table, his hands clasped upon it, and his head bowed: he is either praying or in deep despair or exhausted (or some combination of the three). There is an empty metal folding chair opposite Henry at the table, and we are stationed just behind it (the empty chair).

The scene, lit only by what appears to be a flashlight hanging by a string from the ceiling, is, like the last scene, distinctly Rembrandtian. The yellow cone of light cast down from the flashlight is tight and claustrophobic, its edges cut precisely into total outer darkness. The words:

# THINGS FALL APART
# (6 MONTHS LATER)

appear in the yellow-lit space to Henry's left (our right) then fade out, then Emily steps out of the darkness and into that space. She is older now too, of course, and is played by a different actress. She appears to be wearing the same clothes Mother wore in the first scene of the film: the same rainbow tube-top, and it's too dark to be certain, but her pants look like the same bell-bottom jeans.

Emily has a sandwich in one hand and a can of beer in the other. She sets the sandwich down on the table to the left of Henry's hands, walks around behind him, opens the beer, sets it on the table to the right of his hands, and, as she walks over and sits down in the chair opposite Henry, we swing around to the right to look at them equally. Emily looks at Henry; Henry's head is still bowed.

"Henry. *Henry*," she says.

He looks up at her obliquely.

"Well don't just set there cryin'. Eat your lunch and tell me what happened. I's outside and I seen that truck come up. Who the hell come up in that truck, Henry?"

"'Lectric man," Henry says to the center of the table, "from the 'lectric comp'n'y. Name of Trip Click, he said."

"Well what the hell'd he want?"

"Said . . . said he was workin' them lines, up, up on the main road, and 'at he done tracked them wires down to the house and cut 'em. Said he's a monkey's uncle 'cause we been stealin' 'lectricity, and that they's hell to pay for that, and he's fixin' to brang somebody out here tomorrow, from down Rusk."

Emily sits back in her chair.

"And . . . and that ain't all," Henry says, his eyes still locked on the center of the table, "'cause then he got to fidgitin' and said it done stank like maybe somethin' died up in 'ere as well . . .

"I didn't say nothin', but he said he reckoned he's gonna have to call the . . . the health service too, so I closed the door on him and he lef' . . .

"I ain't been over there in a couple days before today, but when I come in there this mornin', it was hot, and I smelt it too, and when Mother didn't say nothin', I come 'round to look, and she was just settin' there in that Lazy Boy with a un-e't TV dinner in her lap and her mouth hangin' open and her eyes just starin' at the ceilin'."

Henry and Emily sit in silence.

Then Emily sits forward, clasps her hands together on the table, and says, half-smiling, "Well, what're you gonna do now, Henry?"

Fade to black and silence.

S CREEN'S STILL DARK but we hear the sounds of someone doing things inside a house: walking around, moving things around, opening doors. Then it sounds like the person is pouring water or some kind of liquid all over the place. He or she is going from room to room, pouring liquid, out of some kind of container, all over the house. The words:

# STATE OF NATURE

appear against the black then fade out. We hear a match strike and fire up. Then we cut to Henry, in his blue gas station suit. We are moving smoothly backwards in front of, and below him as he walks, a large red plastic gas container in either hand. He is walking away from Avery's house, which is now engulfed in flames, orange and yellow against the dusk, the new black of night seeping in behind everything.

We swing slowly around to Henry's left. Then we swing around behind him and follow. There is garbage all around the compound, strewn about everywhere and in large piles here and there, and there are countless mounds of black dirt, like a hundred dug graves, unfilled.

Henry walks through the open back gate at Mother's, down a path cut through piles of garbage, then kicks open the backdoor to the house and goes inside.

The house is dim, lit only by the gray twilight coming from the back window. There is garbage all over the house as well.

Henry sets one gas can down in the kitchen then heads down the hall to his room. We follow then watch from the door as he pours gasoline all over his room.

We move out of the way as Henry pours gasoline from his room, across the hallway, into Mother's room. He pours gasoline from the floor up onto and all over the bed then all over the floor again.

Walking backwards out of Mother's room, he pours gasoline down the hall. We follow.

When he gets to the living room, he empties the container onto the floor, sets it down, and picks up the second container. Behind him, cast in twilight and shadow, we see Mother, sitting motionless in the Lazy Boy.

We follow closely behind him as he pours gasoline all over the couch, the TV, the living room floor. He turns to Mother and pauses.

Her head is hanging back heavily, contortedly on her neck, her mouth and eyes are open, and there is an uneaten TV dinner in her lap.

He pours gasoline all over her and the Lazy Boy, then he moves into the kitchen and pours gasoline all over it.

He empties the container onto the dining room table, sets it down there, then walks back to the open backdoor and takes a box of matches out of his pocket.

We zoom in on his hands as he takes a wooden match stick out of the box and pushes the tray back into its sheath.

He strikes the match. It flares up. It settles. Then he drops it and disappears out the backdoor. We stay and watch it fall.

When it hits the floor, fire spreads like blue-orange water all over the house until everything is lit beautifully from the bottom up.

Then, through upward-lapping waves of flame, we walk over to the big back window and look out. Henry is walking away. He is walking away, down the path cut through the garbage in the back yard.

When he passes through the back gate and into the darkening field beyond, all at once, a thousand burning points of light ignite all around him, little ornaments of flame, flickering, in the grass, in the trees, everywhere . . . cicadas . . . lighting his way down to the creek.

But we . . . we remain, standing in the back window of the house, looking out, more and more consumed by fire.

Graham Guest is originally from Houston, Texas. He is interested in exploring ways of combining fiction and philosophy. He also plays in a band called Moses Guest. He currently lives with his family in Glasgow, Scotland.

# BLANK PAGE BOOKS

are dedicated to the memory of Royce M. Becker,
who designed Sagging Meniscus books from 2015–2020.

They are:

**IVÁN ARGÜELLES**
*THE BLANK PAGE*

**JESI BENDER**
*KINDERKRANKENHAUS*

**MARVIN COHEN**
*BOOBOO ROI*
*THE HARD LIFE OF A STONE, AND OTHER THOUGHTS*

**GRAHAM GUEST**
*HENRY'S CHAPEL*

**JOSHUA KORNREICH**
*CAVANAUGH*
*SHAKES BEAR IN THE DARK*

**STEPHEN MOLES**
*YOUR DARK MEANING, MOUSE*

**M.J. NICHOLLS**
*CONDEMNED TO CYMRU*

**PAOLO PERGOLA**
*RESET*

**BARDSLEY ROSENBRIDGE**
*SORRY, I BROKE YOUR PROMISE*

**CHRISTOPHER CARTER SANDERSON**
*THE SUPPORT VERSES*